The River Home

Shelly Johnson–Choong

Published and Distributed by:

Granite Publishing and Distribution, LLC
868 North 1430 West
Orem, Utah 84057
(801) 229-9023 • Toll Free (800) 574-5779
Fax (801) 229-1924

Cover Design by: Tammie Ingram
Cover Art by: Tammie Ingram
Page Layout and Design by: Myrna Varga • The Office Connection • Orem, Utah

ISBN: 1-930980-89-2

Library of Congress Control Number: 2002112675

First Printing September 2002
10 9 8 7 6 5 4 3 2 1
Printed in the United States of America

The River Home

Sequel to *Finding Home*

by

Shelly Johnson–Choong

Chapter One

Desperation flooded through Tye as she looked at Kyle. Gently, she placed her fingers over his lips. "Don't," she whispered through new tears as she caressed his face. "Please don't ask this of me."

Kyle took Tye's hand, kissing her palm. Then he crushed her hand to his chest. "Marry me," Kyle said as he looked into Tye's deep green eyes. He pulled her close with his free arm, placing his hand on her neck. Gently he stroked her long, honey blonde hair.

The gesture was familiar to Tye, and she immersed herself in the strength and tenderness of his touch. But today, it broke her heart as she struggled for words.

Kyle continued, "We can be married right here at home. Then we can move back east and work together."

Tye shook her head. "Our dreams have never been the same, Kyle. You're the one who wants to ride in the Olympics. Not me."

Kyle moved away from Tye, settling on the fence. He looked out over the clear western Oregon landscape. The early August heat was ebbing out of the day, along with the sun. Shadows grew in the gilded light, softening the evening. "I know," he said thoughtfully.

"You would stay here and teach children how to ride horses."

"When I'm finished with school that's exactly what I hope to do. I've always wanted to run my own barn. But there's more to it than that, Kyle, and you know it."

Kyle nodded quickly. "I've been thinking about the temple. I know how important that is to you, Tye. I'm prepared to make a deal."

Tye shook her head again.

Kyle held up his hand. "No, listen." His voice took on new urgency. "We can be married civilly this fall, get the next Olympic Games out of the way, and then you can have your temple wedding."

Tye blinked. "It's not *my* temple wedding, Kyle. Besides, you told the missionaries you didn't want to join the church."

"I told them I didn't want to join at this time." Kyle pushed away from the fence and began to pace. "Too many things need my attention right now. I wouldn't be able to give the church a full commitment. One thing that the missionary lessons taught me is that the church requires a lot. I don't have that to give. I train the horses six days a week during the off-season. When I'm competing I work every Sunday." He turned and faced her. "I am so close to the Olympics I can taste it."

"And I'm happy for you, Kyle, but I can't make a deal with a temple marriage. This isn't a game show or a deck of cards. It's our lives. How can I put my dream of a temple marriage on hold while you pursue what's important to you? I don't see that as an equal partnership." Tye lowered her voice, speaking deliberately, "If you're not prepared to give the church a full commitment, why should I think you're prepared to give our marriage a full commitment?"

"That's not fair, Tye. They're two different things."

"Not to me," Tye replied.

"You know my Olympic goals will only be for a little while."

Tye became thoughtful. "No, Kyle. I don't know that. Maybe I'm not being fair, but wouldn't it be better if we both started out with the same definition of glory? We should both be working toward the same goal. Instead, you're working toward the Olympics while I'm working toward a family that's sealed in the temple, which involves a lot more than just the ceremony, Kyle." She paused. "We've always been going in different directions. It's as if we come together for these short bursts of love only to be pulled apart by the reality of who we are." She looked away from him and took in the summer valley that spread before her. It was lovely and peaceful with long shadows that softened the edges of the hot day. Tye longed to run into one of those shadows where it would be cool and still. A hawk cried overhead, shattering the still summer evening. Tye glanced at the Redtail before turning back to Kyle.

Kyle began to pace. "I don't see it that way at all. This isn't a short burst of love. I have loved you from the moment I set eyes on you back at Oregon State all those years ago."

"And I love you, Kyle." She paused, and then whispered, "But I can't marry you."

Kyle stopped and blinked. He opened his mouth to say something and then looked down. Tye went to him, touching his face. He clenched his jaw and pulled away.

"Please, Kyle. Just let things be. Can't we do that? Let's pretend this conversation never took place."

Kyle shook his head. Then he looked at Tye. "I'm going to miss you, Tye," he said. Then, before Tye could speak, Kyle turned and strode away.

Chapter Two

*T*ye fumbled with the knots that held her horse, Trapper. Finally, she undid the rope and led out of the trailer. "You do understand, don't you, Trapper?" she asked. "I couldn't marry him. It just wouldn't be right."

Trapper flicked his ears in Tye's direction. He always listened. Quietly, she stroked his neck as he she moved him into his stall and unbuckled his halter. Glancing at her watch, she considered taking him for an evening ride. No, that wouldn't be appropriate. He had worked hard in today's competition, and the ride home had been tiring. She fed Trapper his apple before leaving him to rest.

Once outside, she noticed a quiet dusk settling over the Umpqua valleys. The sky was an ever deepening purple as a yellow moon began its ascension over the mountains. The symphony of crickets, frogs, and the occasional coyote serenaded Tye as she walked back to her truck. She breathed deep. The feather light night air was perfumed with the lingering scent of wildflowers and sun warmed dust on ripening wild blackberries. The earthy aroma of warm horses and hay mixed with the other scents of the lengthening twilight, creating a bouquet that was unique to Tye's beloved Northwest.

The peaceful evening taunted Tye. Had Kyle really asked her to marry him? Did she turn him down? Tye brushed away her tears and got into the truck. It all seemed so improbable. Putting the truck in gear, Tye drove the short distance to her home. When she pulled into the driveway she was pleased to see Meggie, her best friend, come running from the front door.

"Oh, Tye, I have the best news! We were able to get the house we wanted in Provo. We'll be sharing with two other girls. You and I will have to share a room, but there will only be four of us in the whole house. We'll be just blocks from campus. Doesn't it sound perfect?" Meggie came closer. "What's the matter, Tye? You don't look so good. Is Trapper okay?"

"Trapper is fine," she replied quietly. "Kyle asked me to marry him."

Meggie's eyes grew large. "Oh, Tye ... what are you going to do?"

"I told him no." She looked at Meggie as she pulled herself out of the truck. "I'm glad about the house, Meg."

"We'd better tell your folks about Kyle," Meggie said as she put her arm around her friend. Together they walked into the house.

Rex and Trudy Jorgenson greeted Tye, then listened to the afternoon's events.

Tye added, "How could I say yes under the circumstances? He knows the importance of the Church in my life. He's even taken the missionary discussions. He danced around the idea of a temple marriage—promising me that I could have it in a little while." Tye paused. "Apparently he doesn't mind waiting until his own goals are achieved." Her words were laced with bitterness.

"How did you leave it?" Rex asked.

"He left it," Tye said. "He said he would miss me, and then he walked away. I guess it's best that way. A clean break."

"But that's not what you wanted?" Trudy asked.

Fresh tears stung Tye. "No," she said in a shaky voice.

"What do you want?" Trudy asked.

"I don't know anymore, but I know I didn't want Kyle to walk out of my life like that. It hardly seems real."

"Well, you and Kyle have a very unique history," Rex said. "The horses have always drawn you together. You met at Oregon State University, and the two of you were really keen on each other. Then he took Trapper and competed with him back east while you went on your mission to San Antonio. He even paid you two-hundred dollars a month to lease Trapper to help support you on your mission." Rex shook his head. "I really like Kyle. I truly admired him for his willingness to see you through your mission. But he can't quite seem to grasp the importance of it all."

Suddenly Tye became thoroughly fatigued. She sighed. "If he had believed the gospel was true, he would've been willing to be baptized. He would've found a way to make it fit into his life. I don't think he ever gained a testimony. Isn't that right, Mom?"

Tye's mother put her arm around her daughter. "Yes, Tye. You know how hard it's been for me to give up cigarettes. But once I came to believe in the truthfulness of the gospel, I knew I had to make changes. I'm not saying it was easy, but you're right. Once I gained my testimony, the cigarettes had to go."

"Kyle will never give up horses," Meggie said.

"I don't think he would have to give up horses," Tye replied. "Or even the Olympics. He would just have to make room for the gospel, and if he had a testimony he'd be willing to do that." Tye began to sob. Her mother drew her into an embrace. Tye could feel Meggie rubbing her knee. The support of her friend and family was the only thing that made her feelings of loss bearable. How would life feel without Kyle? It was as if she was throwing off a familiar article of clothing just as a cold wind had hit her. Often, her relationship with Kyle felt like a scratchy coat, but Tye was used to the feeling. It was just always there. Even through her mission, Kyle's presence had been with her. He had stated that he could not wait for her while she was away on her mission, but he had taken her horse; the one thing that would bind them together through her eighteen-month service to the Lord. Trapper had thrived under Kyle's care, and when Kyle had returned him, Tye couldn't determine whom she was more pleased to see: Kyle or Trapper. She had hugged Trapper, who had pulled in her scent and nickered softly. Then she had hugged Kyle, a longing, lingering embrace.

Kyle had asked if he could stay close by through the summer instead of returning back east. Tye had readily agreed. They had spent the summer together. He had helped her get back into riding shape so they could compete together in the local three-day-event shows. Kyle and his horse, Ben, almost always won. His tenure out east was turning him into one of the premier riders in the nation, and Tye enjoyed being a part of that team.

"We had such a good summer together," she sniffed. "The competitions were fun, even though I've lost my competing edge." She became thoughtful. "Competing is no longer important to me. My mission gave me other priorities. In a way it made Kyle and I a better team. I could step away from the event and help him as someone who wanted to see him succeed, instead of someone who was competing against him. Trapper and I competed for fun and it gave me a whole new perspective, which enriched my relationship with Trapper and Kyle." She grew quiet. "After the show, Kyle and I would find a quiet place to let the horses graze while we would enjoy a picnic dinner one of us had made. It was during one of our first picnics that I asked him if he wanted to take the missionary discussions."

"And he really took to the missionary discussions," Rex said. "I was surprised when he said he wouldn't be baptized."

"He shouldn't have proposed," Tye said. "If he wasn't going to join the Church, he shouldn't have proposed. It's ruined everything."

"No. It's best this way," Trudy said. "Now you can go to school without any questions."

School; it seemed so far away and distant, but she and Meggie would be leaving in two weeks.

Tye dried her eyes. School would offer a whole new set of challenges. She would be working part-time; teaching children the joys and hard work of horseback riding. She had never worked during a school year, but her mission had drained her account. She needed to supplement her living expenses, not to mention pay for Trapper's oats and stall in Oregon while she lived in Provo. Her parents would help as much as they could, but most of the responsibility would be Tye's. She looked forward to the challenge. Already she had a job waiting for her at Three Creek's Ranch in Orem.

Tye looked at Meggie, who patted her knee again, her eyes mirroring concern. "I'm so sorry, Tye."

Tye nodded. "Thank you Meggie." She drew in a deep breath. "At least I won't be alone at BYU. You'll be with me."

"We'll have fun, and we'll work hard. You'll heal. I promise."

Tye smiled through her tears.

Later that night, after Meggie had left and her parents had gone to bed, Tye sat at the computer and stared at the blank screen. She wanted to write an e-mail to Kyle. What should she say? In a flurry of words, she reminded him that she was leaving for school in two weeks. She gave him her new street location and informed him that her e-mail address would stay the same. She closed her eyes while pressing the send button.

Chapter Three

Obsession gripped Tye as she drove up Provo Canyon. Pulling the truck into a lower gear she listened as the engine whined, gathering more speed. Ever since her arrival in Provo, chasing storms had become Tye's new past time. In the afternoons she would watch the sky, searching for the dark clouds that rumbled through the valley and funneled through the canyons. Her desire to run the storms down and meet their dark fury wasn't something she could explain. She didn't even try when Meggie questioned her craving for the darkening skies and fierce thunder. Tye had no explanation. All she knew was that she was searching. Although she wasn't exactly sure what she hoped to find.

"Just around this bend," Tye whispered to herself. She slowed down as she rounded the gentle curve in the road.

The storm was still out of reach. Tye pulled over and thought for a moment. Then she turned around and followed the road back to Bridal Veil Falls Park. Maybe if she sat long enough the storm would come to her.

When she reached Bridal Veil Falls, she parked the truck and walked the paved pathway to the falls. She barely recognized the river with its sluggish movement and brackish water. Pain contracted in Tye's heart when she reached the falls that were supposed to gush into the Provo River. Instead, the falls trickled down the wet face of the rock, bringing little to the thirsty river below.

Tye looked around. Young families were studying the sky and packing their picnic lunches early, while at the same time trying to corral children toward the parking lot. The sky did look ominous, but Tye expected that the pregnant clouds would only unleash a pent-up ferocity of thunder and lightning. There would be no rain.

According to those who had been raised in Utah, this was the worst drought the state had seen in recent history. Even the mountain tops were void of life-giving snow. Forest fires were popping up everywhere. From the valley Tye could see their smoke signals rising from the land to the sky like a lost traveler desperately pleading to be found and quenched.

It never occurred to Tye to worry about fire, even though the storms she chased were the cause. She still ran after them. A thrill would rise inside of her whenever she saw the clouds gathering en masse for an assault on the countryside. Then, when the timing was right she would drive up the canyon.

Like the landscape and the fires, Tye looked for rain. She longed for a full river that could invite her with the green canopy of shady banks and a cool touch that would soothe her aching hot wound. Instead she found a dry scorched wind, heavy-laden with dust and heat while dark clouds gathered in a mocking congregation at the dead brown landscape.

Still, she never gave up hope of replenishment. As the clouds rumbled along the mountain walls she would race up the canyon, looking for the dark center of the storm. Often it eluded her. The storm was quick, and it covered terrain she could never reach.

Tye began hiking the steep trail that would lead her right to the falls. From her position beside Bridal Veil Falls, she could see the pitiable river below. Sorrow stabbed at her as she looked at the Provo River which had been reduced to the size of a small, sluggish creek. How much life depended on this river?

Thunder rumbled above. The last of the families scurried toward the parking lot. Tye wished them away. She wanted to mourn alone with the waterless riverbed. She knew how it felt to be so dry and parched. She, like the river, waited for relief.

Thunder rumbled again as Tye settled on a rock by the falls. This time the sound was closer. Its echo from the canyon walls called to something deep within Tye. She turned to the darkening sky, hoping for rain, but the only water that was released came from Tye. Tears rolled down her cheeks and landed on the hard stone at her feet. They dried immediately in the dry wind.

Lightning threatened, but Tye remained still. She breathed deep, hoping for the scent of rain, but her hope was met with dust. Lightning cracked above her as it hit the mountainside, accompanied with another deep pulse of thunder that shook Tye. She felt as weak as she had on the day Kyle had left her.

It had been a month since Kyle's proposal and abandonment, but it could've happened yesterday for all the healing she had done. The wound was deep and slow to close. Every day it was with her; the slow pulsing ache that only relinquished its hold during sleep and the few blessed seconds she had in the morning when she awoke without any memory. Then it would press in on her like a demanding and unwanted guest, touching her spirit and flagging her emotions. Nothing could break through the impenetrable memory; not the happiness she carried over her mother's conversion and the dream they all shared to be sealed, or her happier memories from her mission. Her present life was filled with her new job and schoolwork but even through all her activity the wall of Kyle's memory was still there. It was as if the blessings of her life belonged to someone else.

For weeks, Tye had anxiously cruised her e-mail and street box for some word from Kyle, but it never came. She was sure he was back east by now. This time he didn't have Trapper to bind them. He had taken nothing of hers except her love. But it wasn't enough. It had never been enough.

The wind died down. Tye looked up at the sky. The clouds were passing now as the storm pressed south. The sun, with its relentless heat, broke free of its prison. Particles of dust floated through the air as the only sign that anything had stirred. It filtered the sun and gave the sky a tired look. Sighing, Tye pushed her hair from her face. She looked down to the river that was fed by the falls. According to the calendar, it would be autumn soon. Maybe the change of season would break the lock of the drought. But wouldn't winter bring its own kind of bitterness in its sterility and bone-numbing, brutal cold?

Tye rose from the rock, giving the river one more pitiful look. "I'm sorry," she whispered. But she wasn't exactly sure for what.

Chapter Four

ye opened her truck door and was greeted by the scent of horses and hay. She closed her eyes as the down-to-earth and comfortable aroma came to her through the drought tinged air. It was the familiar smell of warm horses and alfalfa that brought back Tye's happier memories of Kyle. The barn also gave her hope in her future. She was grateful for this job. Horses were the constant in Tye's life. Their independent and noble natures had always been a part of her refuge. Her love for them, and her knowledge of them soothed her troubled spirit. As she walked into the cool of the barn, a calm strength buoyed her. She knew this place, and she was going to teach others about the wonders of it.

When her eyes adjusted to the change in light, Tye saw her young student saddling the pony, Patches, in the crossties. Patches stood patiently while the seven-year-old struggled with the saddle.

Soon, Tye was standing next to Trista.

"Mrs. Holt helped me get Patches out of his stall," Trista said, making reference to the barn owner.

"You want some help with that saddle?" Tye asked.

Trista shook her head. "I can do it," she said as she lifted the saddle once again. This time she managed to get it on the pony's back.

"Good job," Tye said as she brought the saddle forward against Patches' withers.

Trista grinned. Her front teeth were too big for her mouth, making her smile lopsided. She reminded Tye of herself when she was Trista's age. Tangled blonde hair sticking out of a riding helmet and bright green eyes with a sprinkling of freckles across her sun kissed nose.

Tye handed the youngster the bridle. "Okay, can you show me how you would put this on Patches?"

The girl took the leather strips, and with her tongue pressed against her upper lip, she carefully put the bit into the pony's mouth.

"Great job," Tye said. "Now what do we do next?"

"We check the cinch to make sure it's tight so the saddle doesn't fall off. Then we lead Patches into the arena."

Tye nodded her approval before helping the young girl lead the pony into the arena.

Tye looked up into the empty stands. She remembered when she was a child how her mother would sit and wait for her to finish her lessons. "Is your Mom here today?" she asked.

Trista shrugged. "She had to run some errands. She thinks horses smell bad."

"I see," Tye said. "Now, can you mount by yourself, or do you want help?"

"I can do it," Trista said. She proved it by placing her foot in the stirrup and settling herself into the saddle.

Tye patted her knee. "Good girl. Okay, now let's get warmed up."

After the warm-up, Tye spent the next thirty minutes trying to teach Trista to post by rising out of the saddle with the rhythm of the horse's trot. The youngster would get the hang of it for a few paces, then her heels would fly up, forcing her out of balance. She would lose Patches' rhythm. Her tongue would come out against the upper lip, and she would knit her brows together in determination as she tried again. Tye liked Trista's resolve. Many of her students would become frustrated and get impatient with themselves or the horse. But Trista would simply refocus and try again. After the lesson, she congratulated the young girl as she led her and Patches to the crossties. Once Patches was settled, she began coaching Trista in her attempt to untack Patches. She didn't see the young mother until Trista was finished.

"Hi Mom," Trista said. "You should've seen me today. I posted."

Tye turned to face Trista's mother, who was wearing an absent grin and silk blouse. "That's nice honey. Are you almost finished?"

"Yeah. I just need to put the tack away and give Patches a rub down. This is my teacher."

Tye put her hand out. "I'm Tye Jorgenson."

Trista's mother barely took Tye's fingers in her hand. "Nice to meet you." She turned her attention back to Trista. "Triss, honey, can you hurry? Mommy has a manicure this afternoon. I don't want to be late."

"But I still need to brush Patches. He needs me to rub down the sweaty spot from the saddle."

Trista's mother wrinkled her nose. "I'm sure Patches will live if you forego the brush this once."

"No, Mommy. Patches needs to be brushed."

Tye stepped in. "Tell you what, Mrs. Um … I didn't catch your name."

"Mrs. Brannon. Celia Brannon."

Celia was pretty with her blonde hair cut to a blunt shoulder length, defined cheek bones, and brown eyes. Fashionable clothes clung to her thin but well-shaped figure. "Tell you what Mrs. Brannon. I'll brush Patches this time, but our lessons are forty-five minutes long for this very reason. It allows the student to learn all aspects of horse care. We want to make sure you get your money's worth."

"I'll remember that next time. Come along, Triss."

"But Mommy!" Trista began to protest.

"Quit your whining. We need to go." She squeezed Trista's shoulder as she steered her toward the exit.

"See you next week, Miss Jorgenson!" Trista yelled as her mother hurried her out of the barn.

Tye waved before turning the brush onto the pony. After she retired the pony, she glanced at the clock. Her next student was due in fifteen minutes. Pulling out Candy, a small gray, Tye began brushing the older mare for her next student. It was going to be an interesting year.

Chapter Five

*T*ye squeezed behind Meggie in the bathroom as her roommate brushed her teeth. "Just stay in that position for a minute while I finish braiding my hair," Tye said to Meggie as she was leaning over the sink.

Meggie protested as she rinsed out her mouth. "I was here first," she said with a mouthful of toothpaste. "Go use the mirror in the bedroom."

"The light isn't as good."

Down the hall, Tye and Meggie heard an anguished cry.

"What's that all about?" Meggie asked after she rinsed her mouth.

Tye secured her braid. "I don't know, but I bet we're going to find out."

Soon, their two roommates, KayLee and Dianna, appeared at their open bathroom door. "Have you seen my earrings?" KayLee asked.

Tye shook her head and looked at Meggie, who said, "No."

"How do you know when I haven't even described them?" KayLee asked.

"I just know I haven't seen anything that doesn't belong to Meg or me," Tye replied.

KayLee blinked. "That makes sense." Then she wailed. "What am I going to do? I can't leave without those earrings!" She hurried down the hall.

"Why not? They'll still be here when we get home," Meggie said, looking at Dianna.

KayLee's best friend just shook her head. "Devin is walking KayLee to church. She needs those earrings."

Meg and Tye looked at each other. Only KayLee would consider church as a date.

A triumphant cry came from the other room. "I found my earrings!"

"Let's see them," Meggie said.

KayLee hurried before the two girls and moved her hair aside, showing two ruby studs surrounded with small diamonds.

"Are they real?" Tye gasped.

KayLee nodded. "One-half carat each. Rubies are my birth stone. Don't they just knock your socks off? My folks bought them for me when I graduated from high school. Think Devin will be impressed?"

"Devin?" Meggie asked.

"My date." ·

"Oh, right," Meggie said.

"He should be here any minute. He's walking me to church."

"But church isn't a date," Meggie said.

KayLee shrugged as she moved away. "Why not?"

Meggie didn't know what she found more surprising; the prospect of using Sunday meetings as a date or the fact that KayLee had actually lost a pair of half-carat ruby stud earrings.

The doorbell rang.

"Oh. Oh no." KayLee turned and ran past Dianna, back into the hall. Dianna followed. "I don't want him to think I'm standing around waiting for him to show up. Tye, could you please get the door? Call me when he steps inside, okay?"

Tye looked at Meggie and suppressed a giggle. The two girls hurried downstairs and opened the door. She was greeted by a clear-skinned young man with precision cut brown hair and blue eyes framed in brown lashes. He looked like KayLee's type.

Devin smiled politely. "Is KayLee ready?"

"I'll go see," Meggie said.

Tye began putting on her jacket as she waited for Meggie to reappear.

Meggie returned down the stairs. Dianna was behind her.

"She'll be down in a minute," Meggie said.

Giving Devin a friendly wave, Meggie and Dianna met up with Tye and hurried out into morning. The first crisp snap of autumn greeted Tye. Still, she didn't smell any moisture. The chill in the air did not bring the valley any relief.

"Do you think KayLee and Devin will be on time?" Tye asked as they walked through streams of sunshine bouncing off fire red leaves. All three girls were wearing light jackets.

Dianna shrugged. "I doubt it. She's always late." Then she waved the girls off. "I'll see you at home. I'm supposed to meet Doug at his place. We're going to walk to church together."

"Do you think of church as a date?" Meggie asked.

Dianna shook her head. "Naah," she said. "Doug and I don't

date anymore. We're engaged. All we do is talk about the wedding." She moved toward the apartment houses down the block. "See you girls later."

Tye and Meggie hurried to campus. Soon both girls were scrambling into their chairs two minutes before the meeting. "We made it," Tye said quietly.

"I'm glad you did," the young man next to Meggie said. "My name is Mark Olson." He offered his hand to Meggie.

First Meggie then Tye shook his outstretched hand as they introduced themselves.

"Nice to meet you both. You must live close by," Mark said.

Meggie gave him their address.

"I'm not too far from there. In fact I'm right down the street." He studied Meggie. "I think I've seen you at the cafeteria."

Meg nodded. "Yeah. I work there every Wednesday and Thursday evening and Saturday morning."

"I work there also. Last week I ran the Belgian Waffle machine," Mark said.

"Oh! Now I know why you look familiar," Meggie said. She was about to say something else, but the conversation was cut short when the meeting began. Tye and Meggie both looked around for their roommates but didn't see either girl.

After sacrament meeting was over and the congregation headed toward Sunday School, Mark picked up the conversation. "I'm majoring in culinary arts, so my work is a part of my class-time."

"Me too," Meggie replied. "This is my last year."

Mark grinned. "Mine too." He paused as they found seats in the Sunday School classroom. "Hey, why don't you two come over for lunch? I'm making omelets. Then we're going to have a scripture chase. Keeps us old missionaries on our toes," Mark said.

Tye and Meggie looked at one another. "That would be fun," Meg spoke for both girls.

After church the two girls hurried home. They changed clothes quickly. When they came back downstairs, they found Dianna and KayLee sitting on the couch in deep conversation.

"Where are the two of you going in such a hurry?" Dianna asked.

Tye explained.

"Sounds like fun. I wish I could come," Dianna said.

"Why don't you?" Tye said. "We'll share our omelets with you."

KayLee looked excited. "I'd love to come."

"How did your date with Devin go?"

KayLee shrugged. "He was kind of boring."

"It would be really hard to get to know someone in church, KayLee. There isn't any opportunity to talk," Meggie said.

"Maybe," KayLee said. "Besides, it's not exclusive. I'm dating just for fun." She flashed her fingers that held several CTR rings in front of Tye and Meg. "Maybe I can collect another one of these."

"You look like you have plenty already," Meggie said.

KayLee giggled. "I'm trying to see how many I can collect."

Dianna looked down at her hands. "I won't be able to go," she said. "Doug and I had a fight." She fidgeted with her engagement ring. "He wants to patch things up this afternoon."

"I'm sorry," Tye said. "It sounds pretty traumatic." She wasn't sure if she should ask, but she didn't have to wait long.

"Oh, this kind of thing happens between them all the time," KayLee said with a snap of her gum. "I keep telling her she should ditch the guy. The two of us could have a blast."

"But an engagement is a serious commitment, KayLee. It's a promise to be married," Meggie said.

"Yeah, maybe. But Doug isn't worth it." She rose from the couch. "I'll hurry and change so I can come with you."

"It's his mother," Dianna blurted out after KayLee left. "She just wants to run the whole wedding and reception. Doug and I have planned a simple reception with about three hundred people. We want to serve cake, some hors d'oeuvres, and finger food. I know it doesn't sound like much, but my folks don't have a lot of money. This is about all they can afford. Well, his mother says that since Doug is her only son and he's only getting married once, she wants to have this huge sit-down dinner with four-hundred-and-fifty people. And of course, they'll pay for everything!"

"How does Doug feel about it?"

"He wants to let her have her way. He actually agrees with her. I told him that this isn't some road show his mother gets to direct. This is our wedding, and since I'm the bride and my folks are primarily responsible for paying for the event, we should do it our way."

"But weddings are becoming less traditional all the time," Meggie said. "Maybe your folks could agree to allow Doug's parents to help with the expenses. Then there could be some kind of compromise about the event."

Dianna shook her head. "Oh, no," she said. "If that happened then Doug's mother would think she could run the whole show. The word compromise isn't in her vocabulary." Dianna lowered her voice. "And that's not the worse of it."

Tye gave her an inquiring look.

"He says he wants to invite as many people as possible so that we can get more gifts. That's why he wants the four-hundred-and-fifty guest list. I had no idea he could be so greedy." She paused.

"Then there are the dresses."

"What about the dresses?" Meggie asked.

"His mom doesn't like the dress I've chosen for the brides-maids. Doug's sister, Pauline, is a bridesmaid, and Doug's mom thinks that Pauline should have a say in the dress."

"What does Pauline say about that?"

"I saw her choice. It's all shimmery and pink. It looks like a piece of cotton candy with a big hoop skirt and enough chiffon to choke a school of fish."

Tye bit her lip to keep from laughing.

"It's okay. Go ahead and laugh. I did. Unfortunately, I was the only one who saw any humor in it. I told everyone it was way over the top, especially compared to the wedding dress which is very simple in its design."

"Has Doug's mother seen the wedding dress?" Meggie asked.

"Absolutely not! I told the store where we bought it back home that if she comes in to ask for it, they are to tell her that no one is to see it except the bride and her mother. And what do you think happened? As soon as I was at school she marched to the shop, insisting on seeing the dress. They refused. That made her mad, but I don't care."

"What does the dress look like?" Meg asked.

"It's so pretty with a streamlined fit, a mandarin collar, and pearl buttons that go up the back. The material is white silk with a pattern of flowers that catches the light while still being subtle. I've been saving for it all my life."

"You don't think Doug's mother would like it?" Tye asked

"I think she would want Pauline and me to be twins."

"Two sticks of cotton candy?" Meggie asked.

"Something like that," Dianna said wryly.

Tye started to laugh. Then she bit her lip. "I'm sorry. This kind of thing must be very distressing. I shouldn't laugh."

"Well, if it weren't my wedding I'd probably find it hilarious," Dianna said.

KayLee came bounding down the stairs wearing jeans and a white turtleneck. Her lush blonde hair brushed up into loose curls that fell around her freckled face and stunning blue eyes would make any young man hand over a CTR ring. Tye noticed for the hundredth time how pretty KayLee was.

The doorbell rang. Dianna closed her eyes. "Thanks for listening to me," she said. "Maybe it'll make it easier for me to talk to Doug."

KayLee gave Dianna a hug. "Good luck," she said.

Meggie and Tye opened the door. Doug walked in with barely a greeting. Tye, Meggie, and KayLee slipped out into the bright sunshine. The day had lost its earlier chill.

"What do you think will happen?" Meggie asked as she quietly shut the door behind them.

KayLee shrugged. "I hope she dumps the guy."

"Well, you know him better than we do, but maybe they'll find a way to compromise," Tye said. But her thoughts were elsewhere. What if she and Kyle had become engaged? Would it have become a tug-of-war? Somehow she didn't picture her and Kyle fighting over dresses and hors d'oeuvres. Anxiety filled Tye. No, they would've been tense over completely different matters. Tye would've resented the civil ceremony. It wouldn't have been a good way to start a marriage.

For years, she had struggled with being a part-member family. Her father had joined the Church when Tye was six while her mother had steadfastly refused, until Tye had gone on her mission.

They still weren't sealed as a family. It was the one thing Tye had yearned for as long as she could remember. Now that her mother was a member, Tye finally believed her most precious dream would come true, but she didn't dare think about it too much. She was afraid it would dissipate into thin air like the Oregon mist.

Kyle knew of Tye's desire for a sealed family. She had shared it with him during their tenure at Oregon State. But for him, the Olympics always came first. That was his dream.

The girls found the house that Mark had described and rapped on the door. Mark answered. "I was beginning to wonder if you were going to show," he said. "The omelets are finished. Who did you bring with you?"

"This is KayLee," Meggie said. "She's one of our roommates."

Mark threw the door open wide. "Well, c'mon in. We've got plenty."

The three girls walked into a living room that must have been filled with at least twenty people. Quick introductions were made. Tye watched as KayLee twirled one of her rings, smiling at the boys.

"How are you managing to feed so many?" Meggie asked Mark as they walked into the kitchen. She began helping him serve.

"Everyone donates."

"Of course," Meggie replied. "I used to do that when I cooked for a group of friends at OSU, but there were never this many people." She paused. "We didn't bring any money today, though."

Mark placed his hand on Meggie's arm. "No worries." He smiled. "You can help with the dishes."

"Oh, now that is sneaky," Meggie said. "First you lure us over here with the promise of food and fun. Then you turn us into slave labor. What kind of restaurant are you running?" Meggie laughed.

"The cheap kind." Mark threw her a devilish grin. "Besides,

why do you think I asked you? I had to recruit some labor. I'll let you off easy this time though. Your roommates don't have to do the dishes. I think the two of us can handle it."

"Well, some friend you've turned out to be." Meggie grinned. "I'll have to watch you every minute."

Mark nodded. "Yes, you will."

After everyone was finished, Meggie rolled up her sleeves and stood next to Mark. She was up to her elbows in soapy water. One by one everyone filed by, handing Meggie their plate and silverware. She would wash. Mark would rinse, dry, and put away the dishes. When Tye filed by, she handed Mark three dollars.

"What's this?" he asked.

"It's for the meal. I don't expect you to feed me for free."

Mark laughed as he looked at Meggie. "You've got her well-trained."

"It's not that," Meggie replied. "She just doesn't want to do any dishes."

Tye grinned.

After Meg and Mark finished with the dishes, Meggie moved toward the stove.

"Don't worry about the pans," Mark said. "I'll take care of them after everyone has left."

"These didn't come with the house," she said, touching the top quality pans.

"Nope. I brought my own with me."

"I wish I'd done that," Meggie replied wistfully.

"It might be easier for me since I don't have to worry about my roommates wanting to use them. These guys have no interest in boiling water so they leave my stuff alone. I think that might be harder with girls."

Meggie nodded. "You're right. Still, I miss my good pans," she said slowly as she fingered one of the pans.

"I'll let you use mine if you'll cook me dinner," Mark said.

Meggie smiled. "You are very clever, Mark."

"Do we have a deal?"

Meggie thought for a moment. Then she nodded. "I really want to get my hands on some decent pots and pans."

Mark grinned. "My offer is always open." He nudged Meggie's elbow. "Let's join the others." They walked out into the living room where captains were being chosen for the scripture chase teams. Soon, the room was divided. One person stood as referee and the challenge began. Tye and KayLee were on one team while Meggie and Mark on the opposite team. The two sat side-by-side helping each other when one would get stuck. There was much laughter and joking as the teams remained close, but in the end the team that Mark and Meg had joined prevailed, winning by three points.

One of Mark's roommates started handing out bowls of ice cream as Mark and Meggie moved closer to Tye. KayLee got up to join one of the boys from her team. When Mark took her spot on the floor the conversation turned to missions. Mark had plenty of stories about his mission to Alabama which encouraged Tye to talk about San Antonio.

"You know what sent chills up my spine?" Tye asked.

"Probably the same thing that sends chills up every missionary's spine," Mark replied. "Dogs."

"Yes! Dogs. I love dogs, but on my mission I learned that not all dogs love me."

"Did you ever get bit?" Mark asked.

"No, but my companion threw her scriptures at a dog once. She had to get a new quad. The folks weren't home, and we left the scriptures there. The dog hovered over them like a bone. My companion wasn't very happy about that because her scriptures were all marked up. She was pretty much useless for the first couple of week as she tried to break in a new set of scriptures." Tye laughed. "I had a dress ruined by a dog. He was friendly though." Tye smiled at the memory. "It had been raining so everything was muddy. My companion and I were tracting out this one house. As soon as we were inside the gate, this beautiful, huge dog comes lumbering at us from the porch at top speed. I could tell he wasn't mean. He was just jubilant. Anyway, before I could even move he ran right up to me placing his paws on my shoulder like he was hugging his long lost best friend. I just about fell over. His owner called him off, and she was very embarrassed. The dog's name was Pepe, and he immediately obeyed his owner when she called him off. But the dress was ruined. I had paw prints on both shoulders made with Texas mud. I could never get those stains out." Tye laughed again. "The lady felt so bad she let us in to teach the first discussion. Then she offered to have the dress cleaned, but it was okay. We baptized her and her thirteen-year-old daughter three months later. I loved that dog. He was always so happy to see me."

"Blessings come in mysterious ways, don't they?" Mark grinned.

"You're going to think this is really silly but when I got home, I cut out the paw print stain, and I framed it."

"Why didn't you bring that with you?" Meggie asked. "I don't see it hanging on the wall."

Tye thought for a moment. "I forgot, I guess." That was sad. Tye hadn't thought about Pepe and his master for weeks. Now the memory of the mud stained dress and her happy visits with Pepe and his family came shining through the dry dust that had filled her mind since Kyle's proposal. It was such a relief to think about something else.

"I don't think that's silly. I wish I had that kind of memento," Mark said.

Meggie studied Mark. His rich, dark brown hair wasn't cut in any particular style. It looked as if it wouldn't obey any laws that tried to govern it anyway. It hung in straight layers, stopping short just above his ears and eyebrows which framed deep, dark brown eyes. If Meggie looked carefully she could see small, fine lines around his eyes, but his olive complexion kept them hidden. Still, he looked older than most seniors.

After all of the ice cream had been eaten Meggie stood with Mark to help him with the dishes. He gave her a warm smile. "You stay here. This won't take but a minute." After he was finished, Mark offered to walk the three girls home. Tye and Meggie agreed, but KayLee decided to stay. She was in a deep conversation with one of Mark's roommates.

Stepping into the afternoon, the threesome was greeted with dark clouds. A few raindrops scattered themselves on a shiftless, cool breeze. Tye longed to race up the canyon, but it was Sunday.

"We could use the rain," Mark said as he looked up at the sky.

Tye wrapped her sweater close to her body as she followed Mark's gaze. No thunder came with this storm.

When they reached the front porch, a gentle rain started to fall.

Mark thanked them for coming. Then he turned to Meggie. "When can I plan on dinner?"

Meggie sat down on the wicker chair that was protected by the big front porch. The rained drummed on the roof. "I'll have to think about this for a minute," she said.

"Your social calendar is that busy?" Mark teased.

"You have no idea," Meggie said with a wry smile. "I think I can fit you in on Friday night at about seven." She turned to Tye. "Does that work for you?"

"Are you cooking?" Tye asked.

"Yes. Mark tempted me with some really great pans."

Tye laughed. "I'll be there, Meg. You just tell me when and where."

Meggie looked at Mark. "Can you bring the pans over to my house?"

Mark nodded.

"We'll eat here on Friday night at seven."

"How much do you charge?" Mark asked.

"Five bucks for dinner. How many will be there?"

"Just the three of us, unless Tye wants to bring a friend."

Tye put on a face of mock distress. "I don't have any friends."

"Well, you do now," Mark said as he stood.

"I'm not sure that's an honor you want," Meg said. "Look what happened to me. I ended up doing the dishes."

Tye giggled. "You're right. I'll have to think about that."

"Oh, I can tell we didn't get off to a very good start," Mark said. He tapped his chin with his index finger for a moment. "I've got an idea. Let me make it up to you. On Friday night I'll clean every piece of your kitchen after dinner."

"You're on," Meggie said without hesitation.

Mark turned to Tye. "Do you want to rent one of my roommates for the evening? They're free."

Tye shook her head again. "No, thanks. I'll fly solo." She looked out over the brown lawn. The rain had stopped. Already the clouds were pushing away from each other and fanning out over the sky.

Tye's observations were interrupted by pieces of a loud conversation from inside the house.

"I guess they haven't patched things up yet," Meggie said.

Mark became concerned. "Do you think I need to step inside and take a look around?"

Just then, Doug came bursting out of the front door, hotly walking down the stairs. Dianna came to the door; her tear streaked face red from crying.

"He said we'd do it his way or not at all," Dianna said to those on the front porch. "So I told him not at all." She called out loud enough for Doug to hear. She showed the girls her left hand. The ring was missing. Her eyes filled with tears as she turned from the door and ran up the stairs.

Mark looked at the girls.

"It's a long story," Meggie replied.

"I bet it is," Mark said. "Will you girls be okay here? That guy didn't appear very stable."

"We'll be fine," Meggie replied. "Thanks for lunch, and thanks for walking us home."

Mark moved off the stairs. "I'll look for you at the Cougar Eat," he said with his final wave.

Chapter Six

Meggie pulled the breakfast torte out of the oven before popping in the cinnamon rolls. Since her summer's employment at Farmer's Bed and Breakfast, she enjoyed the rich tastes of the morning meal. So when she thought of the theme for Friday night's dinner, she considered breakfast. The torte was a heavenly concoction of black forest ham, scrambled eggs, cheese, and thinly sliced potatoes wrapped up in a puffed pastry. It was a customer favorite at Farmer's. Tonight it would be accompanied with snow peas and carrots in a honey glaze. The cinnamon rolls with almonds, raisins, and cream cheese frosting would be the dessert. Already their aroma was mixing with the heavier scents of ham, cheese, and eggs.

Meggie stirred the honey glaze and checked the carrots before adding the snow peas. She really liked Mark's set of cookware. The pans were heavy and well designed with a thick coating of Teflon. She wished she had brought her own set of pans, but realized Mark was right. It would have been difficult to keep KayLee and Dianna away from them. Since KayLee couldn't be trusted with ruby earrings, Meggie doubted she could be trusted with someone else's cookware. She would just have to settle for borrowing Mark's whenever she had a desire to cook with good pans.

Meg glanced at her watch again and wondered about Tye. She should be here. As if on cue, the front door opened. Meggie walked from the kitchen to find Tye peeling off her jacket.

"Smells good," Tye said. "Let me guess, breakfast for dinner?"

"Uh-huh," Meg replied.

"Have you seen KayLee or Dianna?" Tye asked.

"Dianna's on the phone with Doug, and KayLee is hitting a couple of the BYU dances," Meggie said.

Tye nodded, then said, "Oh, guess what? I got a letter from Toni today. She gave me her new e-mail address."

"I hope she's okay," Meggie said. "I really worried over her decision to quit school and spend a year on the farm." She paused. "I guess I'd hoped that she would want to come here to BYU with us."

"Maybe next year," Tye said. "I think Toni had some things she needed to work out with her family relationships, and the farm was the only place she felt she could do that." Tye pulled the letter from her coat pocket and scanned the contents. "She says that she likes living on the farm with her Uncle Chad and his family. I guess they accepted her into their home right from the beginning, and she feels like a part of their family. Her cousin Jackson has sent in his papers for a mission call, but they haven't received an answer yet."

Tye continued, "She sees her mother almost every weekend. Sometimes her mom goes to church with her but not always. Now that summer is over and the harvest is in things have settled down. I guess they had a huge cherry crop this year."

Meggie smiled. "I'm sure that made her happy. She loves cherries. Remember the tree we planted in the backyard of her Corvallis, Oregon home?"

Tye grew wistful. "We said we'd meet at that tree for a reunion, but we never did. By the time I got home from my mission, Toni was already in Idaho." She sighed. "I hope we have that reunion someday. I sure do miss her."

Meggie wiped her hands on the towel she had thrown over her shoulder. "I do too," she said. "Well, I'm glad she's doing okay. Now that we've got her e-mail address it'll be easier to communicate."

Tye agreed as she folded the letter and returned it to her pocket. Toni had been Tye's first contact as a stake missionary. Her influence had been subtle yet dramatic. Tye had taken her missionary calling seriously and felt a strong sense of duty to teach Toni. What had caught Tye by surprise was how much she had learned from Toni, who had taught Tye how to love and accept people without conditions. It was a powerful lesson.

A conversation being held upstairs grabbed Tye's attention. She could hear Dianna crying into the phone. "I thought Doug and Dianna made up. Didn't she take the ring back?"

Meggie shrugged. "I thought so."

The doorbell rang.

"That must be Mark," Meggie said as she opened the door.

Mark entered the house, handed Meg a five-dollar bill and a bottle of sparkling cider.

"Those cinnamon rolls smell just about done," Mark said.

Meggie agreed as she hurried into the kitchen.

"Okay everybody, let's eat," Meggie said as she pulled out the rolls. "These can cool while we're having dinner."

Mark walked into the kitchen while Tye settled at the dining room table. "What do you think of my cooking gear?" Mark asked.

"I think it's the greatest. Thanks for letting me use it." She handed him a knife. "Would you mind cutting the torte?" she asked.

Mark placed his nose close to the torte, breathing deep. "Meggie this is wonderful. Is it your own recipe?"

Meggie beamed as she nodded. "So are the cinnamon rolls. They have just a hint of apple in them. I hope you like them."

Meggie watched as Mark prepared the plates. She smiled at the reverence he had for food. He wiped up all excess crumbs and cut an apple into wedges and sliced a banana to create an impromptu fruit salad. It gave the plates a splash of color and texture. Then he carried two plates while Meggie carried hers to the dining room table.

After the blessing on the food, Mark took one bite of the breakfast torte. "Oh, Meggie, this is delightful," he said.

"It's my favorite," Tye said. "And it was one of the things I missed while I was on my mission."

"I can see why," Mark said. "I doubt I'll ever view breakfast the same again."

Meggie blushed. "What made you decide to cook?" she asked Mark.

"My Italian roots, I guess. My mother is Italian. She can do more with pasta than any woman I know. As I grew up I came to admire her ability to prepare good food for a lot of people on a tight budget."

"What do they think about you being a chef?"

Mark was thoughtful. "I think they struggle with the decisions I've made for the last ten years. You see, my family is Italian Catholic. At one time I was going to be a Catholic priest. So, it's hard for them to accept anything else."

"I see," Meggie said. "That must've been hard on everyone. I'm sure they had a lot of pride and hope placed in your decision to become a Catholic priest."

Mark spoke slowly. "You're right. When I made my decision to become a priest my family was very proud. My mother even called her family back in Italy to tell them. Everyone celebrated! So, you can imagine the devastation when I changed my mind."

Tye held her fork in midair. "What made you change your mind and join the Church?"

"I was studying to be a priest when I met the elders."

"That must be some conversion story."

Mark shrugged. "I guess I don't see it as all that remarkable because it happened to me. I hadn't been in the seminary very long when I saw these two young men riding bikes in the middle of a snowy January day. I wondered what would compel them to ride a bike in such bad weather. They stopped at the corner where I was standing, so I asked them." He grinned. "That was my first mistake." Then he continued, "I had heard about Mormons, but I didn't know that much about them. I decided that if I was going to be a Catholic priest, I needed to know about other religions and other people. They gave me a Book of Mormon, and I took it—mostly out of curiosity since I had only been exposed to Catholicism."

"What did your teachers say?"

"I never told them. After I had read the book and had met with the missionaries a couple of times, I decided that I couldn't be a priest. It wasn't that I knew that the LDS church was true. I just wasn't sure about my own beliefs. I felt the need to get away from the seminary for a short time in order to figure everything out. I told the priest who was in charge of my education that I needed to go home for a while. He referred me to the bishop who was in charge of the seminary. Both of them really put me to the test. They asked all kinds of questions. When I told him I had been exploring the LDS faith, I was threatened with ex-communication." Mark continued more slowly. "I told him that I didn't know if the LDS faith was true, but what was more important to me at the time was the need I felt to explore my own roots in Catholicism before I could become a priest. The bishop informed my parish priest back home, and when I arrived back in Seattle, we spoke at length over a long period of time. He taught me a great deal, but there were some questions he couldn't answer. That bothered me. I didn't understand why nineteen- and twenty-year-old young men could answer my questions satisfactorily, but my priest could only tell me that I would have to wait to have certain things explained to me." Mark paused. "Now I understand that there are some things that can only be taught by a loving Heavenly Father, but I also believe that we have access to many answers here on earth. I've always believed that. So did the missionaries. And a lot of those answers are made clear in the Book of Mormon. One thing that really impressed me was the way the Book of Mormon explains the Fall of Adam. It made the connection between the fall and the atonement so clear. It allowed me to view the fall as a necessary thing that precipitated the progress of man." His eyes shone with enthusiasm. "That's just one example."

Then his voice grew quiet. "My parents didn't understand any of this. They were simply concerned for my soul. They still are. They're sure if I die before I come back to the Catholic faith I'll wander the dregs of purgatory for eternity. It's a huge worry for them."

Meggie nodded slowly. "Yes, of course it would be." She paused. "Did you ever go back to the seminary to explain?"

"No. Once I got home and started working with my parish priest, I didn't see any need. He kept them informed of all our meetings, and he told let them know that I was continuing to meet with the LDS missionaries." Mark furrowed his brow. "I went through several sets of elders during an eighteen-month period, but it wasn't wasted time."

"My interest in cooking also grew during that time. Seattle is known for some of the greatest restaurants in the nation. There's this wonderful coming together of different foods from Asia and the Northwest. I love the availability of fresh seafood and produce, and the Pacific Northwest coast offers so much fresh variety. We have access to everything from fresh Hawaiian Ahi flown in from the islands to Columbia River sturgeon, not to mention a variety of fresh shellfish along with local and Alaskan salmon."

Meggie laughed. "I know! I feel the same way about Oregon. The summers are full of local fruits and vegetables which you can buy at any roadside stand. Blackberries are wild. And you're right about the seafood. It's the best! So, did you go to work in a restaurant as a cook?"

Mark laughed. "No. This is very unglamourous, but I started out as a dishwasher. I was busy, but I would watch the chefs put together these incredible masterpieces, and I decided that I wanted to do that. Gradually, within that eighteen-month period, I worked up to line cook."

"Did you live at home during those eighteen months?"

Mark nodded. "I wasn't allowed to have the missionary discussions at home though. I always met the elders at the church."

"What did your parents say when you decided to serve a mission yourself?" Meg asked.

Mark leaned back in his seat. "They didn't like that idea one bit. It was very difficult because it fed into their concept of a cult. They felt the Church was taking me away, and that I would never come back. I tried to explain that I would only be gone for two years, but they thought that the Church was lying about that. They were afraid that once I left home, I would be gone forever. My mother was beside herself. I also think there was some shame for them associated with my mission. Like I mentioned, the whole family had made a big deal about my decision to become a Catholic priest, and they were very proud of that. Then I become a Mormon missionary. That was a difficult thing for them to explain—especially to our Italian relations. And no one was interested in my explanations." Mark paused. "I hardly heard from my family while on my mission. It was the closest I ever felt to being orphaned. They never sent me any letters or care packages. That was hard because my companions were always getting letters and boxes from family members while I never received anything. Christmas was the worst. I would call, and no one would answer the phone. I would leave messages on the machine wishing them a merry Christmas and telling them how much I loved them. I knew they were home, because my family never goes anywhere on Christmas day. It hurt that they didn't want to talk to me. I just tried to be kind in those messages. Then on my last Mother's Day in the mission field, my mother answered the phone. We both cried. We talked for a long time. She actually started to believe I was coming home. After that I knew they were beginning to accept my decision."

"Oh Mark. That must have been very difficult," Tye sympathized.

"It was. I tried hard to understand, but it took a long time for all of us to feel better."

"Did they meet you at the airport when you came home?" Tye asked.

Mark nodded. "I was surprised to see them there. But the whole family showed up—even my married brothers and their wives flew in from back east. It was a great reunion; all of this Italian hugging and kissing. I think that's when they realized that I hadn't joined a cult, and that my two-year mission was not a lifetime sentence in some obscure religion. I also think they began to respect my decisions and start to accept that I was LDS. I truly began to feel like we were family once again." He paused and grinned. "Hence my late start in school. I spent some time in the seminary before my mission.

I didn't start at BYU until I had finished my mission at twenty-four. I'm twenty-seven now."

Meggie asked, "Have they accepted your decision to become a chef?"

"Yeah. Now that they've accepted the fact that I'm not going to be a priest, they're happy with the decision I've made to become a chef. When I come home my mother hurries me into the kitchen so I can show her what I've learned. We talk pasta, and Marinara sauce, and clams. She loves it. Cooking has really brought us closer together. It gives us something to talk about when we can't talk about the Church."

"Do your folks know about temples? You had to receive your endowments before your mission. How do they feel about those ordinances?" Tye asked.

"We've talked a little bit about the temple but only in broad strokes. I tell them I've made certain promises to the Lord. They accept that. We haven't talked a lot about temple marriages though. They know about temples, and they know that's where I'll be getting married. I've explained that only church members in good standing can be admitted, but we've never discussed it in personal terms." He became thoughtful. "I expect it will be hard for them. Catholics are known for their huge, wonderful church weddings. My brother married a good Catholic girl from a solid Bostonian Catholic family. They held a full mass during the ceremony. The wedding took two years to plan. I was the best-man. It was an incredible affair."

"Was it hard for you? I mean, there are all these traditions that go back generations in your family. Latter-day Saint weddings are kind of low-key in the world of weddings. You've grown up expecting one thing. Now you have to adopt a whole new set of expectations," Meg said.

"My brother's wedding wasn't hard. It was actually nice to steep myself in the traditions of my family and their church. It's all so familiar to me. I enjoyed it. When it comes to my own wedding though, I don't want the same thing. I see a temple marriage as the highest expression of love for God and love for a chosen mate. I worry more for my family. I'm hoping they will be able to trust me enough to make the proper decision for myself and not get all caught up in what they expect or want. I think it will be harder for them because they don't understand the LDS perspective on weddings." Mark paused. "I try not to worry about it too much anyway. I don't plan on getting married for a while."

Meg cocked her head to one side. "Why not?"

"I've gotten used to the idea of being alone. I decided at the age of seventeen that I wanted to be priest. After that I abandoned all ideas of marriage. Even though things are different now, I'm not in any great hurry."

"You're one of the few," Tye said wryly. "Everyone around here sports an engagement ring."

"I thought your roommate gave hers back."

"Oh, they made up this week," Tye said. "The wedding is back on. But she's upstairs crying into the phone as we speak. KayLee isn't very happy. She was hoping that Dianna would remain single."

"They decided on a compromise," Meggie said. "His mother gets the reception she wanted. Dianna gets the bridesmaid dresses she wants." Meggie paused. "He was over here, pounding on the door at one o'clock in the morning the other night. He scared us all to death. We wouldn't let him in the house. Dianna stepped out onto the porch. I guess he begged her to come back. He said he was sorry for his temper. She took the ring back. I don't know what she's crying about now."

"It's scary, really," Tye said. "I don't want to get married if that's what I have to deal with on a regular basis. Just watching Dianna and Doug go at each other makes me tired."

"I don't think it has to be that way," Mark said.

"I hope not. When Kyle and I …" Tye sucked in her breath. Unbidden tears surfaced. Tye hurriedly brushed them away. "I—um. I think I … um—Excuse me." Tye got up from the table and walked through the kitchen into the bathroom. Quietly, she shut the door before taking several deep breaths. She hadn't meant to bring Kyle to the dinner table, but there he was, right below the surface of any conversation. She closed her eyes and tried to tap into the stillness of the house. She could hear murmuring voices, and then the front door shut.

Her eyes flew open, and she hurried out into the dining room to find Meggie clearing the dishes. "Mark didn't have to go. I just need some time …"

Meg placed the dishes in the sink. "It's okay, Tye. Take your time. Mark just left for a few minutes. He's going to bring over some strawberries and cream along with a crepe pan. We're going to make some crepes. You will join us, won't you?"

"The flood of emotion that rushes through me every time I think of Kyle always surprises me," she said. "I never expect it."

"I'm sorry, Tye. I wish there was something I could do."

"You're doing it. You've helped just by being here. You and Mark both have helped. I've really enjoyed this evening. It's been fun."

Several minutes later, Mark returned with beautiful strawberries, a pint of cream, and a crepe pan. He didn't mention Tye's earlier departure.

Meggie picked up one of the berries. "These are gorgeous. Where did you get them?"

"A produce market out in Payson. I don't know how much longer they're going to be selling though." He showed her the tag. "They're from California, and I think the fall berry crops are about finished. The market was already selling pumpkins by the truck-load."

Meggie stirred the crepe batter while Tye sliced berries. Mark began whipping the cream. Soon, all the ingredients were ready. Meggie turned on the gas burner before moving out of the way so Mark could use his crepe pan.

"Do you have any plans after graduation?" Meggie asked as she watched Mark swirl butter in the pan.

"I hope to go back to Seattle for starters, but I doubt I'll stay. There are great restaurants and chefs on every street corner in that city. It's very hard to stay in business. I just want the experience. Then I'm not sure where I'll go, or what I'll do. I may move to a resort along the coast. It all depends on what opens up to me. Right now, I'm working on some pasta sauces I'd like to perfect. I don't think much past that."

"Can you tell me about them or are they trade secrets?"

"I keep the recipes under strict lock and key." Mark pointed to his head. "But I'll give you the basic idea. My favorite sauce includes butter, cream, capers and lemon, and a touch of white pepper. It's perfect for shrimp. It's lighter than Alfredo, because it doesn't have any cheese in it. The lemon compliments the heavier dairy products and brings out the flavor of the shrimp."

Meggie's eyes widened. "That sounds delightful."

"It is good, but I'm still working on it. What are your plans after graduation?"

Meggie shrugged. "I haven't decided yet. Sometimes I think I'd like to work in or own a small inn, but I feel I need more experience in business." Meg told Mark about her summer job at Farmer's Bed and Breakfast. "It started out because their main breakfast cook went on maternity leave. Then, after she had the baby she didn't want to work as much. So, every summer I take over, and she gets to spend the summer with her little girl."

"That sounds like a nice arrangement."

"It works out for everyone. But I'll be graduating this June, so I'll need something more permanent."

"What about you, Tye?" Mark asked. "You're the non-cook in this equation."

"I hope to finish my degree in animal science and then either own a barn or work in one where I teach horseback riding lessons."

"You teach now. You don't need a degree for that."

"No, but I want a degree. For some reason that little piece of paper means a lot to me. I'll be the first in my family to graduate from college."

Mark flipped the crepes onto a plate. Tye filled them with berries. Meggie piped whipped cream onto the dessert before folding them. For a finishing touch she sprinkled the crepes with powdered sugar and shaved chocolate.

"A work of art," Mark exclaimed as they carried their plates to the table.

Once seated, Mark said, "Hey, I've got an idea! Why don't we all go skiing on opening day?"

"No thanks," Tye said. "I don't ski. I ride horses, remember? One expensive hobby is enough for me."

"I'd love to go," Meggie said. "I even brought my skis, hoping I'd get the chance at least once during the fall semester."

"Thanksgiving is the usual opening weekend around here. Maybe we could go up that Friday. I know that's still several weeks away, but it's never too late to plan. Are you girls going home for the holiday?"

Meggie shook their head. "No. The drive is sixteen hours. If the weather turns nasty it can be hard to get back. But if we go skiing, nasty weather would be perfect," Meggie said. "I sure hope the snow cooperates."

"Me too," Mark replied. "But let's not wait until the snow starts to fly to go out. What other things do you like to do?"

"The movies are real cheap," Tye replied. "And we could go hiking in the canyons. The trees are mostly bare but the days are still clear." She thought for a moment. "I haven't been to the temple since I've been here. Maybe we could do a session."

"Meggie can't come though," Mark said.

"No, but if the weather is decent, I'll wait for you outside," Meggie said. "Maybe we could go up to Salt Lake Temple. While the two of you are in a session, I could spend some time in the visitor's center. I've never been there."

"How does next Friday afternoon sound?" Mark asked.

Both girls agreed. "I have to go to work Saturday mornings though, so we can't be out too late," Meggie said.

Tye and Mark agreed as they began to enjoy their strawberry crepes.

Chapter Seven

*T*ye waved to Celia Brannon as she passed the woman's car. She didn't look up from her book. Tye could hear the radio blaring.

Walking into the cool of the barn she found Trista in the tack room, picking out Patches' bridle. Tye liked the young girl. She was a self-starter who was willing to work hard. She wished her mother would show more interest in Trista's riding. Not everyone liked horses but Celia should be able to put that aside for a few minutes each week while her daughter rode.

"Finding everything okay?" Tye asked.

"Yes, Miss Jorgenson. I've already taken the saddle out along with the bucket of grooming supplies. I didn't think I should get Patches out of his stall without a grown-up around though."

"Good thinking, Trista. Safety always comes first."

"I wish my mom could be a grown-up."

"I'm sorry, Trista. It would be nice if your mother could come and watch you ride."

Trista removed Patches' bridle from the peg. "She says this

horsy thing is just a phase. She thinks that just because my dad left I need to be a tomboy now. She forgets that I was begging for a horse long before Daddy ever left. Daddy tells me I used to ride when I was little, but I don't remember." Trista placed the bridle on her arm as she walked out of the tack room.

"How long has your father been gone?" Tye asked.

"I don't know. He left a while ago."

"Do you ever see him?"

Trista shrugged. "Sometimes. He visited a little while ago but that was before you were my teacher. He came to watch me ride. I don't get to see him very often though. He lives in Colorado. I used to live in Colorado."

Trista picked up Patches' lead rope and halter. Tye followed her into the horse's stall and watched as she haltered the pony and led him out into the crossties.

"Do you have a horse, Miss Jorgenson?"

"Yes, I do. His name is Trapper, and he lives back in Oregon."

"Do you miss him?"

Tye thought of Trapper. "Yeah, I miss him a lot."

"I miss my daddy too," Trista said. "Mom says that Daddy wants me to go and live with him in Colorado, but that won't happen unless it's over her dead body."

"I see. It sounds like your mom and dad are mad at each other."

"They've always been mad at each other," Trista sighed. "I miss my daddy though."

"I'm sure you do, honey."

Trista brushed Patches in silence and then prepared the pony to be ridden.

Once they were in the arena, Trista checked the girth before mounting. Tye was proud of the progress her student was making.

"Do you think that someday I'll be able to ride outside in the open fields?" Trista asked.

"Would you like that?" Tye asked.

"Oh yes!" Trista exclaimed.

"Let's work toward that goal, Triss. If you make good progress maybe you'll be ready for outdoor lessons by next spring. Wouldn't that be fun?"

Trista nodded enthusiastically. "I would love to have my lessons outside. Can I, Miss Jorgenson?"

"We'll see, Triss. I hope so."

〜

The following Monday, Tye sat in her favorite class; Livestock Physiology and Anatomy. She already knew a lot about horses, but in this class she was able to learn about cows, sheep, and goats. It would provide her with an overview of all livestock and barnyard animals. When Tye had received the textbook, she had excitedly thumbed through it to find she would also be studying chickens and geese.

Even though this was Tye's favorite class, there was something better coming next semester. Livestock Physiology and Anatomy was the prerequisite for the class that she yearned to take; Livestock Reproduction. Next semester, she and a partner would be responsible for a pregnant animal. She hoped she would be able to care for a mare. She loved pregnant mares with their big round bellies and quiet dignity.

She thought back to the day she had helped Jade give birth to her new filly, Gypsy. It had been the moment that had brought her and Kyle together. It created a bond that had lasted through a rocky school semester at OSU and a mission.

Tye pushed the thought away. That bond was broken now. Nothing could change that.

Looking out over her class, Tye hoped she would be partnered with a woman but her chances were slim. There were only four other women in her class. Still, Tye wasn't sure she wanted to share another bonding experience with a man.

As if reading her mind, the professor stood and told the class that they were going to announce the partnerships for next semester's Livestock Reproduction class. He wanted to give people the opportunity to work out any scheduling problems before the winter semester started.

"Those who will not be taking Livestock Reproduction next semester, can you please raise your hands?" The professor asked.

Two hands went up. They were both women.

Tye's heart groaned. That left three women in a classroom of ten men. Within a minute, the professor paired up the other two women, leaving Tye with a man named Preston Taylor. The professor then asked that the partnerships sit together so they could introduce themselves to each other. There was a general buzz in the classroom as people moved from their seats.

Then Tye received her second disappointment of the day when Professor Gates handed Tye and her partner a slip of paper with black ink. It read: Bovine. Number: 8217. Due Date: March 10. Tye and Preston would be taking care of a cow that was expected to give birth in March. They weren't responsible for her care this semester. That was being taken care of by another partnership who was caring for her during her gestation period. However, Tye and Preston were welcome to visit Bovine Number 8217 anytime.

"Well, I guess that answers all the questions," Tye said.

Preston nodded.

Tye studied the man sitting next to her. His eyes were a startling crystal blue, and his hair was streaked with strands of blond that spoke of many hours in the sun. His face was weathered with fine wrinkles that appeared around the edges of his eyes. Laugh lines some would call them. Tye saw them as squint lines that came from working in the summer sun and harsh winter wind. It was hard to guess his age.

"What do you know about cows?" Tye asked.

"I know quite a bit about cows. I was born and raised on a ranch around Missoula, Montana."

Tye was surprised at his soft and gentle voice. It was his most pleasant feature. She wanted to hear more from him. When he spoke it was as if the noise of the crowd dropped away.

"Then you must know quite a lot about pregnant cows. Have you birthed many calves?"

"Yeah. When I'm at home I help with the calving season every year. How about you?"

Tye shook her head. "No. I've never worked with cows before, but I've helped with mares."

"There are the obvious differences, but most of the time they can take care of it themselves. It's only when there's trouble that a person will interfere."

The class settled, and Professor Gates began his lecture. Tye concentrated on the lecture taking studious notes.

Then as the class ended, Preston stood. "I know you would prefer a woman as your partner."

"How could you tell?" Tye asked, startled at the revelation.

"I saw the look on your face when two of the women dropped out." He continued, "I won't bother you though. We won't even have to start working together until next semester. Then we'll be meeting in class about twice a week for lectures. The lab will be up to us though. We can look in on Number 8217 separately."

"I prefer to give our cow a name," Tye said.

Preston raised his eyebrows.

"What?" Tye asked. "Didn't you ever name your cows at home?"

"We never named the beef cows," Preston replied. "But I did name the milk cows."

"Well, number 8217 is a milk cow. Don't you think she should have a name?"

Preston sat down on his desk. "Sure. Why don't you take a look at her when you get a minute? Then we can decide what we'll call her."

Preston didn't seem so bad. He appeared quiet and gentle in his speech and mannerisms. He certainly was observant. "I'm sorry about my earlier misgivings," Tye said. "I didn't realize I was so easy to read."

"It's okay," he said. "I can understand."

Tye wondered how he could ever understand her desire to stay away from men who helped birth animals. It was all too close for Tye; too personal and meaningful. She and Kyle had helped bring Jade's little filly, Gypsy, into the world. The memory of that morning was as vivid as her present conversation with Preston. Then before Tye could reply, Preston moved away from his desk, and with a wave he walked out of the room.

Chapter Eight

Preston slipped into the pregnant Holstein's stall. He liked cows. People always complained about the smell, but it never bothered Preston. He had smelled the many pungent odors of cows since birth. In some ways being here with number 8217 was familiar and comfortable. He liked her warm, wide body. It reminded him of working at home.

The birth of Number 8217's calf would not be new to him. He had watched several family cows drop their young. In spite of the lack of sleep and messy circumstances, he loved the experience of bringing new life into the world. It satisfied something deep within his soul that defied explanation.

Some of his earliest memories were of helping his favorite house cat give birth to her first batch of kittens. He had watched her for weeks before the birth as she searched out the right den. Then, when she had chosen the corner behind the dresser, he filled a box with shredded newspaper and rags. Muffin had visited the box several times and seemed to understand and accept Preston's help. Then the magical day arrived, and Preston woke up one morning to find Muffin contently nursing five new kittens. He was sorry he had missed the birth, but pleased that she had chosen to use the box he had prepared. After the birth, he tended Muffin; always making sure she had enough water by her bed and watching the kittens when she needed out. The whole experience had left him a reverenced awe for the process of a mother bringing forth her young.

Moving closer to Number 8217, he whispered softly as he gave her a quick pat. It was getting late, and he needed to get busy on his homework. He was about to open the stall door when he noticed Tye. Her presence surprised him. "Oh, Tye. I didn't hear you."

"You looked occupied. I didn't want to interrupt."

Preston scratched the cow between the ears. "She likes company."

Tye opened the stall door to let herself in. "How is she looking?" Tye approached the cow, giving her a soft pat on the shoulder.

"She's in fine shape. I don't see any reason why she won't give birth to a perfectly healthy calf." He scratched her again. "She likes to be scratched behind the ears."

Tye smiled at Preston. "Does she?" Turning back to the cow Tye moved her hands over 8217's body before getting down on her knees. "She's not swollen yet."

"It'll be a while before we start to see some changes in her."

Tye stood and faced him. "How long, do you think?"

Preston shrugged. "Months. She won't show any changes until next semester."

"I'm glad you know what you're doing," Tye said. "I'm very comfortable around horses, but all I know about cows comes from books and study notes."

"When I lived at home the milk cows were always my responsibility. They always meant more to me than the beef cows out in the field."

"Did you have to milk them?"

Preston smiled. "Every morning including Christmas."

"What do you think we should name number 8217?" Tye asked.

"I'll leave that to you," Preston replied. "I get to name the milk cows at home."

Tye thought for a moment. "How about Elsa?"

Preston agreed. "I have a milk cow at home named Elsa."

"Do you like her?"

"She's my favorite cow. She's an old gal by now, but she still gives plenty of milk."

Tye was brimming with more questions about ranch life but didn't feel like she should probe any more. She didn't want to do anything that would disrupt the comfortable feeling between them. Preston appeared to be relaxed here in the barn compared to his demeanor in class. Thinking on her class, Tye realized that Preston was always there, but he never called any attention to himself. Throughout the lectures he remained attentive and studious. When it came to the other students, however, he seemed aloof. Stroking Elsa's neck, Tye gave the cow her attention. "Maybe you could show me what to expect about the time of delivery."

Preston moved closer to Elsa. "Well, she'll just get bigger and wider at first. But that will probably be the only outward change until a day or two before delivery. The breeding date is June 10th. That means that she should deliver around the beginning of March. Then when her time comes she'll bag up, and her udder will look very uncomfortable. The calf will drop down, and the pelvis will begin to spread. You won't be able to miss that."

"The first week of March," Tye said softly. "That seems like so far off." She turned to Preston. "Doesn't it?"

"Well, it's almost Thanksgiving now, so it'll be about four

months." He went to the door of the stall and picked up the chart that hung on a nail. "This is her feed chart. We won't have to pay that much attention to it until next semester, but you may want to look it over."

Tye studied the writings of the feeding crew. It told her what type of food Elsa was getting, as well as how much she was eating. A small thrill pulsed through Tye. New life. She looked at Preston. "Isn't it exciting?"

"It is. No matter how many times I'm involved in this sort of thing it's always new to me."

"I've watched a lot of foals being born. I've even helped a time or two, but I've never been involved with a cow." Tye was suddenly glad that she was caring for a bovine instead of a horse. She would enjoy the new experience. "The variety is kind of nice," she said.

"So you're more involved with horses?"

"Yes. That's one reason I decided on animal science as my major. I'd like to run my own barn someday."

Preston leaned up against Elsa. "When I go out on the range with my dad I take care of the horses. I started doing that because I was young, and it was a good way to learn the basics of range work. Even after I got the hang of the routine I liked it so much that I continued."

"So you must ride a lot then."

"Yeah. When we're on the range we're in the saddle all the time."

"What do you do here to keep in riding shape? Aren't you afraid of going home and being rusty?"

Preston shook his head. "No. I ride here every two or three weeks. It's not the same but my horse back home, Mayday, is a good mount. She'll take care of me my first couple of days back." He opened the stall door, allowing Tye to move in front of him. She returned the feeding chart. They began the walk to their cars.

"Would you like me to save you a seat in class?" Tye asked.

"That would be nice. Thank you. I'm coming from PE, and sometimes it's hard for me to get there."

As he opened the barn door Tye studied her partner. He wasn't very big, but his body was lean and solid. It was obvious that he was used to hard work.

Once outside Tye sucked in her breath as the wind bit at her nose and fingers. It was as if the chill of winter had crept into the valley overnight. The sun still shone brilliantly, but the light had lost its summer yellow and autumn gold. Now it was white and harsh. A thin layer of clouds began to move across the sky, obscuring the sun. A chill settled over Tye.

"It'll snow soon," Preston said as he squinted up at the sky.

Tye looked at him. "Are you sure?" She shivered elaborately. "I'm still not used to this cold, dry wind."

"Where are you from?"

"Western Oregon. It gets cold there, but not like this." Tye pulled at her jacket as she stepped inside her truck.

"Well, I won't keep you out in the cold," Preston said.

"I'm glad we met out here," Tye replied.

"Me too," Preston said. Then he shut the door to her truck before waving her out of the parking lot.

Tye drove home slowly, her mind on Preston. He seemed so relaxed and confident around the barn. It was obvious that he was in his element when surrounded by animals. Tye enjoyed that quality in him. It spoke of his poise in working with animals that outweighed him by hundreds of pounds. Many men never gained that quiet self-assurance and ended up trying to strong arm or rough up an animal in order to prove their dominance. Tye had witnessed that behavior many times in the horse shows she attended. She despised men who felt the need to bully animals. She preferred to work from a firm foundation of knowledge. Through understanding an animal's behavior, she had a better chance of making that behavior work for her. She wondered if Preston felt the same way.

Tye put the truck in fifth gear. It was lucky for her that she had a partner that was so well-versed in cows. It made her wonder. What was he doing in school? He obviously knew a lot about animals. She decided to ask him that the next time they met.

As she pulled onto her street she immediately began to look for a parking place. Finding one not far from her house, she quickly claimed it and stepped out of the truck. The wind continued to bite. Tye tugged at her scarf as she looked up at the sky. The thin layer of clouds that had moved in from the northwest was beginning to thicken. These weren't the dark thunderheads Tye remembered from the dry summer storms. These clouds were a solid mass of white-gray that covered the sky as they lowered themselves over the valley, obscuring the mountains that had become so familiar to Tye. Tye shivered and scowled. The clouds had brought with them a bitter wind, and it was obvious by their descent over the peaks that they were going to stay awhile instead of rumbling on as their darker summer cousins had done. She stood for a moment and watched as the mountains disappeared behind a curtain of white. She had to bite the curse that came to her tongue. She loved the mountains. Now winter would take them away. It would obscure them in one storm after another, making it difficult for her to find solace and comfort in their lofty peaks. She would hate winter for that.

Tye walked down the sidewalk, pulling her jacket close. As she turned toward her house, the first snowflakes of the season brushed against her shoulders.

Chapter Nine

Mark sat behind the steering wheel and guided the car onto the northern bound lanes of I-15. A fresh layer of snow covered the ground but the roads were simply wet. In spite of the intermittent snow that had fallen during the week, the morning dawned bright and sunny.

"This snow is a good sign," Mark called to Meggie, who was sitting in the back seat. "I think we're going to make our opening day!"

Meggie shared his excitement. "Oh, hey when we get home, can I borrow some ski wax?"

"Sure," Mark replied.

Tye punched him lightly in the shoulder from the passenger side of the car. "You should be paying attention to the road."

"The road has my full attention. By the way, Tye, why don't you come with us? I know you don't know how to ski, but you can just hang around at Sundance Lodge. It's really rustic and comfortable."

Tye shook her head. "No. Thanks anyway."

"She'd rather spend her Saturday in a barn full of cows and horses," Meggie teased.

"That's absolutely right!" Tye replied.

Forty-five minutes later, the threesome arrived in downtown Salt Lake City. Mark found a parking place within walking distance of Temple Square. When they arrived, they were immediately greeted by two sister missionaries who offered them a tour of the grounds. They accepted the invitation.

As they walked around the beautiful grounds, Tye whispered in Mark's ear. "I wonder what it would be like to serve a mission here. Wouldn't it be wonderful to be in the shadow of the temple all of the time?"

Mark agreed.

After their temple session was finished, Tye met Meggie. While both girls waited for Mark, a wedding couple emerged from the temple.

Tye watched the couple. They beamed with love and hope. They seemed completely unaffected by the cold winter day. The cold seeped through Tye's jacket. She sighed and then turned to Meggie. "If I did the right thing by giving Kyle up, why does it hurt so much?" she asked.

Meggie pointed to the young couple, who were now posing for pictures. "Kyle wasn't going to give you this, was he? He wouldn't give you eternity. He was only willing to give you his time on this earth."

Tye brushed away bitter tears. "No."

"Look around you, Tye. Think of where you are. Look at them."

Tye shook her head. It was too hard.

"Look at them," Meggie insisted.

Tye turned toward the couple.

Meggie's voice became soft. "Sometimes we have to sacrifice something or someone we really love for something of a higher understanding. You did that when you walked away from Kyle."

Tye brushed away her tears as she watched the young couple. She was grateful when Mark emerged from the temple. "There's Mark," Tye said as she wiped her eyes. They hurried to meet him.

Once they caught up to him, Mark stopped to look at the young couple, who were now moving to another part of the grounds. "Don't they look happy?"

Tye bit her lip and kept quiet for fear the tears that would catch in her voice. Instead, she simply nodded before turning away and walking towards the car.

Mark turned to Meggie, who whispered, "It's a long story, and it didn't end that long ago."

"Well," Mark said as he and Meggie caught up with Tye. "I'm starved. How about you girls?"

"Famished," Meggie replied.

"C'mon, Tye, let's feed Meggie." Mark put his arm around her shoulder.

Suddenly, the tears came at a rapid pace. Tye could no longer hold on to them. She didn't want to cry. She wanted to say something sarcastic and witty, but only the tears came, unbidden and unwelcome. Quickly, she wiped them away, but more took their place. Oh, how she missed Kyle in this cold place. She longed for their summer of warm comfort and love. She missed his gentle spirit and the loving familiarity that had bonded them. In this place of snow and chill, Tye had no place of reference. Kyle did not exist here. They had never shared this place. She looked at the temple; the spires reached up into a deep cold blue sky. The gray solid rock of the temple was immovable and firm in its glory to God. Tye had just spent the last few hours within its walls that were filled with love and a deeper familiarity. Oh, how she had wanted to share that place with Kyle. But she could not hinge her hopes on some obscure promise he made about an uncertain future. Why couldn't he understand that?

Still, when Tye thought of her morning session, something settled inside of her. She had glanced at Mark a couple of times and had been grateful for his companionship during their ordinances. Working within the walls of the temple had brought a new stillness to Tye's soul. It calmed her and allowed her to exhale. In the temple she felt as if her summer chase of storms was over. Here, she could drink, and there was plenty.

Mark stopped. "Are you okay, Tye?" he asked.

Tye closed her eyes and shut out the cold.

Mark gently enfolded her in an embrace, and Tye willingly went to him. She breathed in the scent of basil and olive oil. It was comforting. Hugging Mark was like hugging Meggie. But not quite. She pulled away. "I'm sorry," Tye muffled out.

"It's okay," Mark whispered. People were staring at the threesome, but Mark didn't care. Tye wiped her eyes.

Mark reached for his handkerchief and gave it to Tye.

"Oh, Mark, I got make-up and mascara all over your white shirt." Fresh tears came to the surface as she tried to brush off the make-up, only smearing it. "I'm so sorry."

"Don't worry, Tye. It's not a tragedy. In fact, I'll never wash it again, okay? I mean, it's not every day someone cries on me. I feel honored." He smiled.

Tye smiled through her tears. "You would've made a good Catholic priest," Tye said. "And I'm grateful you chose another field of work."

Mark put his arm around her. "Me too. C'mon, let's eat. How does Italian sound?"

Meggie fell into step. Soon they were looking for a restaurant.

Chapter Ten

"I can't find my sweater!" Meggie exclaimed as she pulled out clothes from the drawer. "I need that sweater."

Tye got up from her bed and began sorting through the clothes in the laundry basket. "Is this the one you want?" she asked, holding the sweater at arms length.

"Yes!" Meggie snatched the sweater. "Now where are my jeans?"

Tye dug deeper in the basket and pulled out the jeans. "Thanks, Tye," Meggie said gratefully.

"Why are you so nervous, Meg? You're acting like this is your first date in your whole entire life?"

"I don't know. It is my first date since moving here."

"What about Mark?"

"That's not a date. Mark is a friend. I don't care for him in that way."

"I hope you told him in kinder words."

"I don't have to tell him. It's just the way things are. He knows it. I know it. Besides, I was with Mark when I met Joel. He's from southern Utah, and he's so cute!" Meggie giggled.

"What did Mark say?"

Meggie made a face. "He teased me all the way home."

"Sounds like Mark." Tye paused. "You're forgetting one thing, Meg. We were all supposed to go out together tonight. Remember?"

"Oh, yeah. I did forget. Mark didn't say anything at the book-store."

"Maybe he didn't want to get in between you and Joel. I still can't believe that this guy named Joel would even approach you for a date when you were with Mark. Don't you think that's tacky? I mean maybe you and Mark are an item. How would he know any different?"

Meggie put her sweater on over her head. "No. It's obvious Mark and I are simply friends. We don't walk around hanging on each other, and we don't give out those love vibes."

Tye laughed. "Love vibes. What the heck is a love vibe?"

Meggie went to the mirror and ran a brush through her brown shoulder length hair. The curls danced. "Oh, you know. You see couples walking around campus giving out these love vibes. I'm surprised they don't run into walls since they never look where they're going. They're too busy looking at each other. Mark laughs and points them out to me all the time. He's the one who made it up. In fact right before we made it to the bookstore, we were trying to spot couples who were caught up in those love vibes." She changed the subject. "Look, would it be okay if I cancelled out this time? You and Mark can go. He already knows I won't be there tonight."

"Okay. I wouldn't want to get in the way of any love vibes."

Meggie broke out into a grin. "Neither would I."

Both girls heard the doorbell ring. "That's probably him,"

Meggie said in a hushed tone. "Why don't you come down and meet him?"

"Are you sure?" Tye asked.

"Of course I'm sure. C'mon."

Tye followed Meggie to the door.

"Hi Joel," Meggie smiled.

"Hi. You look great."

"Thanks." Meggie moved to one side, making the introduction between Tye and Joel.

They smiled and shook hands. Tye looked him over quickly. His thick brown hair had some curl to it and his green eyes shone in the porch light. He looked warm in a pair of jeans and a forest green parka that gathered at the waist before falling at mid-thigh. The green parka set off his eyes nicely. Joel was a man who was nicely put together.

Joel spoke first, "Would you like to come along, Tye?"

"It's nice of you to ask, but I have plans. Thanks anyway."

"You're sure?"

Tye nodded. Then she looked at Meggie. "I doubt Mark would be very happy if we both deserted him."

"Mark?" Joel asked.

"I was with Mark in the bookstore when we met the other day. The three of us were supposed to go out tonight," Meggie replied.

"Oh, right," Joel said. "Are you ready to go, Meg?"

A twinge of irritation pulsed in Tye. Joel sure seemed willing to dismiss Mark in a hurry.

Meggie began walking down the steps. "I'll see you later," she said as Joel escorted her down the walk.

It wasn't long before Mark came to pick Tye up. Once they were settled into a comfortable pace Mark broke the silence. "Did Meggie go out on her date?"

Tye nodded. "I met him. He seems like a nice guy."

"I sure don't understand why all of a sudden she's dating. And why couldn't she go out with this Joel guy tomorrow night? We had plans."

"If it bothered you why didn't you say something?"

"I don't know, I guess I should have. I mean I know she can't read my mind. I guess I just would've liked for her to choose us instead of him. Besides, I think it's pretty brassy of him to ask her out in front of me, don't you?"

Tye stopped, facing Mark. "Well, yes, I do," she admitted. "I said that very thing to Meggie tonight, but she told me that the two of you don't give off any love vibes when you're together."

"She told you about those love vibes?"

Tye grinned.

Mark laughed. "That was a fun afternoon. Meggie and I were walking around trying to decide which couples were in love, and which ones just thought they were in love." He became serious. "Then Joel appeared and ruined everything."

Tye looked at Mark. "Do you have romantic feelings for Meg?" she asked.

"Me? No. Gosh no," Mark said. "No love vibes for us. We're just friends. You know that Tye. I guess I feel things aren't complete without her. We're usually a threesome."

They fell into an awkward silence. Tye hadn't expected Mark to have so many opinions about who Meggie dated.

Later in the evening, after Tye had beaten Mark in a round of miniature golf, they were sitting in the Cougar Eat. The usual noise was escalating due to the several dances that were in full swing on campus. It made it difficult to talk so they ate in silence. Tye and Mark finished their fries and were about to leave for the quiet walk home, when Tye spotted Joel and Meg. She waved them over to the table she shared with Mark.

"Hey, Mark and Tye. What are you two doing tonight?" Meggie asked.

"Just finishing up," Mark said as he crumpled his paper dish.

"Do you want to join us?" Tye asked moving over.

Meggie was about to answer when Mark cut in, "I really need to study. Maybe some other time." He looked at Tye. "You can stay if you want."

She scooted out of her booth seat. "Oh no. I'm coming with you." She looked at Meg. "I'll see you when you get home."

"It won't be long," Meggie answered.

Tye glanced at Joel as she hurried to catch Mark. "Nice seeing you again."

Joel smiled and waved. "The pleasure's mine."

Tye placed her arm through Mark's, who was waiting at the end of the aisle. Once they were out of the building Tye turned to him. "Why did you take off like that?"

"I didn't mean to be rude. It's just that I really need to hit the books tonight. I forgot about my statistics test I have on Monday. I really hate statistics. I've been putting this off for a couple of weeks now. Do you think Meggie will be mad at me?"

"I wouldn't blame her if she was," Tye answered. "You were very abrupt."

Mark squeezed Tye's hand that she had placed in the crook of his arm. "I guess I'll just have to apologize."

Tye nodded in agreement. "I guess you will."

Mark was silent for a moment, then he blurted out, "It's just that I finally found a cooking buddy, and I don't want to lose her to the first guy who comes along with straight teeth and curly hair."

Tye looked at Mark. His teeth weren't straight, but his hair was. "Are you jealous?" Tye asked.

Mark huffed. "No. Not in the way you think. Like I said, she's my cooking buddy, and I like the way things work between us." He calmed down. "I just don't want someone horning in on our cooking time together. That's all."

The walk continued in the silence of a new snowstorm until they got to Tye's doorstep where Mark bade her goodnight. He didn't linger, and Tye didn't invite him to stay.

The house was quiet when Tye entered. KayLee was doubling with Doug and Dianna.

Tye went up to the bedroom and switched on the computer to check her e-mails. She still hoped for some word from Kyle. Sitting down, she scanned the list of waiting mail. Thelma was sending her weekly updates on Trapper. He was getting a lot of time off and spending it in the pasture. Thelma was working him three times a week so that he would still be somewhat fit when she came home for Christmas. Tye read with detached interest. She was grateful for Thelma's loving care, but she dare not feel too much for Trapper. Somehow those feelings were tangled up in her sorrow and hurt over Kyle.

Guilt washed over her. It wasn't Trapper's fault. Tye hit the reply button and dashed off a short note to Thelma, thanking her for the regular updates and her consistent, good care. Pushing the send button, Tye breathed a sigh of relief. At least she never had to worry about Trapper. He was in a weather tight stall, was fed the best, and got regular fresh air and exercise.

Tye turned off the computer and rose from the desk. She

walked to the window where she watched the falling snow. In the streetlight it swirled gracefully; like dancing ladies in white dresses who knew their steps and swayed to predestined music. They never ran into each other, instead, they moved together, in complete synchronization. She thought of Kyle; their relationship was nothing like the peaceful falling snow. They ran into each other all the time as they bumped off of each other's priorities. She still missed him though. She missed the connection they shared; the love for Trapper and Ben that had kept their love alive.

Turning away from the window, Tye settled into her flannel pajamas. She picked up her physiology and anatomy textbook, deciding she would study until Meggie got home. She heard KayLee and Dianna come home, giggling over their evening. Soon after that her eyes got tired. It wasn't long before the words on the page blurred. She put the book aside and closed her eyes. Memories of she and Trapper with Kyle and Ben rose up from behind her eyes. They attended local competitions almost every weekend, but that wasn't Tye's fondest memories. She loved the beach walks. The foamy white capped waves that pounded relentlessly on miles of sandy shore. Those memories were washed in the bright hues of sunshine and the rhythmatic sound of the ocean. Retreating into herself, Tye could almost go back and relive them; the warm horse underneath her and the warm man beside her. She could sense Trapper's easy gallop and after the run, hear Kyle's generous laughter and gentle conversation.

Other recollections began to crowd around her. Tye opened her eyes and stared at the cold, dancing snow flakes that were illuminated by the street lamp. Brushing tears from her eyes, she allowed the summer memory faded to a whisper of a dream. Rising from her bed, she went to the window. Watching the snow-covered walk, she saw Meggie and Joel. They were strolling slowly through the snow arm-in-arm. Tye's heart flinched. How often had she and Kyle walked arm-in-arm; rambling as if they had nothing but time together? Tye leaned against the window frame as the recollections began pulling her towards them. She resisted. In spite of the realness of Tye's memories, they truly were as unsubstantial as the snow; yet they would bury her if she allowed it.

Tye walked back to her bed and wiped away the tears as she cleared her throat. Even though she couldn't see the front porch from her window, she didn't want to appear to be spying. Several minutes later, Meggie walked through the bedroom door, smiling.

"You must have had a good time," Tye said.

"It was great!" Meg plopped down on her bed. "I had fun. We went bowling and had something to eat."

"You're not much of a bowler, Meg. In fact, I can remember when we went for our activities in the young women's program, you hated it."

Meggie giggled. "Joel doesn't bowl either, so it was humorous." She sighed. "But it was his company I enjoyed. He was pleasant and easy to talk to." She grinned. "And he skis. That's the best part."

"Mark skis," Tye replied.

"A girl can't have too many skiing partners," Meggie said.

"Are you going to see him again?" Tye asked.

Meggie nodded. "If he asks."

"Well, if the slow walk in the snow I witnessed is any indication, I'd bet real money he asks. I'm surprised the two of you aren't frozen statues."

Meggie walked to the window. Then she turned to Tye. "You should come with me sometime."

"Then it's not a date, Meggie. It's a group activity."

"No. We could make it a double date. I bet Joel has a friend."

Panic flooded Tye. "No, Meggie. I'm not ready for that yet."

"When do you think you'll be ready?" Meggie asked. "This semester is almost over, and you haven't even been on a real date. Don't you think you've sat in this bedroom long enough?"

"I don't sit in this bedroom. We went to the temple just last week. And earlier this week I went out to the barn—."

"Cows hardly count as dates," Meggie said.

"I met my cow partner, who happens to be a man. Then I went out with Mark this evening. Just because I got home before you doesn't mean I've been here all night."

"Did you and Mark have a good time?"

"Yeah, it was fun—until you and Joel showed up. Then Mark got a little testy."

Meg brushed off the incident. "Maybe he just felt awkward. If the circumstances had been reversed I'm sure that I would feel strange too."

"Why? If you're just friends, why would it matter?"

Meg shrugged. "I don't know. I've just never seen him with another girl. It would just feel weird."

"You've seen him with me," Tye said.

"Yeah, but that's different."

"Why?"

"I don't know. You and I are best friends. I don't worry about you messing up the cooking partnership between Mark and me."

"That's what he said."

"What do you mean?" Meggie asked.

"He said he didn't want Joel horning in on your cooking time together."

Meggie was quiet for a moment. Then she replied slowly, "Cooking is a fine art. The partnership Mark and I are forging could probably create some wonderful culinary treats." She sat down on her bed. "It's all in how we work together. There aren't any egos or prima donna stuff between the two of us. When we're in the kitchen, we work like a well-tuned machine. It happened the first time I helped him do the dishes."

"Kind of like Trapper and me."

"Yeah!" Meggie replied enthusiastically. "Now your relation-ship with Trapper is much older than my relationship with Mark, but the basic essentials seem to be there between Mark and me." She giggled. "Well, Trapper's your horse. So that makes a difference. But I can feel that Mark and I trust each other in the kitchen just as you and Trapper trust each other in a competition. For instance, I couldn't believe that he shared with us the basic elements of his recipe for a new pasta sauce he's working on. Chefs aren't usually that willing to tell another chef about something they're trying to master on their own. Competition is fierce, and it often feels like it's copyrighted."

"Is that what you think prompted Mark to be so short when you and Joel appeared?" Tye asked.

"Yeah. He doesn't want anything messing up the team dynam-ics that work so well between us when we're in the kitchen. I would feel the same way."

"He said that he was sorry, and that he would apologize in the morning. He didn't mean to be short with you. He just suddenly realized that he needed to be studying for some test in his statistics class."

Meg began to yawn. "I'll talk to him in the morning." She moved across the room. "I think I need to get ready for bed."

Tye agreed. "I'll see you in the morning," she said as she slid between the sheets.

Chapter Eleven

eggie ignored the piped in music that came over the speakers of the grocery store and concentrated on brushing the dirt from the potato. She eyed it carefully. Thanksgiving was one of her favorite holidays, and she loved to shop for the big meal. The displays of pumpkins, Indian corn, and other colorful autumn squashes always put Meggie in a celebratory mood. She was glad Mark had been able to join her for this shopping trip. It made it more festive. "Do you think we could just use bakers for the mashed potatoes? Maybe we should consider the Yukon gold or baby reds? Do you want to keep the skin on or off? If we added garlic—."

Mark laughed as he moved away from the onions.

Meggie looked at him, puzzled. "What's so funny?" she asked.

"Nothing really," Mark said, as he continued to grin. "It's just that I enjoy watching you."

Meggie turned to Mark with the baking potatoes in her hand. "Why you're no help at all, Mark," she said. "You're not supposed to watching me. You're supposed to be paying attention to the potatoes. We've got important decisions to make." Her eyes sparkled with a smile.

Mark held up his hands. "I know. I know. Okay. Potatoes. I think if we're going to leave the skins on, we should use the baby reds. The skins will add a bit of color to the table. If we use the Yukon Gold or regular bakers, then I think we should peel them. Bakers can have a tough skin, and Yukon Gold will just look like lumps. Garlic will work with all three, but the baby reds have a smoother texture that may be more able to carry the garlic a little better."

Meggie nodded as she weighed the potatoes in her hand. "Perhaps you're right," she said as she put the bakers down and moved toward the baby reds.

"They hold their shape better while they're being boiled too," Mark added. Then he said, "You know, we don't have to mash them at all."

Meggie looked at him. "What are you proposing?"

"We can cut them into quarters and boil them until just done. Then give them a quick toss in a frying pan with garlic, rosemary, butter, onions, salt, and pepper. Then we could broil them for a minute—until they're toasty brown. After we pull them from the oven we could add a touch of parmesan cheese."

"That sounds really good, Mark; simple too. What do you think we should do about the gravy?"

"We could still make it for the meat and stuffing if you want, but it wouldn't be necessary."

Meggie agreed as she began picking out baby reds. "I love potatoes for that very reason. You can do so much with them. You know what else would be good?"

"What's that?"

"We could add cream cheese for an even smoother texture along with some garlic, American cheese and chives for a bit of color. That would look nice with the red skins."

"That's a good idea too."

Meggie placed a bunch of red potatoes in a sack. "I like the idea of a quick fry with some butter though. It's a little bit different from the traditional approach. We could add chives just before we place them on the table. It would add a mild flavor and look nice with the rosemary and against the red skins of the potatoes."

After they picked out the potatoes, Meggie and Mark pushed their cart toward the celery. "By the way, how did your statistics test go?" Meggie asked.

Mark's throat tightened. He had meant to apologize to Meggie about his behavior, but it had been hard to pull out the words. Instead, the whole incident of Meggie's date with Joel went underground, but it never completely left his mind. Now, as he stood in the produce department, he studied Meg for a minute. Was she angry with him over his rude behavior when she had been with Joel? Meggie was looking over bunches of celery with a careful eye. There was no indication that the question was anything more than friendly conversation.

"Oh, fine," Mark said casually. "I got a B. I hate statistics. Look, Meggie, I'm really sorry for the way I behaved the other night when we ran into you and Joel. I don't know what came over me."

Meggie looked up from the celery. "Oh, it's okay, Mark. I understand. Tye told me you had a statistics test that you had forgotten about. I'm glad you got a B. I'd be happy with that. I hate statistics too." She turned the celery over in her hand. "What do you think about this bunch? It looks pretty fresh."

Mark took the wet celery out of Meggie's hands and turned it over. A snappish feeling came over him. It was obvious that Meggie didn't care what Mark thought of Joel. "It's fine, Meggie. Maybe we should move on to the turkeys or we'll be here all day."

Meggie placed the celery in the basket. "Okay, Mark. Are you in a hurry?" She began wheeling the basket toward the meat section of the grocery store.

"Aren't we always in a hurry?" he asked with a quick grin, trying to cover his sudden urge to retort sarcastically. "It's part of being a student. Besides, I have to prepare another statistics assignment that's due tomorrow."

"Oh, well, I wouldn't want to keep you from your first love." Meggie grinned as she turned her attention to the abundance of turkeys. "I'm so glad we got here early in the day," she said. "We'll get the best choice."

Mark was just glad there was something else to discuss besides his statistics. He wished he hadn't been so sharp with Meggie. But then she didn't seem to notice that either.

For the next several minutes, Mark and Meggie pulled out different turkeys that ranged close to the poundage they needed. They finally settled on a nine-pound bird.

Mark wheeled the cart to the checkout stand, where he and Meggie placed their purchases on the conveyer belt. When they reached the checker, they both pulled out their cash and paid for the groceries. Once in the car, Meggie began put the schedule together. "We should probably do the pies the night before, although I hate to do them too early because then they don't taste as good. The bird will have to go into the oven late morning, then we can work on the bread, stuffing, potatoes, beans, and gravy in that order. What do you think?"

Mark agreed as he pulled out into the traffic. "Don't forget about the relish. We'll probably want to make that early so that the flavors have a chance to come together."

"Oh, you're right," Meggie said. "I can't wait to taste your relish, Mark. Your secret recipe sounds wonderful."

The earlier snappish feeling started to ebb away. "You'll love this, Meg. It has bits of oranges, pears, tangerines and cranberries in it. I mix that all together with some sugar, orange juice and a hint of almond."

"That's what intrigues me. It sounds delicious."

～

On Thanksgiving Day, Mark pulled the turkey out of the brine. Meggie patted it dry, then squeezed a fresh lemon over it. Then she quickly brushed it with olive oil before adding a rub she had made of garlic and onion with paprika and other spices. Mark turned the oven to the correct temperature before joining Meggie in preparing the bird. They had spent the previous evening preparing the brine for the turkey and mincing garlic and onions before folding them into other spices. After everything was ready, they placed the turkey in the brine to sit overnight in the refrigerator. The spice mixture also went into the refrigerator overnight, allowing the ingredients to give of their flavor. Now it was time to put the nine-pound turkey in the oven.

"You won't be sorry we used these spices," Meggie said lowered the oven door. "This is so good."

Mark had to agree. The aroma of garlic mixed with the bland simplicity of olive oil and lemon juice complimented the pungent smell of paprika and sage, stabbing at his appetite.

Mark washed his hands in warm soapy water. He could hear the football game blaring in Meggie's living room. His roommates and Dianna's fiancée Doug were sprawled out in the living room cheering for their favorite team. Mark's thoughts were far away from the noise of the television though. He was thinking about the afternoon he had spent with Meggie in the grocery store. He enjoyed every process of food preparation. Choosing the ingredients was one of the most important aspects of cooking and something he had always preferred to do alone. That way he wouldn't be distracted from choosing the very best the market had to offer. But when

Meggie had asked him to go shopping with her, he jumped at the chance and had enjoyed it—until he made a complete jerk of himself by snapping at her over celery.

Meggie interrupted his thoughts. "Let's see, this bird will probably take about two hours to bake."

"Have you already made the pie?" Mark asked.

Meggie nodded as she began to tick off the other items. "I made the apple pie last night. The bread is on its first rising. We'll wait until the last minute to make the potatoes and gravy. Did you make the pumpkin pie yet?"

"No, I'm going home to do that right now. Then I thought while that was cooling we could finish the stuffing and put it in the oven at my house."

"Good idea. Maybe we can put the sweet potatoes in there too. What about the cranberry relish?" Meggie asked.

"I haven't started yet, but I have all the ingredients ready to go."

Meggie's eyes lit up. "Maybe I'd better come to your house to help."

"I was hoping you'd offer," Mark said. Then he looked around. "Where's Tye?" he asked.

"She went to the barn." Meggie began washing her hands before wiping the counter tops with hot soapy water. "Tye found out a couple of weeks ago that she's going to be in charge of a cow that's giving birth next quarter. She's really excited. She spends as much time as possible out there."

Mark laughed. "The only cow I want to visit better be on my plate!"

Meggie smiled. "Don't let Tye hear you say that. She's quite attached to this animal. It even has a name. She calls it Elsa. I think it's a milk cow. She told me the breed but I can't remember."

"Well, as long as she gets home in time for dinner."

Walking into the living room, Meggie and Mark announced their plans to spend part of the afternoon at Mark's house to finish the Thanksgiving meal. Everyone waved them off without looking away from the set.

As they hurried toward Mark's home, he told Meggie of his method for baking pumpkin pie. "I make my pies from scratch," he said. "I put the crust together this morning. It's in the fridge. The pumpkin is baking right now."

"You mean you make your pie from a real pumpkin? You don't use the canned stuff?"

"That's right," Mark said. "You'll be able to taste the difference."

"I can't wait," Meggie said.

As they opened the door to Mark's home they were greeted with the warm aroma of baking pumpkin.

Mark went straight to the oven and pulled out the squash. "We'll wait until it's cool before we start to scrape the inside, and mash it. That's what I'll make into my pie. In the meantime we can get started on the cranberry relish." Mark pulled out the ingredients from the refrigerator. Soon, he and Meggie were chopping pears and peeling oranges.

Chapter Twelve

As soon as Tye got into the truck she knew that she was going to take a detour before seeing Elsa. Now that the snow had come Tye wondered what the river looked like. Was Bridal Veil Falls running? Carefully she navigated through plowed roads. The shoulder of the road was choked with snow and with the new storm that had just moved into the area, the roads were clogging fast in spite of the efforts of the plows. Even though Tye rarely drove in snow back in Oregon, she handled the truck easily as it slowly climbed the canyon road. The snow was falling in big, fat flakes. They hurled themselves at her truck at great speed, only to veer away at the last minute. It was an act Tye found fascinating.

When she reached Bridal Veil Falls she parked. With a sigh she sat back against her seat, taking in her surroundings. It was cold. The place had the air of desertion. Getting out of the truck, Tye was struck by the silence. The marching armies of thunder clouds that had roiled above her in summer's heat had been pushed away by the snapping cold. Now, nothing but a dome of white clouds and deepening snow covered the landscape. It muffled all sound as it covered the wounds of the river.

Her heart had gone silent too. She didn't feel any tears for Kyle.

They were frozen in the snow that covered the tomb of her heart.

Tye walked along the river. It trickled toward the valley. No life-giving autumn rains had come to these mountains—only frozen snow and ice. As she reached the falls, she looked up to find the icy rock face. The little amount of water that came from the falls was also frozen, crystallized in its hope to nurture the river.

A snow filled breeze rushed through the canyon. It was different than the dust laden winds Tye knew from her dry summer storms. This was cold and clean. It carried no burden of dirt or heat. But as she drew in the cold, sparkling breeze it seared her lungs.

Tye shivered elaborately as she pulled her coat close and walked along the river bank. How long would the snow stay? How long would it cover the wounds of bare rock and a desperate river?

She pushed her hands inside her pockets. This was her first winter in Provo. She hated the cold, really. It drove her inside. She longed for the life-giving rain soaked breezes of Oregon that followed the misty clouds through fertile river valleys and fir-covered mountains. It wouldn't be long now. Soon, she would be going home for Christmas.

She glanced at her watch. It was time to visit Elsa. Tye smiled in spite of the cold. She remembered her earlier hope of being able to work with a pregnant mare. Now she was glad for the chance to work with Elsa.

Turning toward the truck, Tye walked with purpose.

After several minutes of careful driving she found herself at the barn. Even on this cold day the smell hit her full force, almost knocking the wind out of her. Tye had noticed it the first time she had walked into Elsa's barn. Cows just smelled different than horses. Their odor was sharper and more pungent. It took some getting used to, but after several minutes Tye could breathe again. Once in Elsa's stall, her nose became accustomed to the odor. Quietly she stroked

Elsa's warm neck and then scratched behind her ears. She had already checked for any new signs of the pregnancy, but nothing revealed itself. Instead, Elsa's placid eye looked at Tye with acceptance.

"I think Preston is right," Tye said softly. "You do like company. Trapper liked company too." She paused as she stroked Elsa's silky neck then ran her hand along Elsa's body. "Not all horses do though. Probably cows are the same way. Trapper is a grand horse," she said. "Kyle took real good care of him while I was away on my mission. You've never met Kyle." Elsa turned to look at her. Tye stroked her face. "I miss him sometimes," she said quietly. "When I got home from my mission we spent hours riding together. I loved him Elsa." Tears began to form. "I don't tell anyone about it anymore. Meggie is sick of hearing about it; especially after I soaked Mark's shirt in Salt Lake City. And who else is there? I had hoped he would write once he went back east, but he never did. I suppose it's for the best." Tye sighed and wiped her tears. "Sorry, Elsa. You probably don't want to hear about it either." She gave the cow a quiet slap on the hindquarters before kneeling down to check Elsa's udder. No changes. When Tye stood, she found Preston standing just outside the stall door. She gave a startled cry.

"I'm sorry. I didn't mean to scare you," Preston said. "I just didn't want to say anything while you were underneath her. I mean what if you got scared, bumped her and then she kicked? She's a nice cow, but she wouldn't like you knocking around down there."

Tye leaned up against the wall, putting her hand to her heart. "It's okay. I'm glad you thought of that."

"Can I come in now?" Preston asked.

Tye opened the stall door. "Of course. I just came for a visit. I thought I should come out and look after her a bit over the long weekend. With it being the holiday and all, I figured she would probably just get minimal care."

Preston agreed. "That's why I came out too."

"I thought you'd be home in Montana for Thanksgiving."

"Montana is too far away for such a short vacation. Besides, Thanksgiving is late this year. We'll all be home in two weeks anyway," he said.

Something new stirred inside of Tye. "Would you like to join me and some of my friends for dinner? My roommate and a friend of ours are both culinary majors so it's bound to be a wonderful meal. There's plenty."

"Thanks. I appreciate the offer. It sounds good, but I already have plans."

"Oh, of course, I mean, yes, everyone would already have plans by now. I mean, I should've asked you sooner. I thought you were going to home to Montana, or I would've asked you sooner. I–um … I was going to clean Elsa's stall. Would you like to help me?"

"I'll get the equipment now." Preston left the stall.

Tye was glad. She felt flush. Her face was burning red in spite of the heavy cold that had settled in the barn. How stupid. What difference did it make if her cow partner had other plans? He probably had a girlfriend.

Preston returned with a wheelbarrow, two shovels, and two bales of straw. Within a few minutes the stall was cleaned out. Preston pulled a pair of wire cutters from his back pocket and cut the twine that held the bale of straw. In silence Tye and Preston began spreading the straw. Elsa seemed immensely pleased and immediately went down in the bedding.

Tye's earlier embarrassment left her as she watched Elsa settle. "It doesn't take much to make her happy, does it?" Tye said.

"No."

"Horses are the same, I think."

Preston nodded. "I sure miss Mayday. I bet you miss your horse too, don't you?"

Tye thought again of Trapper and his connection to Kyle. Melancholy washed over her. She tried to push it away. "I miss him a lot," she said quietly. She turned to Preston abruptly. "Mayday is such an interesting name. Where did you get it?"

"Mayday is my mare. I helped bring her into this world, and it seems like she's been paying me back ever since. She's good at getting me out of trouble," Preston said. "That's why I call her Mayday. She's not big, but she's quick, nimble, and sharp. She won't take any baloney from a cow either. She's got better cow sense than I do. She knows when to push them and when to back off."

"It's a great name. Do you want to return to the ranch when you're finished with school?" Tye asked. "I mean it seems apparent that since you were raised on a ranch there probably isn't much for you to learn here."

Preston laughed. "Oh there's plenty to learn, but I don't plan on going back to the ranch after school. I want to be a veterinarian. I doubt I'll even end up back in Montana, although I love it there. Ranchers don't have much use for vets. They do most of their work themselves."

"Do you know which school you would like to attend for your post graduate work?"

"Right now, I would be really happy to be accepted into the program at Washington State or Oregon State."

"I used to go to Oregon State."

Preston's eyes widened. "You did? What did you think of the school?"

Tye was sorry for the slip. She didn't like talking about her tenure that involved Kyle. She backed away from her thoughts of Kyle and focused on Preston's question. "They have a good vet program," she said. "It's a little odd though because right now they don't have any small animal facilities. They have an agreement with Washington State that allows OSU students to move up to Washington State University to study small animal medicine for a year-and-a-half. It's a strange and difficult arrangement. But that's going to change soon. They've finally received funding to expand their veterinary medicine program to include small animals. Right now they're building the facilities, and they'll be hiring the faculty soon." She paused. "Their equine medicine program has always been outstanding. Trapper has never needed their veterinarian facilities, but I've always found comfort in knowing they were close by." Tye was surprised by her outpouring of words. She rarely spoke of Oregon State. Somehow, by sharing her knowledge of the veterinarian program with Preston, she was able to shrug off a tiny bit of Kyle's memory.

Preston nodded slowly. "Yes, I've heard that their students have to make this move to Washington in the middle of their schooling. But I wasn't aware that things were changing. That's great news. I guess I've always preferred Oregon State, because I prefer working with large animals, but I'd be happy just to stay in the west." He added wistfully, "I would like to go to Oregon State though."

"What made you want to become a vet?"

"I love working with all kinds of animals. I enjoy domestic animals and wild animals. When I was a kid I used to keep a journal of bird migrations in our area. My folks used to ask me why I did that. I didn't really know except that I loved seeing the same birds come to the area to raise their young. So, I kept track of them. Later,

I found out that the Audubon Society was looking for those kinds of records, and I turned mine in. They sent me a thank-you note."

"What kind of observations did you make in your journals?"

"I kept track of how many birds I saw of which species. If I was sure it was a returning bird, I wrote that down. I noted if any were sick or hurt. I watched for everything from finches to migrating geese and ducks. I was outside all the time so I was able to keep fairly accurate records. If I ran across any that were hurt or sick I'd try to help them." He smiled. "I helped a lot of baby robins. Often when they're just starting to fly, they get lost and confused. I'd bring them into the house, feed them a mixture of worms and berries, and let them spend the night in the barn with a warm light on them. In the morning they'd be ready to try their wings again."

"How old were you?"

"I started working with birds when I was nine. I kept my bird journals until I went on my mission. The Audubon Society said it was really helpful for them to have records for ten straight years kept by the same person."

"Did you notice any changes?"

Preston laughed. "Only in my handwriting." He grew serious. "I never noticed a huge decline in any one population, but I did notice a slow steady decline in several populations. That worried me. Also there were a couple of years when house finches got terribly sick and were dying. Their populations always rebounded but I never did find out what was killing them. That really concerned me. It was very frustrating. I felt so helpless. I wanted to help them somehow, but I didn't know what to do."

"So birdwatching is what made you decide you wanted to become a vet?"

"It helped. I don't know. There's something about being able to help a sick, confused, and sometimes dying animal that satisfied me deep inside. Watching birds was a part of the bigger picture for me. Because of the ranch I've been around animals all my life, and I can't picture my life without their presence and companionship. But I don't want to work them on a ranch. I would rather aid them. It's hard to explain."

"I think you've explained it very well," Tye said.

Preston became thoughtful. "I've always been more comfortable around animals than around humans." He paused. "Have you ever noticed how crowded college can be?"

Tye shrugged. "I haven't thought that much about it, I guess."

Preston sighed as he opened the stall door. He stepped out after Tye and closed the stall door behind him before walking with her down the aisle.

"What is it?" Tye asked. "Don't you like crowds?"

"I don't like crowds, and I don't like it here," he said. "I miss the ranch and my family. Provo is far too crowded. My mission in Houston couldn't even prepare me for sharing an apartment with five other men. And it certainly didn't prepare me for all the silly women around here." Preston stopped and looked at Tye. "Oh, I didn't mean you," he said quickly. "I'm sure you're not silly."

"How do you know? I may be the silliest woman in the whole valley." She laughed.

"No one who comes out to check on a cow on Thanksgiving Day is silly," Preston said.

"I don't know," Tye said slowly. "My roommate thought I was pretty silly to come out here on a holiday."

"I'm talking about the girls whose biggest goal is seeing how many CTR rings they can collect from the boys."

"Oh. That kind of silly." Tye thought of KayLee.

They walked outside. The clouds had cleared. Preston squinted into the snow and sun. "I miss the open range and the rugged mountains of Montana. I miss the birds, cows, cats, and dogs. That's probably why I'm out here visiting Elsa all the time. I long for the big-sky summers and the cold, crisp winters. I miss the work." He turned to Tye. "That probably sounds pretty silly to you, doesn't it?"

Tye shook her head. "Not at all. I long for the cool forested hills and wild blackberries of the Oregon summer. I miss eating ripe cherries and pears right from the tree. I used to gather tomatoes from my mother's garden in August. I miss the damp smell of fir and pine in the fall and winter. I even miss the rain! And I miss my horse." Tears came to her eyes. "Yeah, I miss Trapper." It felt good to think of Trapper in this way. It felt connected to Oregon—to her home, but somehow Kyle was separate from her feelings for this moment.

Preston turned to her. "I've never been to Oregon."

"And I've never been to Montana."

A look passed between them that startled Tye as much as when Preston had walked in on her earlier. She swallowed hard and broke from Preston's gaze. He shifted his weight, looking down at his shadow in the bright snow.

Tye gathered her courage. "I teach at the Three Creeks Barn outside of Orem," she said. "I'm there every Saturday morning. You can come and watch if you ever want a dose of horses."

Preston smiled. "I'd like that," he said.

"Well, I guess we should go before we freeze out here," Tye said. But with the warm sun hitting the metal of the barn siding it wasn't all that cold.

"Right," Preston agreed. He walked to her truck. She waved at him as she drove away.

Chapter Thirteen

Mark removed the skis from the rack on the top of his car, and then watched Meggie do the same. Soon, they were in step as they walked toward the ticket booth.

Meggie balanced her skis on her shoulder. "I'm so glad we got some fresh powder last night," she said. "The conditions are perfect."

Mark agreed as he looked up at the white mountain that pierced the cloudless blue sky. The trees were sporting their fresh, dazzling winter coats of new snow that sparkled in the dawning sun. The whole canyon seemed to be showing off the winter season.

Reaching into his pocket, Mark pulled out his sunblock and handed it to Meggie. "You may need this," he said. "I've already used it."

"Thanks. I didn't even consider bringing any sunblock from home," she said as she took off her gloves and spread the lotion on her face.

After they bought their tickets, they headed for the chair lift. Mark's heart was pounding. Nothing was like the opening day of ski season. Once on the chair, he looked around as they glided smoothly above the trees. "I'm glad we came early in the morning," he said. "There aren't too many people."

Meggie giggled. "Most folks are probably trying to recover from a turkey hang-over. Wait until this afternoon."

Sliding off the lift chair, they found themselves at the top of the ski run. The surrounding mountains threw long morning shadows over the snow. For several minutes, they stood and let the morning fill them as the sun began to spill over the fresh, unmarked powder. Meggie lifted her face to greet the light of the new day. "Isn't it great?" she asked.

"It's perfect!" Mark agreed. "Hey, I'll race you!"

"You're on!" Meggie said as she pushed off.

Mark fell behind as Meggie's skiing skill became apparent. She was every bit as good as he was; maybe better. Picking up his speed, Mark fell in beside Meggie. The rush of the race and the sound of skis gliding on clean snow made Mark's heart thump hard in his chest. There wasn't anything like the first run of the season, and he was thrilled to be able to share it with someone who obviously enjoyed the sport as much as he did.

When they got to the bottom of the hill, Mark lifted his goggles. "Whoa! Where did you learn to ski? I thought I'd have the upper hand. I've been skiing since I was a baby, but I can tell that doesn't count for anything. I can hardly keep up with you."

Meggie pulled off her goggles and grinned. "When I lived at home we used to ski all the time. When I went to OSU, I could only go during Christmas break so I was glad for the move to Provo. Now that I live here I plan on going as often as I can." She exhaled a heavy mist. "This might be a little ambitious, but I hope to go once a month."

Mark's heart thumped wildly. He hoped he could go with her, but he also worried about the cost. He would have to look over his budget and see if he could come up with some extra skiing money. Then he thought about Joel. He cursed that thought away. Nothing would ruin this brilliant morning with Meggie. "Well, I'll have to practice when I go home for Christmas if I want to keep up with you," Mark said.

"Do you want to go again?" Meggie asked.

Mark nodded as he put his goggles back over his eyes. Soon they were on the chair lift again. They spent their day racing down steep terrain, making hairpin turns, and looking for new powder. At lunch, they grabbed a quick bite and went back to the slopes. Their last run of the day was spent becoming airborne over moguls.

"I don't do moguls very often," Meggie said after they were finished. "They're hard on the knees and hips, but I like the challenge." Even in the cold, waning afternoon, she had begun to sweat from her hard work.

"Are you ready to call it a day?" Mark asked.

Meggie squinted as she looked up at the slopes. She nodded. "It's gotten crowded. The snow has deteriorated due to the sun and the increased traffic." She looked at Mark. "Speaking of traffic, if we get started home now, maybe we'll miss most of it."

Mark agreed. "Plus they'll be a whole new crowd up here for night skiing so this would be a good time to leave."

"I've never been night skiing," Meggie said. "Because we lived some distance from the slopes, we always had to leave before it got too dark, or we would be traveling the mountain passes late at night. My dad didn't like to drive on those icy roads after nine."

"Well, maybe after the Christmas holiday we can come up here one night. Would you like that?"

Meggie's eyes sparkled like the new snow. "I would love it!" She slung her skies over her shoulder. "Let's plan on it."

Moving towards the car, they were stopped in the parking lot.

"Meggie?"

Meggie looked up. "Calum? Hey, what are you doing here? Are you just heading in?"

The young man with soft, sandy blonde hair nodded as he made his way toward Meggie. "Yeah, it took us all day to recover from yesterday's turkey feed. Are you leaving?"

Meggie nodded. "Yeah, we got here early this morning." She nodded toward Mark. "This is my friend, Mark. We beat the crowd and had a great day."

Calum nodded in Mark's direction. Then he turned back to Meggie. "Too bad you're leaving. You could join us." Calum pointed to the carload of young men who were still unloading their equipment.

"Some other time," Meggie replied.

Calum nodded, giving Mark a quick glance. "Well, I hope you saved some good snow for us."

"No promises. If you wanted good snow you should've been up here this morning," Meggie said.

"I'll remember that," Calum replied as he moved off, giving Mark another nod.

Once Meggie and Mark were in the car, Mark asked, "He sure seemed friendly. Who was that?"

"Oh, that's Calum McIntyre. He's from my religion class. He sure looks Scottish, doesn't he? His green eyes and freckles really stand out." Meg replied.

"I thought you were seeing what's-his-name, Joel?"

"I've gone out with Joel once. That hardly makes for exclusive relationship. Besides, I'm not serious with anyone, Mark. I like to go out and have a good time."

"It sounds as if Calum will ask you to go skiing. Do you think you'll go?"

Meggie shrugged. "Sure."

Mark didn't reply as he slowly began to maneuver the car through the rapidly filling parking lot.

"You're worried, aren't you?" Meggie said quietly. "You're afraid that if I date a lot it'll ruin our cooking partnership."

Mark shook his head vigorously. "No. That's not it! I just wonder how Joel would feel, that's all." The words sounded tinny in Mark's ears. He geared the car down. "No, that's a lie," he said. "I do worry about our cooking partnership."

Meggie smiled, placing her hand on Mark's arm. "Don't you worry about that," she said. "I recognize how important it is. Wasn't Thanksgiving fun?"

Mark nodded. "I have the best time in the kitchen with you, Meg."

"I feel the same way, Mark. I won't let anything or anyone get in the way of our team spirit. Besides, someday you'll probably get a steady girlfriend and forget all about me. That's how you strong, silent types are."

Mark laughed. He had never pictured himself as the strong, silent type. He was about to ask Meggie what she meant, but she spoke again.

"Whew! I'll sleep well tonight. Aren't you tired?"

"Yeah, I'm pretty tired," Mark said. He shifted the car into a higher gear as he moved out of a curve. Mark thought back to Thanksgiving Day. He and Meggie's work had been streamlined because of their team approach. It was as if they could read each other's thoughts. He would hand her the next ingredient for her recipe just as she looked up from her work. And she seemed to know just when he needed that spatula, or just how much spice was required for the pumpkin pie. She had never made a pumpkin pie from the actual squash, but without measuring, she had prepared just the right amount of sugar, cinnamon, cloves, allspice, and nutmeg.

Mark geared down as he slowed around a curve. In spite of Meggie's comforting words, he hoped Calum, Joel, or some other man wouldn't upset the delicate balance that existed between the two of them as they cooked. Their teamwork was such a fragile thing. And it was new. Mark had never enjoyed that kind of kinship with someone in the kitchen. It reminded him of some of the feelings he had experienced on his mission. Often, when he and his companion were getting along, and the work was going well, Mark would often feel connected to his surroundings, his companion, the people he was teaching, and his Heavenly Father. When he cooked with Meggie it was the same feeling; a grand connection that included him, Meggie, and food, which was one of the greatest gifts that came from God. There was an invincibility that came with that feeling. He wondered if Meggie felt it. He wondered if she understood.

Meggie reached over and turned on the radio. "Do you mind?" she asked.

"No. Good idea," Mark replied. He was glad for the distraction. They had already shared their thoughts about their cooking relationship. Maybe talking about something as fragile as their teamwork would ruin it; make them aware of something that simply existed on its own.

A song came on the radio that he and Meggie both knew. Mark looked at Meggie, who grinned. Within seconds, they were both singing to the music. Mark tapped on the steering wheel, and Meggie swayed with the music as they sang. When another song blared through the speakers, they continued to sing, tap and sway. They harmonized in places as Mark took the tenor voice and Meggie sang soprano. As Mark negotiated the curves of Provo Canyon, the car seemed to fly. Soon, he was pulling up in front of Meggie's house. He killed the engine. The music died.

"I'll help you with your stuff," he said.

Meggie shook her head. "No. That's okay. I can handle it. One thing my father insisted on whenever we went skiing is that each of us had to take care of our own equipment. He didn't want to be saddled with everyone's gear." Meggie got out of the car and rustled around in the back seat, grabbing her boots and duffle bag. She stopped for a minute. "Next time we go skiing, let's make our own lunch, okay? It'll save us some money, and we can experiment."

Mark warmed to the thought. Maybe Meggie did understand. "Good idea."

Meggie took another look around the back seat. "Give me just a minute to get my skis off the rack." She looked at Mark. "Thanks for driving," she said. "I don't have a car, so I really appreciate it. I had a good time."

"Thanks for coming with me, Meg. It was loads of fun."

Meggie smiled as she shut the door. Within a quick minute she had unlatched her skis and was heading up the walk. Mark watched her go as the last of the winter sunlight ebbed out of the day.

Chapter Fourteen

*T*ye found Trista in the tack room, pulling her saddle and bridle from the wall. In spite of the cold the girl was dressed lightly in sweats and a down vest. Once she got moving she would get warm.

"It's cold, isn't it Triss?"

Triss nodded. "My dad is here today," she said. "I told him to wait in the stands in the arena. He'd like to talk to you after our lesson."

"I'd like to meet him."

Tye followed Trista down the aisle to Patches' stall, where she haltered the pony before leading him to the crossties. As soon as the pony was settled, Trista began brushing his coat. Then she saddled him and placed the bit in his mouth.

"We're ready to go, Miss Jorgenson."

Walking out into the arena, Tye looked up into the stands to find a rugged looking man dressed in a warm coat and jeans.

"That's my daddy!" Trista waved exuberantly.

Tye felt the young girl's enthusiasm for her father's visit. It also showed in her lesson. Periodically, Tye would glance up into the stands to find Trista's father watching his daughter intently. He appeared to be truly interested in Trista's riding.

After the lesson, the man made his way to the arena floor where Trista made proper introductions. "This is my daddy. His name is Kenneth Brannon. Daddy, this is my horse teacher, Miss Jorgenson."

Tye shook his hand and was pleased by the warm, firm grip he offered on this cold day. "Would you have a few minutes after Trista's lesson?" Kenneth asked.

"Of course," Tye said.

With her father by her side, Trista went through the process of untacking and brushing Patches. She went through every step with deliberate motions so that her father could see what she was learning. He was interested and a couple of times corrected Trista as she held the brush to groom Patches. After Trista was finished grooming Patches, Tye helped the youngster lead him to his stall.

Kenneth spoke, "Triss, I need to speak to Miss Jorgenson for a moment. Can you wait right outside the office door?"

"Daddy, it's cold," Trista said. "Can you turn the heat on in the car?"

He looked at Tye. "Can you wait just a minute?"

"Sure."

Trista took her father's hand and walked out of the barn. Tye heard Kenneth give Trista instructions about the heat in the car as she walked into the office. She turned on the office space heater.

Kenneth returned, walking through the open door. Tye closed it after him to keep the warmth in the room.

"I appreciate you taking time to meet with me," Kenneth began. "How is Triss doing in her lessons? She appears to be learning."

"Triss is very determined and extremely focused. She has a healthy respect for horses but she's not afraid. Her progress is encouraging and impressive."

Kenneth nodded. "I'm so glad she's taking lessons. You see, before Celia moved here we lived in Colorado. Trista's Grandma and Grandpa Brannon have always had horses, and she enjoyed them; even as a baby." He smiled. "I used to take her with me on rides. We wouldn't go very far or very fast, but we would just walk around the pasture. Triss loved it. She was always clamoring for more time on the horse. Then, when Triss turned three, my folks bought her a pony. It was just a baby, but they thought by the time Trista grew into riding, the pony would be old enough and trained. Then Celia left, taking Trista with her. That hasn't stopped my folks, though. They have gone through with their original plan. The pony is trained and ready for Triss." He paused. "I'm working very hard on bringing my daughter back to Colorado, but until that day I'm going to be coming out here for some long weekends. Would you mind if I bring her to her lessons when I'm in town?"

"No. I would welcome your presence and your input, Mr. Brannon." Tye was thoughtful. "Colorado isn't that far."

Kenneth shook his head. "No, it's not," he said. Then he added, "It's not the physical mileage that worries me, Miss, Jorgenson. It's the emotional distance. I'm trying to make up for that now." He paused before continuing, "I've made some mistakes in my life, and it's taken me a while to figure that out. Now that I've gotten my priorities straight, Trista has risen to the top. It's where she should've been all along, but I got lost for a while. I've talked to Trista a little bit about that, and I've asked her to forgive me. She's a very forgiving little girl, and I'm hoping we can make a brand new start. I've considered moving to Utah so I can be closer to her, but the custody hearings are in Colorado. My practice is there as well, so for now I'll be flying out here about once a month."

Tye smiled. She looked into the man's face. He was ruggedly handsome with sandy blond hair, hazel eyes, a chiseled nose, and a firm jaw. Tye could see where Trista got her fine looks. She had her father's nose, her mother's rosebud mouth, light blonde hair, and brown eyes.

"I'll be looking for you, Mr. Brannon."

"Please, call me Kenneth." He produced a business card and wrote his home phone on the back. "If Triss ever needs anything, just call."

Tye took his card and studied it. "You're a physician?" she asked.

He nodded. "I'm a cardiologist for an HMO. If I had my own practice it would be nearly impossible for me to take the time away to come down here and see Triss. But as things stand now I'm only on-call once a month. When I come to Utah I have to take a couple of days without pay, but it'll be worth it."

"Trista is definitely worth it," Tye said as she placed the business card in her shirt pocket. "I hope to see you again."

Kenneth stood. "You'll see me often, Miss Jorgenson," he said. They shook hands again. Kenneth walked out of the barn just as Tye's next student arrived.

Chapter Fifteen

ye sat in her Animal Physiology and Anatomy class, concentrating on the diagrams in her book. It was her final exam. Even though she knew she would pass, she wanted to do her best. She glanced at Preston, who sat beside her. He was absorbed in his own test.

Several minutes later, Preston stood. Tye felt a touch of dismay. She was hoping to say goodbye to him before Christmas vacation. She watched him walk to the front of the class; place his test on the stack of finished exams before walking out of the door. Tye let out a sigh and focused on her paper. Oh well she thought. We'll have all of the next semester to say hello and goodbye. She spent the next several minutes going over her answers before turning in her test.

When she left the classroom she was surprised and pleased to see Preston leaning against the wall.

"Hey," she said quietly.

"How did you do?" Preston asked as he pushed himself away from the wall.

They walked toward the parking lot.

"I think I did okay. I hope I got an A. How about you?"

"I feel as if I could build a cow from the ground up," he said. "I also feel like I could do the same with a chicken, a goose, a goat, a sheep, and a hamster."

Tye laughed. "It feels good to be out of school, don't you think? What are you going to do during Christmas vacation?"

"I'll help Dad with whatever he needs done. The winter hasn't been too bad so I doubt we'll have much work. Will you be riding?"

Tye nodded. "Meggie, that's my best friend, goes skiing every year with her family. So I'll have plenty of time with my horse."

Preston opened the building door for Tye as they walked outside. "Maybe you could bring a picture of your horse next semester."

"Oh, I have a picture." Tye grabbed her wallet out of her purse and produced a photo. Then she remembered that Kyle was in the picture. It had been taken right before one of their summer shows. Trapper was polished to a shine and ready for the competition. His expression and the way he held himself showed how keen he was on the day. Kyle was holding the reins when Tye had taken the shot. Too late now. She handed the photo to Preston.

"Wow! He's a beauty. And he's big."

"Sixteen hands," Tye said.

"I think I told you that Mayday is much smaller." Then he added, "She's pretty good looking in the summer though. In the winter, her coat grows out, and she just looks shaggy."

"Is she a quarter horse?" Tye asked.

"Yeah. Typically they stand fourteen to fifteen hands. They're agile though and can call the bluff of any cow. What's Trapper's breeding? He looks like a thoroughbred."

"He is a thoroughbred."

Preston looked at the picture again. "Who's the man? Is he your trainer?"

Tye pulled back into herself. "He was a friend. While I was on my mission, Kyle took care of Trapper." She wished her voice didn't reflect her melancholy.

Preston looked at her closely before studying the picture again. "He did a fine job, I'd say."

"Yes, he did."

Preston handed back the picture. "You've never mentioned your mission. Where did you serve?"

"San Antonio."

"Why didn't you ever say anything? We were practically neighbors—well in Texan terms anyway. I served in Houston."

Tye thought about her mission. "Texas seems like so long ago," she said wistfully.

"How long have you been home?" Preston asked.

"I came home last April."

"It hasn't been that long for you. I've been home for two years now."

"So we weren't exactly neighbors. You were ahead of me."

"Did you like San Antonio?" Preston asked.

"I loved it. The people there are warm and open. They'll invite you into their home without a second thought. But they're more interested in sharing a beer with you and talking about the Spurs, than in listening to a gospel message."

"Sometimes I think that's what a mission is all about," Preston began. "I mean, I know we're supposed to teach the gospel, and that's the sole purpose of our work. But often, I think it is to help us come away with a greater love for our brothers and sisters. In that way we're being taught. While I was in Houston, I walked into some of the grandest mansions I could ever hope to see. I also walked into some of the lowliest hovels I ever hope to see. And yet through those extremes I really came to understand that we're all part of the human family; a part of our Father in Heaven's family."

Tye was quiet for a moment. "We didn't have a lot of baptisms in that mission, but I know what you mean. I came away with a real love for the people. I've never seen such hospitality, warmth, and generosity. I remember on one particularly hot summer afternoon, this woman came running out to the sidewalk and invited us into her home; not because she wanted to hear the gospel, but because it was over one-hundred degrees outside. She had seen us tracting in her neighborhood, and she was worried about us. She gave us cool water. We rested in her air-conditioned home for about thirty minutes. It reminded me of the Good Samaritan. It's as you have said. I often felt that the people of San Antonio were the teachers, and I was the student." Tye broke away from her musing and looked back at Preston. "Have you ever been back to Texas?"

"No, but I hope to go back someday. After my mission I immediately went into school. I was only home for two weeks. Since then my summers have been busy on the ranch. Have you ever thought about going back?"

Sadly, Tye hardly gave Texas or her mission a second thought. These few minutes with Preston were the first time in weeks that she had discussed a piece of her memory she hardly considered. It reminded her of the few missionary stories she had shared with Mark. She never thought about her mission or Texas unless someone else brought it up. She was too focused on the summer she and Kyle had spent together. It seemed to dwarf all of her other life experiences. Maybe it was time she changed that. "No, I haven't given it much thought, but I think I should. It was a good time in my life. There are some folks I would love to visit."

They arrived at Preston's truck.

"Maybe someday we can get together and swap mission stories. I would love to here more about San Antonio."

Tye warmed to the thought. "I'd like that," she said. "And I'd like to hear more about your mission as well." She paused. "Thanks for waiting for me," she said. "I was hoping to get to say goodbye before the end of the semester."

"Me too. I hope you have a safe and relaxing Christmas vacation. And give that pony a nice long ride."

Tye grinned. "You bet I will. You too." She waved Preston off as she began the short walk home.

Chapter Sixteen

ye double checked the girth of Patches' saddle while Trista placed the bit in the pony's mouth. "This will be our last lesson before the Christmas break. Are you ready for Christmas, Triss?"

Triss nodded. "Can I ride outside today?" she asked.

"Not yet. I want your posting to be more stable. Remember to keep your heels down. That will help your seat stay centered, and you won't wobble all over the saddle."

Trista nodded as she took Patches by the reins, leading him into the arena. Tye followed. She looked up into the stands, hoping to see Celia, but instead she found the stands empty.

After Patches was warmed up, Tye began putting Trista through her lesson paces. After the lesson, Tye moved Patches and Trista into the crossties so Trista could untack him. She was met by Celia, who was impatiently walking down the aisle, her heels echoing on the cement floor. The horses watched as she passed by their individual stalls. Tye noticed that their interest didn't wane as Celia came to a stop before Patches.

"Hey, Mom, you should pet Patches. He's warm and soft,"

Trista said as she began to untack him.

"I don't want to pet Patches," Celia said, wrinkling her nose. "I want you to hurry so I can get you home and cleaned up. Mommy has a date this afternoon."

Trista turned to Tye. "Mommy has a boyfriend now."

Tye smiled politely.

"Don't tell people my personal business young lady. Now get a move on."

Trista looked down as she shouldered the reins. "Yes, ma'am," she said quietly before scampering off to the tack room.

Celia turned towards Tye. "Is there any possible way you could finish with her five minutes earlier?" she asked with an edge in her voice.

"Of course, Mrs. Brannon. Would you like to start five minutes earlier?"

"No. I just want her out of here as soon as possible." She checked a perfectly manicured nail. "I don't understand Trista. She should be home playing with dolls and dresses. Instead she wants to roll around in the muck with horses."

"Lots of girls dream of horses, Mrs. Brannon."

"I never did," Celia said. "Trista gets this from her father. I suppose you've met the famous Dr. Brannon. Actually, he should be called infamous. Every nurse in Boulder, Colorado knows him; in the biblical sense."

"I see," Tye said. "I'm very sorry, Mrs. Brannon."

"Oh, don't be. I'm through being sorry."

"What's the biblical sense, Mommy?" Trista asked as she came from the aisle.

Celia colored, and her face softened. "It's just your mommy

speaking out of turn, Trista. It's nothing for you to worry over." She changed the subject. "Don't dawdle, Triss." She clucked over her daughter. "What's Kirby going to say when he looks at you?"

Tye could tell this was testing the outer limits of Celia's patience.

Trista nodded. "Yes, Mom, I'll hurry," she said. Quickly, she finished with Patches and then helped Tye lead him into his stall. "I just need to put the saddle away. I'll be right back." Trista hurried away, and a strained silence grew between Tye and Celia.

"Kirby is my date this afternoon," Celia said after several minutes. Then she turned toward the tack room. "Trista, you get out here this instant!"

Trista came hurrying from the tack room. "Sorry, Mommy. I had to go to the bathroom."

Celia closed her eyes. "Don't ever use the bathroom here. No telling when it was cleaned last. Wait until you get home."

"Our bathrooms are cleaned daily, Mrs. Brannon," Tye said quietly.

"Wow! We only clean ours about once a month," Trista announced.

Celia gave Tye a tight look of warning before placing her hand on Trista's shoulder. "We're leaving now young lady," she said.

Trista shot Tye a hopeful glance before hurrying down the aisle with her mother. Tye waved. Even after Celia and Trista left, Tye could still hear Celia's high heeled shoes echoing in the aisle of the still barn. The horses all seemed to be keeping their eye on Celia's exit, as if they expected her to return. Sighing, Tye turned from the door and pulled out Candy for her next student.

Chapter Seventeen

Meggie stood in the kitchen, watching Mark alternate between two flavors of cheesecake batter. First he poured the white chocolate batter into the chocolate crumb crust. Then he added the dark chocolate batter.

"When the cheesecake is cut, it'll come out like a zebra pattern," Mark said as he worked. "It's really pretty, and it tastes good too." He finished with the dark chocolate. Then he took a fork and gently swirled it in the middle of the cake. "You don't go all the way to the crust when you twirl the fork," Mark said. "That would mess up the pattern. You just lightly dip your fork through the first two layers. That way you get a paisley affect on the top, which brings out both colors and allows you to keep most of the pattern intact."

Mark placed the cheesecake in the oven. "Thanks for letting me use your oven. I think the temperature is more stable than mine, and I really want this to be perfect. It's my final assignment for my class on food critiquing and writing."

"You're welcome, Mark. You can use my oven anytime. It makes the house smell good."

"Hey, maybe while it's baking we can go through some of your religion homework," he said.

"That would be nice, but you know what I'd rather do? Let's go build a snowman in the front yard."

"Meggie, it's snowing like crazy out there."

Meggie grinned. "I know. Isn't it pretty?"

"I was thinking more like cold."

"This complaint is coming from a grand champion skier? I'll make hot chocolate after we're finished. That'll warm you up."

"I have a better idea. Why don't you make hot chocolate, and we'll work on your religion homework. Don't you have a final coming up soon?"

Meggie shrugged. "Yeah, but this afternoon I don't care about finals. I want to play in the snow. In a couple of days we'll be going home. I'll miss this Utah snow." She grabbed his hand, pulling him out into the living room.

"But you said you'd be going on a ski trip. You'll see plenty of snow."

Meggie began putting on her coat. "Let's play," she said.

Mark gave in and began putting on his coat and scarf.

Soon, they were outside, rolling snow into huge balls. They smoothed out the rough spots with their gloved hands until the balls were perfectly round.

KayLee came up the walk. "Hey, can I join you?" she asked. "You guys are doing a great job."

"Sure!" Mark said.

He glanced at Meggie, and noticed a sour expression. But it didn't last long. Soon, KayLee was in the middle of their work with her lively chatter. Mark and Meggie had worked in silence but now the snowy air was buzzing as KayLee talked about the latest school dance. "I'm going to miss those school dances," she said as she helped place the head of the snow man on top. "Home seems so boring now that I've been here. This is my first semester at college, and I love it!"

"Christmas vacation will go by so fast. You'll hardly have time to miss the social activities here," Mark said. "You'll be busy seeing old friends from high school. There'll be parties to go to. You'll have to go Christmas shopping for everyone. It won't be a bit boring."

KayLee looked up from her work. "Why, Mark, I think you're absolutely right. I feel better already. And I do miss my folks and my little sister."

Meggie interrupted, "KayLee? Would you mind running into the house for some chocolate kisses? I want to use them for the eyes. Grab a piece of that rope red licorice too. We'll use that for the mouth. It's all in the top drawer by the refrigerator."

"Sure, Meg!" KayLee bounded up the steps.

"She seems like a sweet girl," Mark said. He pulled a branch from under the snow and gently worked it into the body of the snowman for an arm.

"Oh, she's great; if you don't mind brainless."

"Why, Meggie. I've never heard you say such a mean thing."

"She has no business horning in on our snowman," Meggie said as she continued to work.

Mark glanced at his watch. "Oh, I need to go in and check the cheesecake." He ran up the stairs.

Meggie remained silent as she ran her hands over the snowman. She would not run after Mark like a hovering mother. She wished she would've told him about the CTR rings on KayLee's gloved hands.

After several minutes of working on her own, Meggie stepped

back, admiring the snowman. He was perfect. She had chinked snow into the crevices so that instead of three distinct parts, he looked more like one body. She looked up at the house, wishing Mark would appear. Then she wondered about the cheesecake and trudged up the stairs.

Opening the door, she was greeted with the scent of the baking confection. It filled her and gave the house a cozy warmth. She began to unthaw immediately. She looked into the kitchen where she saw Mark gently opening the oven door. KayLee stood close by. Too close.

Meggie hurried into the kitchen. "How did it turn out?" she asked.

"It just needs to sit with the oven off and the door propped open a crack," Mark said without looking up.

"KayLee did you grab those candy pieces?" Meggie asked.

"Oh, sorry, Meg. I got too caught up in what Mark was doing. Isn't it beautiful?" KayLee asked. "I've never seen a prettier cheesecake. I can't wait to taste it."

"What makes you think—," Meggie began

Mark interrupted, "Unfortunately, KayLee, you can't have a piece of this. It's my final assignment for my food critique and food writing class."

"You mean this mouth watering dessert is going to be wasted on a bunch of chefs who can make their own?" She pouted. Then she asked, "What kind of writing does a chef need to do?"

"Well, if I ever wanted to work as food critic I would have to write articles for magazines and newspapers."

"That sounds like fun," KayLee said. Then she brightened as she turned back to the cheesecake. "Will you make one for me when we get back from Christmas vacation?"

Meggie went to the drawer and rattled the candy wrappings

loudly as she pulled out the necessary pieces to make the snowman's face. She didn't hear Mark's reply. Two Hershey's kisses, and a piece of red licorice would make the eyes and mouth. She pulled a piece of black licorice from its package. It would make a perfect nose. As she was about to leave the kitchen she noticed the puddles of water that were gathering near the stove where KayLee and Mark were standing. "I hope you guys plan on cleaning that up," she said as she pointed towards the floor.

"Oh, I'll do it," KayLee and Mark said in unison. Both of them laughed as Meggie walked back outside.

A few minutes later, Mark joined Meggie as she created the face of the snowman. "Why are you so cranky?" he asked.

"I just don't like the way she hovers and expects you to feed her because she happened to stumble in while the cheesecake was baking," Meggie replied. "I think it's rude."

Mark laughed. "Why Meg, are you getting possessive over my cheesecake?"

Meggie's dark mood lifted a little. Mark's question did put a silly spin on Meggie's behavior. Then she giggled. "I guess I am," she said.

Mark took the red licorice from Meggie's hand and placed it as a frown on the snowman. Meggie laughed harder. She manipulated the licorice to look like a smile. Then she put the eyes and the nose in place. They stood back to appreciate their work. The snow had stopped, and the clouds had lifted showing off the white mountains against a lengthening, gray dusk.

"Do you think it'll be here when we get back from vacation?" Meggie asked as she motioned toward the snowman.

"I hope so," Mark said. "He makes a nice greeter. Now, what do you say about that hot chocolate you promised?"

Meggie grinned as they walked back into the house.

Chapter Eighteen

*T*ye stood in her family's kitchen before a pot of fresh steaming green beans. Gently, she prodded them with a fork. They weren't ready. It was nice to be home, surrounded by her family. Christmas was proving quiet. Meggie's family had left earlier in the week, renting a condominium in Sunriver, Oregon. They had invited Tye and her family to join them any time. But Tye had decided to remain close to Trapper.

"That Christmas ham sure smells good," Tye said as she moved to the oven. Opening the door, Tye took a peek at the roasting ham.

Her mother and father were both in the kitchen working on different dishes. Rex was putting the finishing touches on his favorite sweet potato casserole while Trudy took the scalloped potatoes out of the second oven.

"How is Meggie coming along in her cooking classes?" Rex asked.

"She's very happy with them. She'll graduate this June. I hope she can find a job she likes."

"And how are you and Trapper getting along?" Trudy asked.

Tye prodded her beans one more time before taking them off the heat. "Trapper's fine. Thelma has kept him in good shape over the fall semester. He seems to be getting plenty of pasture time as well."

"But you don't sound completely satisfied," Rex said.

Tye drained the beans. "It's not Thelma really. I think she's giving Trapper the best care possible."

"But it's not Kyle's care. Is that it?" Trudy asked.

Tye brought the beans back to the stove, turning the flame on low. She placed a pat of butter in the pan and stirred the green beans to coat. She added lemon pepper and a pinch of salt. "Kyle kept him ..." she searched for the right word.

"Kyle kept him for you," Rex said.

Tye flinched. "Yeah," she said quietly. "He kept him for me." She turned to her folks. "There was something magical about the way Kyle looked after Trapper. I can't explain it. I never worried about him."

"Do you worry about him in Thelma's care?"

"No, I don't worry exactly ... It's just that when Kyle had him, I felt like a part of me was with him. I know that sounds silly but that's how I felt. I was connected to Kyle through Trapper, and to Trapper through Kyle."

"It can be the same with Thelma. I know she e-mails you weekly with reports on Trapper's care. I think you were connected to Kyle by love," Trudy explained. "In some ways sharing the horses was like sharing kids."

"That's it, Mom! I mean how can Kyle keep silent? Doesn't he wonder about Trapper? I wonder about Ben."

"Have you been expecting him to write or call?" Rex asked.

Tye nodded as she put the beans in a serving dish. "He knows where I live in Utah. He also knows he could always reach me through the two of you, but he hasn't so much as sent an e-mail. I still check every day. I keep hoping he'll get in touch with me."

"Maybe you're looking for some closure. The relationship ended on a very abrupt note. It must be hard to come to terms with it," Trudy said.

"Yeah. On Saturday morning we went to a show together and everything was fine. By that afternoon, it was over. I still catch my breath every time I think about it."

"Is it hard to be around Trapper?" Rex asked. "I guess I wonder about that because I don't want Kyle to come between you and Trapper."

Tye was thoughtful. "Yeah, it is hard to be around Trapper simply because I expect Kyle to appear. We spent my last three months together before my mission. Kyle had Trapper during my mission. Then we spent the first four months together after my mission. Then Kyle left, and I went back to school. So, my most recent memories of Trapper always include Kyle. In fact a schoolmate asked to see a picture of Trapper, and I pulled out a photo of Trapper and Kyle. It was the only one I had."

Tye moved the beans to the table before checking the ham. Her mother was busy finishing the potatoes, so Tye pulled out the ham and placed it on a rack.

"One thing you may want to remember, Tye, is that your life with Trapper goes back seven years. You and Trapper have had five years together before you even met Kyle. He's a relative newcomer in that relationship."

Tye sat down. "I hadn't thought of it like that."

"Maybe while you're here you could take another picture. It might remind you of that reality," Trudy said.

Tye shrugged. "I don't know. Trapper isn't in show shape, and he hasn't had the extensive grooming that goes along with a show."

"So, groom him. You've got time. Spend an afternoon getting him ready for the picture, and then call me. I'll come to the barn and take a picture of the two of you," Trudy suggested.

Rex placed his hand on his daughter's arm. "Trapper is yours, Tye. Take him back. Don't allow Kyle to interfere with that."

Tye felt a stab of guilt. Since she had been home, she hadn't spent as much time with Trapper as she had imagined.

Trudy moved to the table carrying the fragrant ham. "We're ready to have this Christmas feast."

Everyone sat down. Then before they were to say the prayer, Rex said, "We have some good news for you, Tye. We've set a sealing date."

Tye grabbed her father's hand.

"May 3rd." He grinned. "We wanted to wait until you were out of school. We'll meet you in Utah and then all come back together. How does that sound?"

"It sounds perfect!"

"We've asked Meggie's family to join us. They'll come to Utah with us. Then we can bring you girls home together."

A few minutes later, as Rex said the Christmas prayer, Tye's heart filled with gratitude. Her parents were good, strong people who understood how she felt about Kyle. Their words had helped make sense of those feelings, and how she projected her hurt and anger for Kyle onto Trapper. The guilt washed away. It wasn't too late. She could still take care of him. She would claim Trapper as her own.

She peeked at her father as he prayed. So, they were going to be sealed. Before her mission, Tye remembered telling Kyle that her most fervent dream was to be sealed to her family. And now that dream would come true. Joy burst in her heart. When her father ended the prayer, Tye was filled with that joy and love. She squeezed her mom and dad's hands. Finally, they were hers.

Chapter Nineteen

*T*ye changed gears on the truck before turning onto the long muddy road that would lead her to the barn. Mud splattered as high as her window as she inched forward along the pothole-ridden track.

Tye rolled down her window breathing in the heavy scent of fir, pine, and oak mixed with mud and wet grass. When she turned into the parking lot of the barn the odor of fresh wood shavings and warm horse greeted her. Tears came to her eyes. She was home. She got out of the truck, fingering the apple in her pocket.

Arriving at Trapper's stall, she was pleased at how he turned to greet her. She let herself into his stall and handed him the apple. He bit it in two. As he ate, Tye took off his blanket. For a brief moment, she stood and looked at the beauty of Trapper. The lines of his confirmation were elegant and showed his fluidity in movement. Stepping closer, she put her hands on him. She caressed his warm, soft nose and looked into his gentle and intelligent eye. Soon, she was touching him everywhere—his shoulder, neck, and legs. She picked up his feet, checking his hooves. Then, she ran her hands along his back and down his flanks. Trapper turned to watch her in interest. She ran her fingers through his mane and checked his ears.

He was in perfect condition—well muscled and relaxed. She had not done this when she had first come to see him, but now it seemed right. It was as if she was getting to know him again as she slowly stroked his silken neck.

Quietly, she placed the halter on Trapper, leading him to the crossties. She retrieved her grooming gear and began preparing Trapper for their picture. She started at his tail, which was wrapped to keep it clean. She unraveled the wrapping and gave it a blunt cut at the hocks. Then she brushed it until it was silky and smooth. Next she started working on thinning and shortening his mane. After finishing his mane, she ran the brush over his body, feeling for bumps or bruises in his skin. There were none. She spent most of her time working on his feet. Mud clung in little balls to the hair around his fetlocks and pasterns. It was tedious work that kept Tye on her knees for a while. But after a couple of hours, Trapper was ready for his photo shoot.

Tye went to the phone and called her mother. While she waited for Trudy to appear, she stood next to Trapper, quietly talking as she went over him one more time. She whispered her apology for staying so distant. She told Trapper about school and promised him that she would come home to spend the summer with him. Nothing would come between them again. After several minutes, Tye heard her mother's car pull into the parking lot. Soon, Trudy appeared with the camera. Tye led Trapper outside. She was glad it was cloudy. It would make it easier to take a good picture. Soon, Trudy was clicking away.

"I think they'll turn out nice," Trudy said. "There's some Christmas pictures on this roll too, so I'll take it in and have it developed it this afternoon."

Tye gave her mother a hug. "Thanks, Mom."

"Are you going to ride now?" Trudy asked.

"Yes, I still have plenty of light left."

"I'll expect you around dinnertime," Trudy said.

Tye waved her mother out of the parking lot before turning back to Trapper. In a matter of minutes, she re-wrapped his tail and had him saddled for that long ride she had promised herself. But first she wanted to work. Leading Trapper into the indoor arena, she mounted.

Tye began to warm up Trapper in the soft sand-like footing. She melted into the saddle. Oh yes! She was riding! Gently, she asked for a walk. Trapper brightened, sensing it was time to go to work. Tye closed her eyes for a brief moment, allowing the rhythm of Trapper's movement underneath her leg to pull her along. Opening her eyes, she asked him to bend around her left leg. Trapper immediately responded. She asked for figure eights, then the extended trot. Trapper complied willingly. Tears came to her eyes as the cadence of their work took over. She asked for a canter in figure eights and flying lead changes. Trapper obeyed. Dressage—the classical form of riding was always Tye's favorite, because Trapper was so good at it. Nothing felt more right than going through those beautiful moves here in her home. Tye was so engrossed in the joy of her work that the winter chill left her. But after several minutes, she began to tire. She wasn't in competing shape. Trapper wasn't even winded.

Dismounting, Tye led her horse outside. She mounted again and began walking through well-known seasonal creeks and mud. Finally she came to the familiar open meadows of sparse and winter bare oak trees. Their branches reached heavenward toward the sodden sky. A damp wind chased the clouds, always keeping them out of the reach of the lonely oaks. She looked over the scuttling shades of gray that covered the sky. The wet, heavy air moved across her skin and pushed at the ragged and saturated grass. Tye loved this gray, northwest weather. It cleaned the earth, leaving everything rain scrubbed and fresh.

In spite of the familiarity of Tye's surroundings, there was a sense of strangeness. She and Trapper were alone. "I wonder if Kyle came home for Christmas," Tye wondered out loud. She looked over the wet horizon. Part of her expected to see Kyle riding Ben towards her. Her father was right. Everything had ended so abruptly that some inner sanctuary stubbornly held on to their relationship and the manufactured hope that eventually they would be able to work things out. That's where her hope ended though. Her mind got fuzzy when she tried to think of what that meant. How could they work things out?

Tye still checked her e-mail, hoping that Kyle would write because she was coming home. She couldn't help herself. Twice daily, she would turn to the computer screen only to find it empty.

"And it's going to stay empty," Tye said as she turned Trapper towards home. "It's just the two of us now, Trapper. Just us two." Tye reached over and ran her hand along Trapper's mane. She had her warm horse, and even though there was no man, it was enough.

Trapper flicked his ears in Tye's direction. He always listened, and somehow she thought he understood. Kyle was not coming back.

Chapter Twenty

"Hey girls!" KayLee exclaimed from the top of the stairs when Meggie and Tye walked in the door. "How was your Christmas?"

"Good. It was nice to be home. What about yours?" Tye asked.

"Great! Look what my parents gave me for Christmas." She pulled her hair away from her ears to reveal diamond studs. "Each piece is a full carat! Can you believe it?" She lifted her chin. "I'm determined to bring home a diamond on my finger to match by May."

"Have anyone in mind?" Tye asked dubiously. "It seems like when we left you weren't dating anyone particular."

"Oh, I don't have anyone in mind," KayLee said airily. "The Lord will provide."

"The Lord doesn't exactly provide diamonds, KayLee," Meg said.

"Oh, Meg, you're so silly. I don't expect the Lord to provide the diamond. I expect the Lord to provide the man. The man will provide the diamond."

"Ah, I see," Meg replied. Then she asked, "Hey, where are all your CTR rings?"

"I left them at home. It's time to get serious."

"Well, happy hunting," Tye said.

KayLee beamed. Then her face clouded for a moment as she motioned for the girls to come closer.

Both Tye and Meggie leaned towards KayLee.

"Just so that you know ... Dianna and Doug broke off their engagement over the holidays. I think it's permanent."

Meggie raised her eyebrows expressively.

"I'll let her tell you the story, but I thought you should know so that you didn't ask any ... well, you know, embarrassing questions."

"Right," Tye said softly. "Thanks, KayLee."

Once Tye and Meggie were in the privacy of their own room, Tye shut the door and let out a sigh.

Meggie nodded in agreement as they began to unpack.

As Meggie put away the last of her clothes, she said, "I can't wait to see Mark. He'll be so envious of my ski vacation. I'm going to walk down to his house. Do you want to join me?"

"No. I'm tired. I'm going to take a shower and go to bed. My statistics class starts at 9:00 ..., and I want to go to the barn before class and look in on Elsa. Tell Mark hello for me though."

Several minutes later, Meggie was standing on Mark's front porch. When Mark answered the door, she quickly gave him a hug. "I missed you!" she exclaimed.

"Yeah? Well, I doubt you missed me all that much. I got your one and only e-mail telling me you were up at Bachelor for two weeks." Mark opened the door wide. Meggie stepped in. "Did you ski every day?" Mark asked.

"Not every day. We went into Bend for a couple of days of window shopping. We practically ate our way through the city. And we never ski on Sunday. We brought all our groceries with us, so on Sunday we went to church and then cooked in the condominium."

Mark smiled. "Did you do the cooking?"

Meggie grinned. "Yeah. I made up a new recipe. I call them spinach rolls."

Mark made a face as they sat down on the couch.

"I know. They don't sound very good. I'll have to think of a new name for them, but my family loved them."

"How did you make them?"

"Well, tomorrow, let's go to the store and get the ingredients. We can make a batch together."

Mark grinned. "You've got a deal, Meggie." He paused. "Did you drive straight through from home to here?"

Meggie shook her head. "My folks always spring for a motel room in Boise. Tye provides the transportation with her truck. I provide half of the gas, our food, and a motel room. It's a good trade. Our folks don't like the idea of us driving straight through. The weather is dicey, and it's easy to get tired. Did you ski much?"

"Well, not as much as you," Mark said pointedly. "But I did get out with one of my older brothers who came from New York for the holidays. He brought his wife and kids. They stayed for about ten days. We went up to Stevens Pass on two separate occasions and Snoqualmie for one day. That was fun. When do you want to go to Sundance again?"

"I'd love to go tomorrow, but I think it's going to be later in the month before I can afford it," Meggie replied. She giggled. "I wish my folks would give me a skiing allowance."

"Yeah? Well, I wish your folks would give me a skiing allowance too."

Meggie laughed as she stood. "What time should I come over tomorrow?"

"How long do these spinach rolls take?"

"Well, if we use frozen bread dough, which is what I did in Bend, it goes a lot quicker since they only have to go through one rising for thirty minutes after they unthaw. Would it be okay if I came by around four?"

"That'd be perfect. It would give me the opportunity to start some fresh vegetable soup." "Do you want to feed your roommates? We'll make about a dozen rolls."

Mark shrugged. "Sure. I'll collect the usual four bucks."

⌣

The following afternoon, Mark stood by Meggie as he watched her work with the bread dough. She had bought frozen spinach, Parmesan and Monterey jack cheese, along with dill weed, garlic powder and white pepper.

"Do you have any olive oil?" Meggie asked.

Mark went to the cupboard, producing olive oil.

Meggie spread the oil lightly over the dough that she had rolled out into a long rectangle. Then she added the cut and pressed spinach, cheeses, garlic and spices before rolling the dough. She spoke as she worked. "It's the same idea as cinnamon rolls," she said. "Only it's a savory recipe, instead of sweet. If you wanted, you could make your own bread dough and add spices directly to the dough. That would be best."

Mark agreed. "I think I would add a little more garlic, maybe in the form of a little garlic salt. I would also add some dried onion along with pieces of spinach directly to the dough. You could even add small bits of red pepper for some color and a peppery bite."

Meggie nodded as she lightly coated the muffin tin with olive oil. She sliced the rolls, and placed them in the muffin tin before draping them with a towel to rise. "We'll check them in about twenty minutes," she said. "How is your soup coming along?"

"Oh, it's ready to go. Just simmering."

The doorbell rang.

"I bet that's Tye."

One of Mark's roommates answered the door. Tye, KayLee and Dianna stepped in with a flurry of snow, coats, and scarves.

Mark and Meggie came from the kitchen.

"Tye told us to bring some money," KayLee said. She offered four wet dollars. Mark took the money. He noticed how pretty KayLee was in a cream-colored sweater that draped over her petite frame and black pants that accented her small waist. "Hey KayLee. What do you think of our snowman?"

"He looks better than I thought he would. I'd say he's a survivor."

"Meggie and I are going to spruce him up tomorrow. We named him Legs."

KayLee giggled, then said, "If I have time, I'll help you give him a make-over."

Mark moved to Tye and gave her quick hug before re-introducing himself to Dianna. Once he was back in the kitchen with Meggie he commented on KayLee. "I don't think I realized how pretty she is."

Meggie gave him a hard look. "Don't even think about it," she said. "She's looking for a diamond to match the earrings her folks gave her. And I'm not talking about a stud for her nose."

Mark laughed.

Tye joined them in the kitchen. "Hey, what's so funny?"

"Meg is trying to save me from your roommate, KayLee," Mark said conspirationally. "What do you think, Tye? Do I need saving?"

Tye shrugged. Why would Meg be concerned if Mark dated KayLee? He'd learn soon enough how silly she was. Besides, some men liked silly. Mark didn't seem the type, but who knew?

Soon, everyone was around the table, and the meal began. The rolls were proclaimed delicious, and the soup was perfect. The food disappeared within twenty minutes. Tye helped clean up while an impromptu study group started around the dining room table. KayLee, Dianna, and a couple of Mark's roommates were in the same religion class and took the opportunity to start on the semester's work.

After Meggie was finished in the kitchen, she wiped her hands on a dishtowel. "I think I'm going to head on home with Tye, so I can study tonight."

Dianna stood. "I'll come with you," she said.

"How about you, KayLee?" Meggie asked.

She flashed her eyes at Mark. "I think I'll stay," she said. "I would love to learn how to make that vegetable soup. Maybe Mark would be willing to give me some weekly cooking lessons. I still dream about the cheesecake."

Mark flashed Meggie a quick and knowing grin.

Hurriedly, Meggie put on her coat. She stepped out of the door before Tye and Dianna could say a quick goodbye.

Once they were out on the walk, Meggie snapped, "Well, Mark could've at least walked us home. He always does that."

"Oh Meggie, if Mark is special to you just tell KayLee. She'll keep her mitts off. That's one good thing about KayLee. She won't steal someone else's man," Dianna said.

"He's not my man," Meggie said in an exasperated tone. "Mark and I are only friends."

"Doesn't sound so friendly to me," Dianna said.

"Why don't you tell us what happened between you and Doug?" Meggie asked in a softer tone.

Dianna's shoulders slumped. "His mother is what happened," she said. "I hate his whole family. His mother is so bossy; ordering everyone around like we're all a bunch of corporals in her personal army. I've met her before but because of the wedding, we had a lot to do that involved her. I just noticed her bossiness for the first time. She just barged in on the whole thing and even started telling my mother what to do. She did her best to exclude me during family time. I mean I'm the bride for heaven's sake. Well, I was the bride. One night, I was over at their house, and Doug's father announces that we're going out to dinner. And before I can even put on my coat, Doug takes me aside to tell me that this is a "family dinner." At first I didn't understand. I mean, I thought I was part of the family. After all, I'm Doug's fiancée. Well, I was Doug's fiancée. But apparently that didn't qualify as family. Doug told me they were going without me. I was shocked. Most of the time they acted as if I wasn't even there."

"What did Doug think of all this?"

"He went along with it. To him it was perfectly normal. When I approached him about it he said that I was just too sensitive."

"I'm really sorry, Dianna," Tye said.

"I'm just glad that I figured it out before we got married. Can you imagine how awful it would be to marry someone like that and not know it until it was too late?" She continued quietly, "Still, it does hurt. I loved Doug. I still love him, but I can't believe I used such poor judgment. KayLee says we'll have a blast this semester. We'll go to every dance and activity put on by the ward and school."

She sighed. "I hope she's right."

"Oh, KayLee will keep you busy," Tye said. "I don't doubt that."

Chapter Twenty-one

"How was your Christmas vacation, Triss?" Tye asked as she walked beside the young girl, who was leading the pony into the arena.

"It was nice. I got to spend some time in Colorado with Daddy." Her face clouded over. "Not very much time though." She brightened again. "But he's here today."

A warm flush came over Tye. "That's nice," she murmured as she looked into the stands. Kenneth was sitting in his regular place. He smiled and waved at Trista and Tye. Trista waved back. Tye smiled.

"Are you ready to start warming up Patches?"

Trista nodded and began the warm up exercises as Tye moved poles into the middle of the arena.

"Today, you're going to trot down the center of the arena and over these poles," she explained to Trista. "Can you tell me what is going to be important for you to remember as you do this exercise?"

Trista thought for a moment. "I'm going to have to keep Patches' attention." She paused. "Is there anything else?"

"Yes. You're going to need to use as much of the corner as

possible so you can approach the poles straight. No weaving around. Don't let Patches fall into your circle. Keep them nice and wide so he can be straight when you meet the poles."

Trista nodded as she nudged Patches into a trot against the long wall of the arena. As she got to the corner, she rode Patches right into the corner. He stopped. Trista kicked him.

"Wait just a minute," Tye said as she walked to where Trista and Patches were stuck in the corner. "What do you think happened?"

"He's being dumb!" Trista said. "No one rides right into a wall! I want him to use the corner but not stop in the corner."

"Trista, don't take your frustration out on Patches. He rode right where you told him to ride. What do you need to do different so that he rounds the corner?"

Trista gave Tye a dark look. "I didn't ride him into this stupid corner!"

Tye gave Trista a calm but determined eye. "We can cut the lesson short right here if you aren't willing to control your temper. Temper tantrums on horseback only lead to disaster."

Trista was quiet for a moment. "I don't know what happened," she said.

"Okay. I'll tell you," Tye said quietly. "You were so intent on using every inch of the corner that you didn't give him the aid he needs to turn the corner. How would you do that?"

Trista thought for a moment. "More outside leg?" she offered.

"Exactly. More outside leg will help him to round the corner while bending around your inside leg. Try again. And no kicking."

"Yes, ma'am," Trista said.

Tye grabbed Patches' bridle to help start him in the right direction. "Now, you have three corners to practice in before you come around the same corner to the center of the arena." She yelled as Trista came to her first corner. Trista's aids were a little unclear. Patches took a minute to understand but he rounded the corner. By the time Trista was rounding her third corner, her aids were more defined, and Patches was moving better. Trista brought Patches into the middle of the arena with the poles. Patches stepped over them without a bobble.

"Very good," Tye said. "Now, try it from the other side of the arena."

Trista nodded. Again, the attempt went well.

Tye asked Trista to turn Patches around so she could work from the opposite directions. Then the lesson was over.

"Very good work, Trista. That's a difficult exercise," Tye said as she opened the arena gate.

Kenneth joined them and gave Trista a hug. "Good job, Triss."

"Thanks, Daddy," Trista beamed. She grew thoughtful. "I guess I shouldn't have blamed Patches for my own mistake."

"That's an important lesson to learn, Trista," Kenneth said quietly.

Trista turned to her father. "Will you help me with Patches?" she asked.

"Sure, honey."

Trista led Patches to the crossties, and with Kenneth's help began to untack the pony. Tye stayed out of the way as the two talked about Trista's new assignments in school and the snowy weather. "I can't wait until spring!" Trista said. "Miss Jorgenson said I can ride outside in the spring." She paused. "I wish it was spring now."

"We don't have that long to wait, Triss," Tye said.

Kenneth spoke, "Miss Jorgenson, Trista and I are going to the

Dairy Queen for lunch. Would you like to join us?"

"Oh, yes, Miss Jorgenson. We can all eat hamburgers together!" Trista said.

Tye was taken aback by the invitation. But what really surprised her was the strong desire that welled up inside. She wanted to go with them. She shook her head. "I'm sorry," she said. "But I have another student who comes in soon after Trista."

"Why don't you just leave a note," Trista suggested.

Tye and Kenneth both laughed.

"I wish I could Triss, but that wouldn't be fair to the next student. Think about it for a minute. You wouldn't like to come to the barn, all excited for your lesson, only to find a note explaining that the teacher went to lunch at Dairy Queen."

Trista shook her head. "No, I guess I wouldn't like it much," Triss replied.

"Thank you for asking me, though. That's very nice."

"Maybe we can make it for another time," Kenneth said. Then he turned to Trista. "Are you ready to go, honey?"

Trista nodded, and with Kenneth's gentle hand on her shoulder, they left the barn.

Tye fought the desire to follow them to the entrance. As soon as she heard Kenneth's rental car spring to life, she noticed the quiet of the barn. No longer was Trista's laughter and enthusiasm ringing in the aisle with Kenneth's deep voice. She pushed those thoughts away. She had another student coming in a few minutes. It wouldn't do for her to be daydreaming about Trista's father.

Turning back into the aisle, Tye found Candy's stall and began preparing the little mare for her next student.

Chapter Twenty-Two

*T*ye stood in Elsa's stall and ran her hands over the pregnant Holstein. She hadn't changed much since Tye had seen her last.

Tye scratched behind her ears. "I know you like that," she said softly.

With one more pat on her neck, Tye opened the stall door to check the feed chart. Elsa looked good. Everything was in proper order. She was eating properly. Her coat and eyes shone with vitality and health. And she looked genuinely happy to see Tye.

Walking to her truck, Tye was about to step into her vehicle when she saw Preston pull into the parking lot. She waited for a moment.

He emerged from his pick-up and walked to her. "Hey Tye! How are you?"

"I'm fine, thanks, Preston. I was hoping I'd run into you." She had a strong desire to embrace him but pulled her coat close instead. "How was your Christmas?"

Preston shrugged. "We didn't do a lot. There isn't a lot of snow this year so the cows have grass, and we didn't have to worry too much about their water freezing. So, I just sat around and ate a lot. I did ride up into the mountains a few times. It was cold up there. Are you just leaving?"

Tye nodded. "I've already checked on Elsa."

"Do you have time to walk with me to her stall?" Preston asked.

"Sure."

"How was your holiday?" Preston asked as they walked into the barn.

"It was nice. I rode a lot. I enjoyed my folks and Trapper. It was good to be home."

"How does Elsa look?"

"The same to me. I think she's fine." She changed the subject. "So, what do you think this class is going to be all about?" Tye asked.

"I think it's for people who haven't had a lot of exposure to livestock. Vet majors who primarily will work on small animals but need some sort of background in large animals before going into vet school. I doubt there will be too much new information for you and I. Still, it can be a fun class … and an easy A."

"Speak for yourself," Tye said. "I've never worked with cows before."

"You'll be great!" Preston said.

"So, tell me," Tye began. "How do you spend your time when you're not working on an easy A?"

"Well, some classes aren't this easy. So I do study a lot."

"You don't happen to have a statistics class, do you?" Tye asked.

"Nope. I lucked out this semester."

"What about Business Planning?"

"Yeah, I do have that class. It should be interesting. We'll have to put a detailed business plan together and then defend it at the end of the semester."

"Who's your professor?" Tye asked.

"Dr. Maloney."

"Mine too!" Tye exclaimed. "Do you want to study together? I know our business plans would be different, but it could be fun to see how they each work."

Preston didn't answer. Instead, he stepped into Elsa's stall.

Tye wondered if she had been too bold in her request. "Oh, maybe that won't work for you," she said gently. "It was just a thought, but it might be hard for our schedules to match up." She wanted to give him a comfortable out.

"No, I think it'll be fine." He hesitated again. "It's just that I've never studied with anyone before. I know study groups are popular, and this would probably be a big help. You just surprised me, that's all."

"Why don't you ever study with anyone?" Tye asked.

"I don't know. I guess the opportunity has just never come up."

Tye gave him a questioning look. "How can that be? People are always getting together to study. You live with five other men. They must study some of the time."

"But they don't take the same classes I do." Preston stuffed his hands into his pockets. "I'm an only child, Tye. Out on the ranch we're miles from anyone. I learned very early to rely on myself, my family, and my horse. I like it that way."

"I'm an only child too, Preston," she said softly. "But I didn't grow up on a ranch so I would guess that my experience has been different than yours." She smiled and touched his arm. "If you prefer, we don't have to study together. I didn't realize—."

"No, I would enjoy the opportunity to study with you, Tye. Are you free on Thursday evening around seven?"

"Yes. That'll work for me."

"Can I meet you at the entrance to the library?"

"I'll be there." Tye said.

⌢

Tye hurried in spite of all the layers of clothing that protected her from the winter weather but hindered her progress. A furious snowstorm was dumping snow by the inch every few minutes, making the short walk from her home to the library difficult. In spite of the street lights, Tye found it difficult to see through the swirling flakes. At least it wasn't windy. Most of the time she tried not to think about the bitter weather but now, shivering and sweating due to the cold and her exertion, she longed for the soft breezes of spring. Finally, she reached the entrance. Preston was standing just inside the doors, looking for her. She waved as she neared the building.

Preston opened the door for her. Tye rushed in with a flurry of snow and a breath of cold air.

"I'm sorry I'm late." Her words rushed out. "The snow made things slow."

Preston helped her with her coat. "I know. It's a pretty bad storm. The weather report states that we can expect over twelve inches before it's all over. Then there's another storm right on its heels."

Tye shot him a look. "Thanks for the good news," she said wryly.

Preston smiled. "Oh, I specialize in good weather reports. Let's find a computer."

They walked through the maze of tables and rooms, finally

settling on two computers that sat next to each other.

Preston watched as Tye shed her scarf, ear-coverings, and gloves. She looked radiant. Her skin was nicely flushed from the cold, and her green eyes shone with the brilliancy of emeralds. She wasn't very big but he knew she had to be strong if she rode horses. Over the Christmas holidays, Preston had spent some time reading and learning about the sport in which Tye participated. Three-day-eventing could be grueling and difficult. It also looked exhilarating and challenging. It expected tough bodies and minds. It required a unique and trusting partnership between horse and rider. Preston had come away with a new respect for Tye and her work with Trapper.

"Why don't we start by you telling me about your business plan," Tye said. "Are you going to use the ranch?"

"No. That would be a cop out. I'm going to use my veterinarian practice."

"I would think you would have to be very determined to become a veterinarian."

Preston was thoughtful. "It's all I've wanted to do since I was nine." Then he asked, "What is your business plan?"

"I want to run my own barn after I graduate."

"Would you own the barn or just run the program?"

"I could do it either way. I would probably start out by just running the program. Then, maybe after I get some clients and a good reputation, I can have my own barn."

"I would think that most barn owners would also be trainers."

"Not always. Some barn owners just really love horses. They like to ride and they enjoy caring for horses, but they don't know how to teach a rider or train a horse. So they'll bring in a trainer. Once that trainer becomes well-known it doesn't take long for the barn to become full of boarders. That makes everyone happy. The barn owners are happy because their barn is full with people who rent their stalls. The trainer is happy because her schedule is full. Hopefully, the horse owners are getting a good trainer and teacher, along with a good solid barn and good feed for their horse. It works well for everybody."

Tye busied herself by pulling paper out of her notebook. "In our class, our first assignment is to write an essay that tells why we have chosen this specific line of work."

Preston turned to his computer. "I think I already have an idea about how I want to approach the essay. Would you mind reading my rough draft when I'm finished?"

"Sure. Will you read mine?" Tye asked

Preston nodded. Soon, both Tye and Preston were busy on their individual computers. Preston finished first. Tye stopped her work, glancing at her watch. It was nine. She stretched as she and Preston traded places so they could read from each other's computer. After they were finished reading, they both made suggestions and notes. Finally at nine-thirty, they saved their work to disk before printing out their rough drafts.

Afterwards they began walking towards the entrance of the library. When they reached the door, they stopped, and both of them struggled into their winter coats and gear. The snow had not let up dropping several inches since their arrival.

"I'll walk you home," Preston said.

"Don't you drive to campus?" Tye asked.

"Yeah, but I'll walk you home then come back for the truck."

"We could drive," Tye suggested.

Preston grinned. "My truck is about as far away as your house," he replied.

Tye smiled. "Thank you, Preston. I appreciate your willingness to walk me home."

Stepping outside, Tye noticed a fitful breeze starting to push at the snow. It added to the intensity of the cold. Tye sucked in her breath as they walked into the biting temperature. "I'm still not used to this cold. I hope that changes soon."

Preston resisted the urge to put his arm around her and pull her close. "It does get cold, I know."

"Do you want to get together tomorrow and finish up our essays?" Tye asked. "I don't have any classes on Friday."

"I can't," Preston said. "I've got plans."

"Oh, okay."

"I try to go to Payson a couple of times a month. I stay with Martin and Lorena Thomas. They're friends of my parents," he explained. "They own a small ranch outside of Payson where they run a few cows. It's good for me to get out and ride. I don't have any classes on Friday so I spend some weekends out there."

"I bet it's fun," Tye said.

Tye's response made Preston curious. He didn't think it was something that a girl would enjoy. The weather was often harsh. "I really like it," he replied. "But it might be difficult if you don't like the cold."

"I have to admit that I haven't ridden much in the snow, but I do know that riding always makes me warm." She became thoughtful. "If you dress properly it could probably be a lot of fun."

"Maybe you would like to come with me." Preston was shocked at his own words. It had not been his intention to invite her. What would the Thomases say? He hadn't even considered them. What was he thinking?

Tye stopped and faced him. "I would love to go, Preston."

Preston was both glad and anxious. "I usually spend the night," he stammered. Then he quickly added, "It probably wouldn't be a good idea if you spent the night. I'll have to ask the Thomases. I've known them since I was little. Oh, but I'm sure it'll be fine if you come with me. They're always telling me I should bring a friend." A thought startled him. "I just don't know if they meant a girl." He shook his head. "I'm sure it'll be fine. I should come pick you up tomorrow morning."

Tye smiled. "Preston, I don't have to go if you're not comfortable with it. I don't want to tax someone's hospitality towards you."

"No. Oh, no. It's not that. I … um … I, it's … um, I think I just need to call them and check to see if it's okay. I can call you later this evening and let you know."

"It's getting a little late for phone calls." She stopped. "My house is right here."

Preston looked up at the small two-story home. The lights were shining from inside. A porch light beamed over the fresh snow, illuminating the falling flakes.

"Look, Preston. We don't have to do this. I can tell that the invitation was an accident. I know how it is to say something and then wonder how that ever could've happened."

Anxiety melted from Preston. The porch light beamed into Tye's face, making her eyes shine in the snowy light. Her long blonde hair seemed to absorb the light, giving off a soft shine that complimented the falling snow. She truly did understand. An unexpected stillness crept into Preston's heart like a summer Montanan morning. It warmed him in spite of the falling snow and temperature. "I would like you to come with me tomorrow," he said quietly. "I do feel the need to call the Thomases and ask them for permission to bring a guest. I hope you will grant me that. I can call you and confirm first thing in the morning."

"That'd be fine."

"Some of the work will be dirty so you may want to bring some fresh clothes. You can get cleaned up there."

Tye nodded as she began making her way up the snowy walk of her home. When she reached the porch, she turned and waved. Preston returned her wave as he watched her go inside. He looked down at his feet, expecting to see a puddle of melted snow. Instead, his snow boots were firmly entrenched in ten inches of light powder.

Chapter Twenty-Three

The following morning, the snowstorm that had pummeled the Utah Valley had passed through. Although the weather report had talked about the possibility of another storm, Friday dawned bright, clear, and cold. The mountains stood as hushed sentinels over the snowy valley. Tye took notice of them as she got into Preston's truck. She was grateful for their presence and wondered about their canyons. Was winter a bitter season for the rocks, trees, and rivers? Or was it a season of rest, hibernation, and rejuvenation? For Tye, winter was fatiguing. There was no rest; only harsh cold and wind.

As Preston slowly pulled away from the curb, Tye turned her attention turned towards the driving conditions. The roads were treacherous so early in the morning, but Preston carefully negotiated ice sheets on the freeway. The Montanan winters had prepared him for such eventualities. He was comfortable behind the wheel.

Tye spread her hands out in her lap, soaking up the sun that came through the windshield. "So, tell me about the Thomases," she said.

"They're friends of my parents, really," he began. "They've

known each other since before I was born. Martin and Lorena Thomas used to own a ranch in Montana, but they decided they didn't want to work such a big spread. They wanted to raise their kids closer to town and be able to offer them other activities besides ranching. So, they moved here to Payson. Over the years they've accumulated some land and a few head of cattle."

"Is that what they do for a living?"

Preston shook his head. "No. They don't have enough cattle for a full-time ranch. Martin retired from the water company about two years ago. Lorena used to be a school teacher. They're a bit older than my folks. Their youngest girl is about five years older than me. They ranch now because it's what they love." He paused as he turned off the freeway. "I've enjoyed coming by a couple of times a month to help out with chores or whatever else they're doing. I miss the ranch a lot. This helps."

Pulling into the driveway Preston shut off the engine. "It's icy so watch your step," Preston said as he helped Tye out of the car.

A few minutes later, introductions were made as Tye met Martin and Lorena Thomas. The older couple welcomed Tye and Preston into the warmth of their kitchen. The wood stove was burning brightly, giving a cozy warmth to the house.

"Sit down, Tye," Lorena said. "I'll make you a cup of hot chocolate."

Tye took a seat. "I don't know if that's a good idea. If I have a cup of something warm I may never get back outside."

Martin laughed. "Relax all you want. We usually feed Preston before he goes out."

After everyone was seated at the table the dishes of potatoes, bacon, and eggs were passed around. Martin and Lorena asked Tye about her home. She told them about the Oregon coast and forests. Then she told them about Trapper and her riding experiences. "I've never done any western riding, though. I'm a little nervous about today."

"Don't worry," Martin said. "We've got a sure-footed pony for you. She's a great teacher."

Tye was pleased. Usually, she was the teacher. This time she would be the student.

"Are you thinking about Sunny?" Preston asked.

Martin nodded. "If you're finished we'll go out and make some introductions."

"I'm ready, but shouldn't I help Lorena with the breakfast dishes?"

Martin grinned. "No, I can do that when I get the two of you settled on your chores." He chuckled. "Once you get out in that cold, you may wish you had stayed and helped. But don't you worry. You just come on in anytime you want."

Tye stood and followed Preston's lead out to the barn.

Once in the barn, Preston asked, "What's on the agenda today?"

"The fences along the east line need to be looked at. This storm probably pushed some off them down. And you may want to take a torch and a sledgehammer to check those water troughs. I've already checked the troughs once this morning and given the cows their morning feed so we'll feed again later this afternoon."

Martin pulled a little gray horse out of a stall. "This is Sunny. We'll saddle her up for you."

Tye took the lead rope from Martin while stroking Sunny's shoulder. The horse was small and shaggy due to her winter coat.

Martin returned with a saddle and other tack that was unfamiliar to Tye. She placed the bridle Martin handed her on her shoulder while holding onto Sunny. Martin saddled the little gray mare. Then, when Martin was ready, she handed him the bridle. Martin placed the bit in the horse's mouth.

After the saddling up was finished Tye and Preston led their horses outside.

"Aren't you coming with us?" Preston asked of Martin.

He shook his head. "No. The gelding is a little sore in the hind end so I'm giving him a couple of days off. Besides, Lorena needs my help with some chores in the house."

"I can stay at the house, Martin," Tye suggested. "You can take Sunny. I didn't mean to interfere with your work."

He smiled as he shook his head. "No, no no. You and Preston go on. I don't mind staying inside on a cold day like today. It's nice for an old duffer like me to have a day off every now and then." He held Sunny while Tye mounted. "Up you go now."

As they headed into the fields Tye and Preston gave Martin a final wave. Once they were out of hearing range Tye turned to Preston. "Maybe I need a lesson."

"Oh, that's right," Preston said. "This will be different to you." He began by explaining the differences in the bridle. "You won't need much tension on the reins," he said. "These bits magnify the pressure in the horse's mouth. That's why you always see western riders with loose reins."

"In English riding we always keep the pressure between the horse's mouth and our hands. This is a strange feel for me," Tye said as she concentrated on the leather straps between her fingers.

"Hold them in your left hand," Preston advised. He moved to where Sunny was standing, reached over and showed Tye how to hold her reins. "It's necessary to have a free hand when you're working. You may need to use your rope or possibly your shotgun."

"I don't have a shotgun!" Tye exclaimed.

"Chances are you wouldn't need one here," Preston said.

"Martin and Lorena live too close to town to have to worry about too many predators, but in Montana we always ride with a firearm."

It was an unsettling thought for Tye.

Preston continued, "At any rate, use only your left hand for the reins."

Tye did as he suggested and dropped her right hand to her thigh. She gave Sunny a nudge with her legs. The horse moved at a walk as Tye directed her to Preston's side, who continued their short lesson.

"This is how you turn," he said as he executed a turn with Sargeant to the right at a walk. "Lay your reins against your horse's neck in the direction that you want to go. If you want to turn right, lay the left rein on your horse's neck," he explained as he gave her a visual example. "You try."

Tye's efforts were clumsy, but after several attempts she was able to communicate her desire to Sunny. "She's a nice horse," Tye said as she leaned over, giving Sunny a pat on the neck.

"Are you ready to trot?" Preston asked.

"I think so."

"Okay. Remember to keep your hands light."

She nodded as she nudged Sunny into a brisk walk, keeping up with Preston and his mount, Sergeant.

The sun hit the snow, making it look as if they were riding through a field of diamonds but after a minute, the glare became overwhelming. Tye pulled her sunglasses down to shield her eyes. Preston pushed his hat down. The walk exhilarated Tye as she moved along on Sunny. The sky was clear blue, and the bitter cold kept her alert. After several minutes of riding they reached the east fence. Preston slowed Sergeant's walk, keeping his eyes on the wire that separated Martin's cows from his neighbor's property. When he found a place that needed repair he dismounted and taking the pliers from his saddle bag, began the job. Sometimes he would need Tye's help, and she would dismount and follow his instructions. Together they would work the wire and post until Preston was satisfied. "Snow is hard on these fences," Preston murmured. "Drifts form and push them over."

Throughout the morning they continued to ride, looking for weak spots in the fence. The work was mostly done in silence, except for the few instructions that Preston would softly give Tye. She didn't mind the lack of conversation. She was warm from the riding in the sun. The work was satisfying, and she enjoyed being in the field with this quiet young man.

As the morning wore on, the sun rose high. The last repair was made. "I think it's time for some lunch. Are you hungry?" Preston asked.

"I'm starving," Tye said.

"Let's head back. We'll check some of the troughs on our way in but they're probably fine. The sun has warmed the water."

Several minutes later, they dismounted in front of the barn, tying their horses up in the sun.

As they neared the house, Tye smelled the aroma of chicken soup. Lorena greeted them warmly. As they sat down at the table she placed a steaming bowl of soup with homemade biscuits in front of Preston and Tye.

Tye and Preston ate with a hearty appetite. Afterwards Tye stood to help Lorena with the dishes.

"You sit down for a minute," Lorena admonished. "You've been working all morning out in the cold."

Tye realized for the first time that it had been work. She had enjoyed herself so much that she had forgotten that the job she had been doing was work.

"I'm going to head back to the barn and see if Martin has anything else he would like for me to do," Preston said. Then he turned to Tye, "I'll come and get you if you'd like."

"Yes, please."

Lorena took the dishes to the sink and began running hot soapy water. "So, how long have you known Preston?" she asked.

"I met him last semester. Now we're partners in a reproductive physiology class. We're looking after a pregnant Holstein."

"Well, I'd say she's in good hands. Preston has birthed a lot of cows."

"Elsa isn't the only one who's in good hands," Tye said. "I'm glad he's my partner. I've never worked with cows before."

"Are you a pre-vet major, like Preston?" Lorena asked.

"No. I'm finished with school after I have my Bachelors in Animal Science. I want to teach horseback riding lessons."

Preston interrupted with the breath of a storm that followed him into the warm kitchen.

Tye shivered.

"He wants us to check the troughs one last time," Preston said. "The temperature has dropped, and there's a couple that might be frozen over if they're under a tree. Then I'll take you home."

Grabbing her coat Tye followed Preston out the door. She glanced at the sky. The promised storm was gathering. The clouds that had silently moved in during the lunch hour were now lowering themselves in the familiar posture over the tops of the mountains. Tye hurried to Sunny. Within a few minutes she and Preston were on their horses. Preston knew where all of the water troughs were. They checked the few troughs they had seen on their way in to lunch, but some of the water troughs were further in the fields. Preston and Tye broke new snow on their way to them. They came to their first trough. "I don't think the pipes are frozen," Preston said. "There's just a thin layer of ice on top." Dismounting, he pulled the sledgehammer from his saddle and broke through the ice. They moved on to the next trough as the first few flakes began to drift lazily. By the time they were finished, forty-five minutes later, the snow was coming down in small needle like flakes, being driven by a wind that promised stronger gusts soon. Tye was beginning to feel the chill of the day. The warm soup left her, and her feet and fingers were beginning to numb.

Preston noticed the drawn look on her face. "Cold?"

She nodded.

"We're done here. Let's get you inside to thaw out." He mounted once again, and they began the ride back. Ten minutes later, Tye dismounted. Her frozen feet hit the ground, sending shock waves through the rest of her body. She tried to loosen the buckles on her saddle but her numb fingers would not cooperate. Preston watched for a moment then moved beside her. "Don't worry about Sunny. I'll untack her."

Tye shook her head. "I can do it."

Preston placed his hand on top of Tye's, then quickly undid the buckle. "It's not good to be so cold," he said gently. "Go inside."

Tye looked at him with the idea of defending her position, but the soft look in his blue eyes changed her mind. She walked past him and into the house where a cup of hot chocolate and her fresh clothes were waiting.

"Would you like a hot shower?" Lorena asked as Tye stumbled into the house.

Tye nodded mutely. Her frozen extremities cried out for heat.

Lorena handed her a towel before showing her the bathroom.

Stripping off her clothes, Tye tucked her braid at the nape of her neck before stepping into the warm steam. As the hot water flowed over her body, her muscles began to loosen. Tye could not remember when she had been so cold. Twenty minutes later she emerged from the bathroom feeling fresh and alive. She had taken her hair down and removed the braid, brushing out the loose waves of curl. She looked outside. The snow and wind was beginning to howl around the house.

"Where's Preston?" she asked Lorena.

"He should be in any minute now. He's probably feeding the horses."

Preston came into the house. "You look a lot better," he said as he looked at Tye.

"Thanks. I feel better."

He hurried into the shower, while Tye sat at the kitchen table with Lorena.

"Preston must think the two of you make a pretty good team for him to bring you out here," Lorena said. "We've told Preston he can bring any of his friends, but he has always come alone." She became thoughtful. "He's a quiet young man, but it's worth the effort of getting to know him."

Tye sipped her hot chocolate. "How long have you known him?"

"Since he was born. My husband and his father grew up together in Montana. They've stayed in touch ever since. We had three children, and it was a nice time whenever our families would get together around haying time. Preston doesn't have any brothers and sisters. I used to think our tribe was a little overwhelming for him. It always took him a couple of days to adjust to all the hubbub that comes with more than one child."

"Has it been hard for him to be without brothers and sisters?"

"It's hard to say. He can't really compare it because he doesn't know the difference. He spent a lot of his spare time in the mountains. He could've gone into town to hang around with friends or schoolmates, but Preston always chose to be alone. He'd go up into the mountains for days. I guess he's always been a little bit of a loner."

Tye was about to ask Lorena more about ranch life when Preston walked out of the hallway, looking a bit fresher.

He tossed his duffle bag on the couch, letting out a sigh. "I think we got the fence up—at least for now," Preston said. He turned to Lorena. "Thanks for having me. It's a good thing I'm coming out here and staying in shape. Otherwise when I get home I would be in real trouble."

"You're always welcome Preston, whether you work or not," Lorena said.

Preston moved into the living room and sat on the couch.

Martin came through the kitchen door finding the two women sitting at the table. Asking after Preston he found him in the living room. "Why don't you go on and get out of here," Martin suggested.

"I never leave this early," Preston said.

"You never leave until Sunday," Martin reminded him. "This storm isn't going to lighten up. It would be better if you were closer to home. Besides, you have a young lady with you this time. I'm sure that the two of you have better things to do than to spend your Friday evening with a couple of old fogies like me and Lorena."

"Martin—," Preston began to protest.

"I don't want to hear another word about it." He fished around his pocket until he found his wallet. "Here's forty dollars. You and Tye go out to dinner."

Tye walked into the living room during the conversation.

"That's not necessary Martin. I really enjoyed my time here."

"I appreciate that young lady. We hope that you'll come again, but it's almost supper time, and I can think of a lot of nice places up in Provo the two of you should try. They're closer to home, and it'll be a nice change of pace from riding the fence all morning."

"Now Martin," Preston began, trying to give back the money.

"It won't do you any good to argue with me Preston. I've known you since you were pint size."

Preston was silent for a moment then graciously accepted. "Thank you Martin. Tye and I will put this to good use." He put the money in his pocket.

"See that you do," he admonished as he showed them to the door.

Several minutes later, Preston was maneuvering his little truck onto the freeway. The roads were covered in snow, and visibility was limited due to the wind and blowing snow. It made driving problematic and slow.

"You don't have to take me out to dinner if you don't want to," Tye said.

Preston glanced at her then returned his eyes back to the road. "Don't you want to go?"

"Oh, yes. It's not that," she began carefully. "I just don't want you to feel obligated."

"It'll be fun. I haven't been out to a restaurant since I came home from Houston. Where should we go?"

Tye suggested a Mexican restaurant in downtown Provo.

They found a parking spot and were seated by the hostess. Before too long they had ordered, and their meal was set in front of them.

"Lorena was saying that when you're home you spend a lot of

time up in the mountains. Did you ever get lonely out there?"

"I never get lonely in the mountains. They're teeming with life, and I can draw on that energy," Preston began. "I love the mountains. In many ways they're my refuge."

"Refuge from what?" Tye asked. "I thought you enjoyed ranch life."

The question hung in the air as Preston considered sharing a part of him that he had never shared with anyone. He barely acknowledged these feelings himself. "I think I told you that I never had any brothers or sisters."

Tye nodded.

"Sometimes I feel most lonely when I'm in the middle of a crowd. School was always hard. It still is. I much prefer going to the Thomases or spending my time with Elsa. I know that sounds strange. I should want to be around people, but that's never been my nature. I don't know. Maybe if I would've had siblings things may have been different." He paused. "My mother had a difficult time during my birth. There were complications, and she almost died. After I was born she was told that she would never be able to have another baby. I've always felt bad about that."

"It's not your fault for being born. I bet your folks wanted to have you, didn't they?"

Preston nodded. "Yeah. They have always told me how they planned for me and are so grateful that they were able to bring me into the world. But sometimes I felt like I carried all of their hopes and dreams that should've been shared with siblings. So, I used to go up into the mountains. Most kids go to the prom for an escape. I went into the mountains."

"Were you running away? Maybe you're afraid if you get close to someone you'll hurt them like you think you've hurt your mother."

Preston blinked. "I hadn't thought of it like that," he said.

"Well, I'm no psychology major, but it's something to think about."

Preston smiled. "Maybe you should major in psychology."

Tye giggled. "That'll be a hundred dollars, please."

Preston laughed. "All I can offer you is this dinner in a Mexican restaurant, and I'm not even paying for that. Martin is." He changed the subject. "Was it hard for you to be an only child?"

"I don't know any other way. Plus I've had close friends. Meggie is like a sister to me. We've been together since grade school. I'll tell you what has been difficult though." She paused. "My dad joined the Church when I was six. I was baptized at eight. My mother didn't join until I was on my mission. For years I wanted to be sealed to my family." She looked down at the table. "I used to sit in church and feel envious of all the sealed families. I even used to be jealous of Meggie. Then, I came to accept my mother as she was, and when I went on my mission, she quit her smoking habit and joined the Church. We're going to be sealed in the Salt Lake Temple in May."

"My parents were sealed in the temple, so I was born in the covenant. I never had to wonder about that."

"Everyone has their own personal struggle. Even though we were both only children, our experiences were different."

Preston nodded. "I'm glad you're going to finally be sealed to your family. That must be a dream come true."

"I have prayed for this all my life," she said. Then she placed her hands over Preston's. "Thank you for this day. I've had a wonderful time."

Preston met her eyes. "You did?"

"Yes, I did. The Thomases are wonderful people, and I have enjoyed you."

Words tumbled inside of Preston. He wanted to tell her how her company delighted him and eased his pull to be alone. She wasn't one of the silly girls he was used to seeing in his religion classes, who coyly giggled while flashing painted nails and lips. She was warm and genuine. He was relaxed and comfortable in her presence. But none of that found voice. Instead, he said, "Maybe you can come with me again some time."

Tye squeezed Preston's hands. "I would like that."

Chapter Twenty-Four

Walking into the barn, Tye's mind wasn't on the lessons she was going to be teaching. Instead, she wondered about Preston. Would he come to the barn today? They hadn't talked about it. She wished she had given him another invitation.

As she walked to Patches stall, she heard a car drive up and two doors slam. Trista appeared in the aisle. "I'll get Patches," she said.

Tye helped the young girl halter the pony and lead him to the crossties.

"My daddy came again today," Triss said. "He was able to get two weekends off in a row. He likes to watch me ride."

A few minutes later, Tye walked into the arena. She glanced up into the stands to see Kenneth sitting alone. At first Tye was sorry Preston wasn't there. Then she was glad. But what difference did it make? Kenneth was simply the parent of one of her students with a sticky past and a difficult ex-wife. She turned her attention to Trista and started the lesson.

"But Miss Jorgenson, we need to warm up Patches before we begin," Trista said.

A hot fluttery feeling engulfed Tye as a flush began to rise into her face. How could she be so stupidly distracted? "Yes, Trista. Of course, you're right. I'm sorry. Let's start out with a walk."

Patches dutifully began to walk around the edge of the arena. Then Tye asked Trista to bring him into a trot and then a slow canter in each direction. Trista obeyed with all the skill she could muster.

"Now, let's start your figure eights at a walk."

"Do we have to walk?" Trista asked. "Patches likes to trot."

"I know Patches likes to trot, but one of the very important things about riding horses is keeping them disciplined. Patches needs to do as you instruct."

"But I like to trot too," Trista said.

"Patience is the virtue of dressage, Triss," Tye explained. "Besides, you can't let Patches just walk any old walk. He needs to carry himself properly, and you need to help him do that. That takes work. Gather your reins, and squeeze him into an interesting walk. Don't let him poke along."

Trista nodded and began walking Patches. The pony slowed to a crawl. "You need to push him a little, Trista. Nudge him with your leg, but keep your rein steady."

Trista did as she was told. Patches moved better.

"Now, how does that feel?" Tye asked.

"It feels like he's paying attention," Trista said.

"Good. Now do another figure eight at a posting trot. But be gentle in your aids. You want Patches to transition smoothly from his walk into his trot."

Trista nodded but nudged the pony a little too hard. He jumped into his trot.

"No, Triss. Try again."

Trista brought Patches back down to a walk, and after several paces nudged him back into a trot.

"Much better, Triss," Tye praised. "Don't let him drift into the center of your circles," Tye said as the pony began to weave from the pattern of the figure eight. "Keep him focused by applying a little inside leg."

Trista tried but her timing was wrong, throwing off her posting. Her heels flew up and she landed on the pony's neck. Patches stopped.

"Okay, try again," Tye said. "Start at a brisk walk."

Trista nodded as she began again. This time her figure eights were round.

"Good. Let's end on that note. It's always important to end on a positive note."

Trista rode Patches to the center of the arena where she dismounted. For the first time since the lesson began, Tye allowed herself to look into the stands. Kenneth was making his way down to the arena.

He was wearing a camel-colored coat over a rich brown sweater and jeans. The coat matched his sandy blond hair and brought out his deep hazel eyes.

"You look great, Triss," Kenneth said. "I can tell that you and Miss Jorgenson are working very hard."

Trista beamed. "We are, Daddy. Miss Jorgenson is the best teacher ever."

Kenneth put his arm around his daughter. "Yes, I can tell that the two of you are quite fond of each other."

Tye blushed.

"Do you want to help me untack and groom Patches?" Trista asked.

"Sure," Kenneth replied.

After Patches was in the crossties, Tye stood back and watched as father and daughter worked on the horse together. It was beginning to become a familiar pattern. Trista made a couple of trips to the tack room with Kenneth in tow. She was glad Kenneth was encouraging her riding. It was obviously important to Trista, and Celia wasn't interested. It was nice that one of her parents took interest. She wished Kenneth lived closer. Again, the hot fluttery feeling rose up in Tye. She pushed it down. It was simply because she thought it would be good for Trista if she had her father nearby.

"I think we're finished, Miss Jorgenson," Kenneth said.

Tye pulled away from her thoughts. "Trista, do you want to lead Patches back to his stall?"

Trista took the lead rope in one hand before giving Patches a hug. Then she led him into his stall and with her father by her side, took off the pony's halter.

"Okay, young lady," Kenneth said. "Let's get you showered and changed."

"What are we going to do today, Daddy?" Trista asked.

"I thought we'd go up into the canyon and build a snow fort and a snow man to guard it. We'll pick up some lunch along the way. How does that sound?"

Trista's eyes grew large. "Oh, Daddy, I've never built a snow fort before."

"Yes you have, honey. Don't you remember building snow forts when we lived in Colorado? You and I built them all the time."

Slowly, Trista shook her head. "I was just a baby back then. I don't remember."

"Well, we'll refresh your memory today," Kenneth said.

Tye smiled. Building snow forts with Kenneth and Trista sounded like fun.

"Thank you, Miss Jorgenson. Trista is really improving."

Tye blinked. "I'm so glad you're able to be here with her, Ken—I mean, Mr. Brannon."

"No, please, call me Kenneth," Mr. Brannon said quietly. "I prefer it." He held out his hand. "Until next time, Miss Jorgenson."

Tye took his hand and returned the gentle press.

Chapter Twenty-Five

Meggie set her skis against the wall then peeled off her hat.

Tye put aside her business plan. "How did your date with Joel go?" she asked.

Meggie sat down and tried to remove one of her heavy ski boots. She tugged, but the boot clung fast. Her foot dropped to the floor with a thud, and she flopped back on her bed with a sigh. "I don't know," she said to the ceiling. "I think it's beginning to fizzle out."

"What makes you say that?" Tye asked. "Didn't you have fun tonight?"

"I always have fun when I'm skiing," she said. "And this was the first time I'd ever been night skiing, so that was fun. But I could've been with anyone … or by myself for that matter, and it would've been the same experience." Meggie sat up and tried the boot again. It slipped off and fell heavily to the floor. "It wasn't like that when I went skiing with Mark. When Mark and I went skiing over the Thanksgiving holiday we had a blast. I wish he could go with me. We had talked about going night skiing, but he can't afford it, and I can't afford to pay for both of us."

"He would never let you do that anyway," Tye said.

"Probably not."

"So what's that got to do with Joel?" Tye asked.

Meggie worked the other boot free and sat in her stocking feet. "We don't talk much. It's as if we've said all there is to say. The drive home was completely silent. He has absolutely no interest in cooking. Whenever I tell him about my classes, or what I'm doing, he gets this totally bored look on his face. He just zones out. Food just doesn't interest him. He'll eat anything. One day I actually saw him brush mold off a bagel and then eat it!"

Tye swallowed hard. "Didn't he get sick?"

"No, he was fine. I got sick, but that didn't bother him either."

"You'd think he'd be interested in having you cook for him. Is he?"

Meggie shook her head. "He hasn't so much as asked. Like I said, he has absolutely no interest in food. That's just something I can't understand. How can someone go through life without caring about what they eat?"

Tye shrugged.

"Do you think he'll ask you out again?"

"No. I'm not going to give him the chance. I think I'll ask to meet him for lunch tomorrow, and then tell him that I think we should just go our separate ways."

A knock on the door caught the girls' attention. Tye went to the bedroom door to find KayLee standing there. She walked in without an invitation, settling on Tye's bed. "What exactly do you see in that Mark character?"

"What do you mean?" Tye asked.

"He's actually showing me how to cook."

"What's the matter with that? Isn't that what you wanted?" Meggie asked.

KayLee shook her head slightly. "That was just a come-on. I mean if I wanted to make soup, I would open a can."

Meggie's impatience began to show. "That doesn't make any sense, KayLee. What did you expect him to do?"

"Well, a movie would've been nice. I hate cooking. Besides, I don't want someone to cook with me. I want someone to cook for me." She sighed. "Mark seemed like the perfect candidate."

Tye laughed. Meggie shot her a strong look. Tye stifled her next giggle.

KayLee continued, "I thought maybe we'd start to get to know one another a little, and then he'd ask me to go to a movie or something. But instead, we've had all these cooking lessons. He's talked about the difference between canned chicken broth and homemade chicken broth. He tells me the importance of having an oven thermometer and a meat thermometer. Why can't you just use the same thermometer?" She paused. "I don't get it. What do you see in him? He's so serious."

"That's precisely what we see in him," Meggie said. "Look, KayLee, if you've spent time in the kitchen, then you've been getting to know Mark."

"Well, all he talks about is cooking. Then he asks me all these tough questions. How do I feel about the conflict between Israel and Palestine? What do I think about the current presidential administration? I didn't even vote in the last election! And all the while he's wrestling with chicken parts." KayLee made a face. "I hate touching meat, and I've never liked spending time in the kitchen. What difference does it make? It all ends up in the same place."

Meggie sat up on her bed. "KayLee, I think there's someone I would like you to meet."

KayLee looked suspicious. "I don't know. If he's anything like Mark …" her voice trailed off.

"No, he's the exact opposite. His name is Joel."

KayLee brightened. "You mean Joel Baxter? But Meggie, you've been dating him."

Meggie furrowed her brow. "I know," she said. "But it's not working out. Maybe the two of you will have better luck. I'll talk to Joel and see what he says."

KayLee rose from Tye's bed. "Well, okay. Let me know." She gave them both a hug before walking out the door.

"She does have a sweet spirit," Tye said.

Meggie kicked her ski boots out of the way. "She's an idiot. Can you imagine spending your education looking for a man who can produce a diamond that will match a pair of earrings your folks gave you for Christmas?" She rose from the bed. "I'm taking a shower and getting ready for bed."

The finality of Meggie's words made it clear that the subject was closed.

Chapter Twenty-Six

The following Sunday, Tye and Meggie silently traipsed through the snow toward their meetings in the Spencer W. Kimball building. The walk was quiet. It took most of their energy just to keep warm and walk upright on the treacherous ice-covered concrete. The storm that had pushed through on Saturday had finally abated; leaving a weak, gray dawn and ten new inches of snow. The air was still and cold. Snow muffled any sound, giving the neighborhood a quiet hush. That was one thing about the snow Tye enjoyed. When it was new, it covered the world in white tranquility.

After they found their seats inside the auditorium, Meggie and Tye let out heavy sighs as they began peeling off layer after layer of heavy winter clothing.

As the meeting started, Meggie began looking for Mark. He wasn't anywhere in sight. "Have you seen Mark this morning?" she whispered to Tye.

Tye shook her head, still gazing at the speaker.

"I hope he's okay. He was fine yesterday," Meg said. Her voice laced with concern. As they walked home in a lazy snow, Meggie said, "I'm going to go to Mark's house. Do you want to come with me?" she asked Tye.

"I'm starving, Meg. Can't we go after lunch?"

Meg shook her head. "You go on and eat. I need to make sure he's okay."

Tye carefully walked up the steps of the porch. "I'll get some lunch ready for you too," she called.

Meg waved as she hurried down the frozen walk. When she got to Mark's house she noticed that it was quiet, and her concern grew. Her knock was timid. When there wasn't any answer, she knocked harder. Finally she heard steps toward the door and patiently waited while the individual on the other side fumbled with the knobs.

"Just a minute!" Mark called from the other side of the door.

When he opened the door, Meggie's eyes grew large. Mark stood in his bathrobe. His hair was disheveled, and his skin was a pale ashy color.

"Mark!" Meggie exclaimed. "What's the matter with you? You look terrible."

"Thanks a lot," he replied in an irritable tone. "I woke up with it. I feel just awful." He looked at Meg. "What are you doing here?"

"I didn't see you at church, so I thought I'd check on you. I'm glad I did."

"Well, there's nothing you can do. I'd invite you in, but I'm probably contagious. It would be best if you just left me alone for a few days."

"Look, you shouldn't be standing out here in the cold. I'll go home and make you some chicken soup. I think I have a bottle of seven-up somewhere too. I'll bring that with me."

"Chicken soup and seven-up. That doesn't sound like a very good combination."

"You don't mix the two of them together," Meggie explained. "I always had chicken soup and seven-up when I was sick, and it always made me feel a lot better." She began her descent down the stairs. "I'll be back in a little while. Close the door! You're letting out all the heat!"

Before Mark could protest Meggie scurried down the steps. He stood there in the doorway with his mouth open, unaware of the chill he was inviting into the house. Finally an icy blast of wind slapped him. It took his breath away, and the fragile feeling in his stomach gave way to nausea rising in his throat. He slammed the door and hurried up the stairs, reaching the bathroom just in time.

Leaning against the sink, a cold and clammy sweat rose to the surface of his skin. He let out a shaky breath as his knees gave way. Grabbing onto the sink, he sunk to the floor and lay on the cold tile. At first the cool, hard tile felt good against his burning skin. Then he began to shiver uncontrollably. Rising to his knees, he washed his mouth out before standing. Dizziness overcame him as he hung onto the counter. With measured steps, he clung to the wall and inched his way to his bedroom where he crawled in between the covers, shivering. Fatigue washed over Mark in warm waves as he huddled under the covers. Finally, his body began to feel warm again. His eyelids drooped in spite of his effort to stay awake for Meg's second visit. By the time his roommates were home from church he was sound asleep.

When Mark awoke several hours later it was because of the pounding in his head. He stumbled to the bathroom and took a hot shower. It helped clear his head and made him drowsy once again. Instinctively he knew that he needed to get something to eat so he chanced a trip downstairs. His roommates were scattered about the living and dining area. Upon his arrival Darrell stood and walked him to the refrigerator. He showed him the bag Meg had left.

Mark pulled the bag from the fridge and poured the contents

into a pan. The aroma of fresh chicken soup heartened him. The seven-up bottle was half empty, but Mark didn't complain. He was lucky anything was left. Besides, he didn't feel strong enough to argue. Instead he put his liquid diet on a tray and climbed the stairs once again. He could tell that the soup was homemade, and he wished he could taste it, but the illness killed any hope of that. The broth looked delicate and was loaded with vegetables and bits of chicken. The nourishment made him feel better. After he had finished his meal he was about to settle back down under the covers when the phone rang. "It's for you Mark," a voice rang out from downstairs.

Mark picked up the extension in the hall to hear Meg's voice.

"How are you feeling?" she asked.

"Better. Thanks for the soup. It really helped. It's the only thing I've been able to keep down."

"I think chicken soup is a cure all," she said. Then in a more serious tone added, "I hope you feel better."

"Thanks. I'm sure I will in a couple of days."

"If you'd like I can try to talk to your professors tomorrow and see if they'll give me copies of their notes."

Relief flooded through Mark. "Meggie, I would really appreciate that. I was worried about attending class."

"Consider it done. Now, I'll let you go so you can get some rest."

They both said a farewell before hanging up. Mark felt a comforting new warmth come from his center. He wasn't sure if it was the chicken soup or the fact that Meg had looked in on him and was helping him through this illness. He climbed into his bed with a smile in spite of his fever. She really is a good friend. he thought as he drifted off to sleep once more.

Chapter Twenty-Seven

*T*ye rose early and checked her e-mail. But along with looking for word from Kyle, she was scanning for news of Trapper. Thelma still wrote weekly updates, and Tye was reading them with enthusiasm. She embraced the news and no longer tried to disengage her feelings for Trapper from Kyle. Trapper had come first. After pushing the send button on her reply, Tye looked for any new mail. Some stubborn part of her believed that Kyle was still out there, thinking of her. After all, his leaving had been so abrupt that it never felt completely final. She couldn't help but continue to watch for some word. But at least it wasn't keeping her from Trapper. And eventually the desire to hear from Kyle would fade away. Already it wasn't as potent as it had been before Christmas. Some part of her understood that he wasn't coming back. With time, she would make that knowledge her reality. She could sense it happening even now.

Rising from the computer desk, Tye said a quick goodbye to Meg before hurrying to the shower. She was brushing her hair into a pony tail when the phone rang. KayLee was still in bed, and Dianna was off to class. Tye picked up the phone in the hall, hoping the ring didn't wake KayLee. She forgot all about her roommate when she heard Meggie's worried tone.

"Tye, can you come over to Mark's?" Meggie asked. "He doesn't look good. I'm really worried. I think we may need to take him to the hospital."

Tye grabbed her keys and purse before jogging the short distance to Mark's house. One of Mark's roommates let her in. The house was hushed. There was none of the usual Monday morning rush. Mark's roommates lined up close to the door. "We just gave him a priesthood blessing," one roommate said.

Tye could tell by their demeanor that it was serious. She hurried up the stairs and found Meggie and Darrell in Mark's room. Meggie was sitting on his bed, caressing Mark's forehead. "He's burning up."

Darrell looked worried.

Mark's eyes were bright with fever, but he said nothing.

Tye walked over and touched Mark's face. Fear spilled from the pit of her stomach. "Let's take him to the hospital," she said. "I'll go get the truck and meet you out front."

She hurried to the truck, where she turned on the ignition. The engine sprang into life. Putting the truck in gear, Tye drove to the front of Mark's house. A minute later Mark appeared with Meggie and one of his roommates. He was wrapped in a blanket and leaning against Meggie and Darrell. Against the white snow, his flushed cheeks and glittering eyes looked frightening.

Meg placed him into the truck next to Tye. Mark didn't speak but Tye could hear his teeth chattering and ragged breathing. She turned on the heat. Meggie sat down next to Mark and as she slammed the door, Tye put the truck in gear and hurried the short distance to the hospital emergency room. Once there, the nurse took one look at Mark and directed the three of them to a curtained off room. She took his blood pressure and his temperature. "I'll go get the doctor," she said. "He's treating a sprained ankle. Meanwhile, I need you to fill out some paper work." She handed Meggie a clipboard.

Meggie did her best. "I don't know his insurance," she said as she gave Tye a desperate look. "I don't even know his middle name."

"Just do the best you can. We'll figure the rest out later," Tye said.

Meggie turned back to the clipboard as the doctor walked in. He went right to Mark before looking at the chart. Then he checked the chart and barked some orders to the nurse, who immediately grabbed an IV bag, some tubing, and a needle. Deftly, the nurse placed the needle in Mark's arm, spiked the IV bag, and adjusted the tubing. Meggie and Tye watched the liquid drip into Mark's vein.

The doctor turned to the girls. "How long has he been sick?"

"Yesterday morning," Meggie replied.

"What are his symptoms?"

"He told me that he's vomited but mostly he has this fever that really scares me. He says he has a hard time breathing sometimes."

"We'll take an x-ray, but I'm guessing he has pneumonia. This is the third pneumonia case I've seen this morning, and it's by far the worst. I'm going to have to ask you to wait out in the waiting room now. I'll have the nurse come tell you when he's stable."

Tye and Meggie hurried out into the waiting room. Minutes ticked by and turned into hours. The receptionist took the papers from Meggie. There was a television on, but no one was watching. The noise drove Tye crazy.

"What are we going to do?" Meggie asked.

"What do you mean?" Tye asked.

"Oh, Tye. He looks so sick. Do you think he'll make it? People die from pneumonia."

Tye placed her arm around Meggie. "Mark will be fine," she said gently. "He's young and strong."

Tears came to Meggie's eyes as she clung to Tye. "He's so sick," she said quietly.

"I know," Tye replied.

Finally, the nurse came out. "Mark is stable now," she said. "We were able to bring his fever down. He's been admitted, and we'll most likely be keeping him for a couple of days. He's in room 302 if you care to see him."

Meggie sprang from her seat. Tye had to jog to keep up with Meggie, who rushed for the nearest elevator then down the hall, until she came to Mark's room. Tye watched as Meggie stopped just outside Mark's hospital room. She gave Tye a scared look.

"It'll be okay," Tye whispered.

Meggie swallowed, took a deep breath, pressed her lips together, and walked in calmly. Tye followed.

Mark was sitting up in bed, still hooked up to an IV line. His cheeks were still flushed but the glittery look was gone from his eyes. His skin had lost some of its parched, drawn appearance. It was obvious that he was tired and worn.

"Well, they say you're going to live," Meggie said as she smiled and took Mark's hand. "Guess so," Mark said throatily.

Meggie sat down on the edge of the bed.

"They think I have pneumonia," Mark said.

"I know," Meggie replied. "I'll stay with you, Mark. Don't worry."

He nodded quietly and laid his head back on his pillow.

Tye sat in a corner chair. This moment seemed to belong to Meggie and Mark.

Tears came to Meggie's eyes again. She tried to bite them back.

Mark saw them. "Afraid you'll lose your cooking buddy?" he asked quietly.

Meggie nodded quietly. "You really scared me, Mark."

Gently, Mark reached up and caressed Meggie's face. "I'm not going anywhere," he said. He closed his eyes, and his hand dropped to the bed.

Meggie took his hand. "Neither am I," she said.

Mark fell asleep.

Tye moved toward Mark and Meggie. "Maybe you should catch a couple of classes while he's sleeping," she suggested. "I can stay for another hour or so."

Meggie shook her head. "I want to be here when he wakes up."

"Then I'll go on to school," Tye said. "I'll try to catch yours and Mark's professors, and let them know what has happened. If I can, I'll pick up notes and assignments. I'll bring your books if you'd like."

"Thanks," Meggie said.

A few hours later, Tye returned with Meggie's books and some lunch. Mark was asleep while Meggie quietly sat by his side. When Tye walked in, Meggie put her finger to her lips. Tye crept stealthily into the room.

"How is he?" Tye asked.

"He's sleeping a lot. And he's on his third IV bag. I think they slowed the rate though. The nurse messed with the buttons, and the liquid has slowed."

"He must've been severely dehydrated," Tye said.

"His face has lost that pinched look. Don't you think?"

Tye agreed.

"He woke up once and seemed to be stronger, but after we talked for ten minutes he drifted back off to sleep. He woke up an hour later but only for a minute."

Tye placed the books on the small table and stood by Mark's bedside. "Do you want me to sit with him for a little while so you can take a break? Maybe you can catch an afternoon class."

Meggie stood, glancing at her watch. "If I leave now I can catch my religion class." She picked up her books. "Thanks for bringing them, Tye."

Tye hugged Meggie before she walked out of the door.

After Meggie had gone, Tye settled in the chair by Mark's bedside. The color in his cheeks had paled considerably. His breathing was regular but not very deep. Tye found herself wishing she could breathe for Mark. Quietly, she placed her hand over Mark's. It was going to be a long recovery.

⌒

Mark sat on the couch and took a sip from his water bottle while Meggie fed the VCR the newest release. Meggie returned to the couch as Mark pushed the buttons on the remote. She touched his knee. "Are you feeling okay?" she asked.

Mark nodded.

Tye sat on the other side of Mark. "If you get the least bit sick, just say, and we'll call it an early evening. We don't have to watch the entire movie in one sitting."

"Make sure you drink all your water," Meggie said.

Mark laughed. "Okay, Nurse Tye and Nurse Meggie. I'll let you know if I feel sick, and I'll tell you when I run out of water. But I think I'll be okay. I'm not ready for a nursing home, yet. After all,

I did study a little this afternoon."

"Yeah, and it ruined you," Meggie said. "You should've seen his coloring, Tye. He was as green as moss."

Tye laughed. Then she grew serious. "And you've dropped some weight, Mark. Pneumonia is very serious. It's a good thing Meggie came along and decided to take you to the hospital."

Mark barely recalled the trip to the emergency room, but he did remember receiving an IV and spending the night in a noisy room. He had been discharged the next day. Since then, Meggie had been doing her best to give him the necessary care. She had made him two pots of soup; beef vegetable and chicken noodle. She had also made him a loaf of home made bread. For six days Mark ate Meggie's soup and bread, complemented with canned peaches. The craving for the peaches had been an oddity, but Meggie had not questioned it. Instead, she had gone to the store and returned with six cans. Tonight, she had made him his first solid food of chicken and pasta with loads of broccoli and spinach in a light sauce. Mark had eaten sparingly; afraid that his body wouldn't be able to tolerate the solid food. But instead, he found it had strengthened him. He was grateful for Meggie's unerring and unflinching care that had included his family. She had called his family in Seattle and kept them informed of his progress while he was in the hospital. Then he had been able to call himself. They had been so relieved to hear his voice and know he was doing better. They had also been grateful for Meggie's help and had sent her flowers for her tireless care.

Meggie had also kept Mark's professors informed and had kept Mark up-to-date with notes and assignments. He was still behind, but the semester wasn't a total loss like it might have been without Meggie's unfaltering help.

It felt good to be home and doing something fun with his friends. But he knew that his activities would be limited for the rest of the semester. He simply didn't have any strength or stamina. He looked at Meggie, "I won't be going skiing like I'd hoped."

Meg agreed. "I think your skiing season is finished," she said gently. "But don't worry. The slopes aren't going anywhere."

Mark grew quiet. He knew the slopes would always be there. He just wondered about Meggie. She would be going places without him. He was grateful when the movie began.

Later that evening, Mark told the girls he wanted to go for a quick walk by himself. At first they had argued with him, but he had insisted. He had been cooped up in the house for one week, and he wanted to breathe fresh air and move his atrophying muscles.

"We'll wait right here on your front porch," Tye said as Mark walked down the stairs.

"Don't go too far," Meggie cautioned.

Mark waved as he trudged in the wet snow. It felt good to be out. The clouds were low and the lights from the city illuminated them with an unnatural glow. The snow and ice crunched underneath his feet as he walked. His pathway was well lit, due to the street-lights that towered above him, but none of that caught his attention. All he could think of was Meggie's vitality. She deserved someone who could take her skiing, and enjoy the outdoors as she did. Their one and only trip had been the highlight of his school year. Unfortunately it would not be repeated.

Soon, Mark's head began to pound with fatigue and cold. He turned around and walked the short distance home. The girls were on the porch, both wearing anxious expressions. He walked up the steps. "I'm tired now," he said. "I think I'll go on to bed."

Meggie put her hand to Mark's face. Without even thinking, Mark covered her hand with his own. Meggie didn't notice.

"No fever," she said.

"Goodnight, girls," he said.

They waved as they walk down the steps.

Mark trudged up the stairs and into his room. "What more does she want?" he asked out loud. The sound of his own voice startled and embarrassed him. Carefully, he sat down on the bed and settled back against the wall. He knew what she wanted. She wanted to ski. She wanted someone who was healthy and capable. She deserved that.

Chapter Twenty-Eight

*T*ye rose in the white gray dawn to find snow being pushed around by a sharp wind. It discouraged her. The early thaw she had enjoyed last night had infused her with hope for an early spring. Sighing, she began preparing for a cold day at the Thomases.

Later, when she looked out the window for the second time, she saw Preston's truck. It was double-parked. Preston was walking to her front door. She glanced at Meggie, who was still asleep. Hurriedly, she scrawled a note, telling her friend where she was and to call her if Mark took a turn for the worse.

Then she grabbed her coat, gloves, and scarf before silently padding downstairs, where she opened the door for Preston before putting on her shoes.

"It looks nasty out there," Tye said.

"It is. It's cold and blowing. Are you ready?"

Tye stood. "Yeah."

Stepping out into the storm, Tye was cut by the snowy wind. For a long moment she felt as if her lungs had been carved out of her. She couldn't find her breath. She was grateful to reach the cab of Preston's truck, which he had kept running. It was warm and snug. Tye relaxed once Preston put the truck in gear and began inching forward on the snow-packed road. Traffic was light. Tye didn't care how long the drive took them. The cab was comfortable and inviting.

"I hope this winter doesn't hang on too much longer," Preston said once he pulled onto the freeway. "It'll be calving season within a month or so."

"If I were a cow, I'd be tired of the snow."

Preston laughed. "I don't think cows think of it one way or the other. It's just the way it is if you're a cow."

"It's the way it is if you're a human too. It can't be helped, but I'm tired of it as a human, and I'm sure I'd be of the same opinion if I were a cow."

Preston laughed again.

"Back home the crocuses are in bloom," Tye said wistfully.

"Already?"

"Spring starts in February in the Northwest." She sighed. "And the daffodils and tulips are beginning to show." Tye huddled deeper into her coat. "It's just not the snow, although I am tired of it. I guess I'm homesick too. I miss my horse and my family."

Preston reached over, rubbing Tye's knee. "I'm sorry," he said.

Tye squeezed his hand. "Thanks."

The rest of the drive was silent. Preston concentrated on the road. Tye watched horizontal snow cover the landscape.

Finally they pulled into the Thomases driveway. Tye didn't want to get out of the cab. She and Preston had created a warm and relaxed atmosphere.

Preston killed the engine. "Are you ready to make a dash for the door?" he asked.

"Do I have a choice?" Tye asked.

"You always have a choice," Preston said softly. "I can take you home if you don't want to stay. I would certainly understand. This is nasty weather."

Tye smiled. "No, it's snowing everywhere. I may as well be here with good company than mope around the house missing the crocus. Let's go."

They both opened their doors and hurried for the house. Lorena was waiting for them and opened the door before they could even knock.

"Such weather," Lorena said as she shut the storm out behind them. "Warm yourselves by the fire while I finish breakfast."

Tye huddled near the wood stove and slowly began to take off her layers of outer gear. "How are things this morning?" Preston asked.

"Well, it doesn't stop because of the weather," Lorena said. "I'm starting to worry about some of my cows. I hope this winter doesn't hold on for too much longer. It's hard on them."

Preston shot Tye a look.

Tye gave Preston a covert smile. "If I were a cow, it'd be hard on me too," she whispered to Preston, who grinned.

Tye held Preston's look and found herself warmed as much by his blue eyes as by the fire.

"Where's Martin?" Preston asked.

"Martin left for California yesterday for his yearly visit with grand kids. He likes to go before calving season. This year he left about a week later than he likes because the weather has been so bad. But he had decided he wouldn't stay the whole week. Now with this nasty storm moving in, I bet he jumps in his truck and leaves California today." She moved to the stove and cracked some eggs into a hot cast iron skillet. "I really appreciate the two of you coming out this weekend," Lorena continued. "This snow has been a big surprise. When Martin left yesterday, the weather report was for some clouds but no precipitation. They were predicting a calm and warming week. Martin never would've left if he'd known the weather was going to turn."

"Have you been out this morning?" Preston asked.

Lorena placed two plates full of bacon and eggs in front of Preston and Tye. "Yes. I went out right at dawn. I fed the cows and broke up the ice in the water troughs."

"What would you like us to do while we're here?" Preston asked.

"The pipes to the troughs probably need to be thawed," Lorena said. "And I haven't been able to clean the stalls yet today. If you wouldn't mind, Preston, could you take the torch out and thaw out the pipes?"

Preston nodded. "Sure."

"Tye, could you help me clean the stalls?"

"Sure, Lorena."

Tye could hear the concern in her voice.

After breakfast everyone bundled up in their coats and boots before moving out to the barn.

Lorena and Tye went right to work cleaning stalls while Preston tacked up Sergeant. Several minutes later Preston peeked into the stall where Tye was working. "I hope you don't mind cleaning stalls," he whispered.

"Not at all. I may not be able to lift a western saddle over my head, but I've had plenty of practice with a shovel and a wheelbarrow. Besides, I'll be warm and dry for the most part, which is more than I can say for you." She grinned.

Preston looked outside. Snow was blowing hard across the landscape, obscuring even the nearest lean-to. He sighed. "Well, I'm off. I'll be back around twelve-thirty for lunch." He led Sergeant outside. Tye watched as he mounted the horse and rode into the driving snow.

For Tye, the morning went by in speedy silence as she filled her wheelbarrow with soiled shavings and then replaced them with fresh woodchips. She dreaded the quick trips into the wind and cold to dump the dirty bedding and load up on fresh. But during every short trip, she would watch for Preston. Snow would sting her face as she would try to look through the white storm. Then she would check her watch. Lunch time was approaching soon. Still she was surprised when Lorena appeared at the door of the stall where she was working; a sheen of sweat on the older woman's face.

"This is the last one," Lorena said. "You look like you're about finished."

Tye was spreading fresh shavings. "I think I'll wait for Preston, though," Tye said. "It's almost twelve-thirty now. He should be coming in any minute."

Lorena placed her shovel inside the tool shed. "I'll go and get lunch ready." She stopped and faced Tye once again. "Thanks for coming," she said. "Your help is making a big difference."

Tye was warmed by Lorena's words of appreciation.

Tye was putting her shovel and wheelbarrow away when Preston walked in leading Sergeant. His jacket was covered in snow, and his jeans were caked with the white powder, except for the creases. Tye went to him and took Sargeant's reins. Preston removed his hat and shook the snow from the ends of his hair. "This weather is brutal," he said.

Tye led Sergeant to his stall. She took the bridle off and replaced it with his halter so that he could drink unhindered. She left the saddle on his back. "Let's get you in the house and fill you up with hot food. Lorena's making lunch now."

"That sounds good," Preston said. "After lunch I'll have to go out one more time. I want to feed them before it gets dark."

"I'll help you."

"You don't need to do that," Preston said. "The weather is really nasty."

"I want to help you," Tye said. "We can saddle Sunny after lunch. The whole thing will go faster if there are two of us," she said.

As they walked to the house Tye picked up several layers of clothes she had set aside as her work had progressed.

At lunch, Lorena served hot soup and sandwiches. "There's a message on the machine from Martin," Lorena said as she sat down. "He's already left California."

"The storm will be gone by the time he gets home. He should've just stayed," Preston said.

"Knowing Martin, he's feeling like he shouldn't have left in the first place. I wouldn't even try to talk him into staying," Lorena said. "But I will try to catch him on his cell phone later today to let him know that the two of you have been here, and that everything is fine. That will ease his mind until he gets home."

"After lunch, I think I'll feed and check the water lines one more time," Preston said.

Lorena nodded. "I'll go out with you," she said. She looked at Tye. "You can come along also, Tye, if you'd like. But please, don't feel obligated. The weather is nasty."

"I want to come along, unless you've got something else you need me to do," Tye said. "I'm dressed for bad weather, and Sunny is a sure-footed pony."

"Good. That'll make the work go faster."

Several minutes later, Preston was helping Tye place the heavy western saddle on Sunny's back. Lorena met them in the aisle, leading the gelding.

Once they were out in the storm Preston rode close to Tye. "Do you think you can remember how to turn?" He asked.

"I think so."

"Let's see it," Preston yelled above the wail of the snowy wind.

Sunny turned in spite of Tye's clumsy efforts.

"Good. Let's go."

"What are we looking for?"

Lorena replied above the howl of the storm, "We'll check the water supplies and get some feed out. We also need to look for any cows that might be struggling with the cold. If they're having a hard time, we'll drive them to the barn. They're usually okay in the weather unless one of them is sick or something."

Together, they headed into the blinding whiteness of the fields and storm. They rode in silence checking water supplies, which due to Preston's earlier work were running clear. As they rode through the storm, Tye noticed that the cows congregated near the hay stacks. It made it easier to feed them and check them over for any signs of weakness or sickness. It was on their way back to the barn that they spotted a cow standing off by herself. Preston and Lorena saw it at the same time and pointed the animal out to Tye. All three riders pushed their horses through the storm until they came to the lean-to, where the cow was standing. As they got closer, Sunny began to shy away from the lone cow. Tye calmed the horse by settling deep into the saddle. As they inched closer Tye saw what was upsetting Sunny. Bright red blood covered the snow in and around the lean-to. A new calf stood shakily on its feet next to its mother. It bawled pitifully. This was serious. Tye edged Sunny closer. The mare snorted and pranced. Tye pushed her lower leg and heels into the mare's side. Sunny inched forward.

Preston had no trouble on Sergeant, who stood quietly as Preston swung out of the saddle and slowly approached the new mother. Lorena also dismounted and followed Preston.

Tye continued to keep Sunny still, although the mare pushed out great clouds of moist, warm air. Tye could feel Sunny's rib cage contract with each exhalation. The mare continued to tremble, but she stood. Tye turned her attention to Preston. Should she dismount? Before she could answer her own question, Preston quickly removed his jacket and wrapped the newborn. Then he picked up the calf and swung it over the front of his saddle. He mounted Sergeant and moved close to Tye. She looked over the newborn. Birthing fluid and blood still clung to the little calf's face, but the fluid wasn't frozen yet. That would mean that the calf was brand-new and its mother hadn't been able to clean him properly. Tye ran her gloved fingers over the calf's nostrils to clear out any fluid.

"Can you fall in behind me with Lorena, and watch the cow?" Preston asked. "They don't always follow like they should."

"What do I do if she starts to walk off?" she asked.

"If the cow turns your way, keep Sunny in her path. She won't let the cow get past her. Lorena will help you."

Tye did as Preston asked, following behind the cow. The new mother trudged behind Sergeant, bawling for her calf.

The calf answered with a bleat of its own. Then it became quiet. The mother panicked and began to trot. Gratitude flooded through Tye. She didn't know what she would've done if the cow had turned belligerent.

When they finally reached the barn Preston dismounted before gently pulling the calf off of his horse. Tye also dismounted and took Sergeant's reins as Lorena opened the gate that led them away from the fields. Tye followed Preston and Lorena, who handed her the gelding's reins as soon as they stepped inside the barn. Preston stopped at the first stall inside the barn and put the calf down. The cow immediately pressed inside and began to lick her little one. Preston removed his jacket.

"Can you please take the horses and tie them up?" Lorena asked. "We'll untack them later. Right now I need towels."

Tye took the horses and led each one to their stalls, where she swung their reins around the bars of their stalls. Then she hurried to the tool shed where she found Lorena gathering towels. The older woman handed several to Tye. "Can you take these to Preston?" she asked. "I need to prepare a bottle, just in case."

Tye ignored her numbing feet and hands that were beginning to burn with cold. "Will the calf die?" she asked.

Lorena looked grim. "I hope not," she replied. "I don't think he was out in the weather for very long."

Tye left Lorena and took the towels to the stall where Preston was working.

Preston took the towels. With brisk motions he began rubbing the calf. "He looks pretty new. I think she had just dropped when we arrived," Preston said as he worked. He shook his head. "I should've seen this cow's distress on my first round this morning. I didn't even notice her."

"Don't blame yourself," Tye said. "You did the best you could."

"Yeah? Well, that won't be so easy to say if this little guy dies. Sloppy work," Preston said as he steered the calf towards a meal. "If he eats, I think it'll be okay."

Tye looked at the mother. She didn't seem the least bit concerned as the youngster began to nudge her udder.

Preston grabbed a teat and rubbed the calf's lips. "C'mon, little guy. Have some lunch."

The calf grabbed hold and began to suckle. Tye leaned up against the doorframe as the tension eased out of her. She looked at the cow, who continued to chew her cud.

Lorena appeared at the stall door, holding a warm bottle. "How is our newest addition?" Preston let out a sigh of relief. "I think he's going to be okay."

Lorena looked him over with a critical eye. "He's eating with gusto. That's a good sign."

She leaned on the opposite door frame of Tye. "I'm glad we went out there. If he'd been out in this weather for much longer I'm afraid we might've lost him." She started to look worried. "We can't afford to lose any calves. I hope we don't have too many early births. Did you see any others that looked like they were ready to drop?"

"No, but I'm riding back out there to look again. I missed this one. I could've missed another."

Lorena looked outside. "I think I'd like to move them closer to the barn. Can the two of you take care of this little one while I go out and bring the herd into the near field?"

"Let me go with you," Preston said. "Tye can finish here."

Lorena thought for a moment. "Okay. It'll go quicker if we work together. Let me get you a clean jacket."

Lorena left.

"You don't mind staying with the calf for a little while, do you?"

"No. Do I need to do anything?"

"No. In fact you can stay in the house if you'd like. I think he's going to be okay."

They both looked at the new calf. He was sucking down lunch with enthusiasm.

"Should I come with you?" Tye asked.

"No. I appreciate you being willing to go back out into the storm, but Lorena and I can do it. Just untack Sunny. I won't be too long."

Lorena returned with a fresh jacket. Tye watched as Preston pushed his arms through the sleeves and buttoned it up to his neck. Then they moved toward the horses. Lorena and Preston untied Sergeant and the gelding before leading them back out into the snow. Tye was left alone in the barn. The sound of the storm wailed around her. It blew through the cracks and open doors. The very building groaned under the unyielding snow and wind. It bit at every piece of uncovered skin. Oh, how she missed Oregon's soft gentle patter of rain and the lush green forests that carried the heavy scent of fir on fresh storms. She longed for the soft aroma of the new spring that dotted her landscape with flowers and nourished it with a gentle mist.

Moving toward Sunny, Tye envied the mare's long winter coat. Slowly she began to remove the saddle. She carried it to the tool shed before filling Sunny's water bucket and placing a flake of grass hay in her feed bin. She checked the other horse's stalls. The gelding's stall and Sergeant's stall were both clean, but they needed fresh water. She would not feed them because she wasn't sure of the amount of work the horses would be doing as they drove in the cows, and it was better to let the horses cool down before giving them their feed.

After she finished her chores in the barn she checked on the calf one last time. He was fast asleep in the deep wood shavings she had spread that very morning. She hurried to the house, where she quickly showered and changed into fresh, warm clothes. She was almost finished cleaning the lunch dishes when Preston and Lorena burst into the house with a flurry of snow and wind.

"Everybody's fine. We've moved them closer to the house so I can check on them easier," Lorena said as she began to unwrap her outerwear. She turned her attention to the weather. "This storm doesn't look like it's going to let up. It might even get worse as night falls. I think the two of you should get on the road very soon."

Preston and Tye agreed.

"I'll go get the truck ready if you want to take a quick shower to warm up," Tye suggested.

Preston handed her the keys. Tye scrambled into her dry jacket and hurried outside where she started the engine to Preston's truck. She turned the heat on full blast. At first the vents blew cold air, but as the engine warmed the cab began to unthaw. It melted the snow on the windshield and hood. Tye brushed the melting snow off the truck before walking back in the house. Preston stepped out of the hallway, looking warm and clean.

"Thank you for coming today," Lorena said. "The two of you have made a huge difference. Martin and I are so grateful."

"You're welcome, Lorena. I hope you'll call me if you need anything," Preston said.

"I don't want you out in this storm any longer than necessary. I'll be fine here. The cows are closer to the house. I can check on them throughout the night if necessary with headlights from the truck. None of them looked ready to drop anyway. But they've got better shelter in case one of them does decide to surprise me. Don't you worry, Preston. I'll be fine. The cows will be fine. You need to get on home before dark." She looked out the window.

Preston and Tye followed her gaze. Even though it was only three o'clock, the light was already starting to fade, leaving a blue afternoon veiled in white.

"The truck is warm and ready to go," Tye said.

Saying a quick goodbye to Lorena, they both hurried to the truck. Preston pulled out onto the road where darkness fell almost immediately like a thick, dark stage curtain. Driving was slow and tedious, but traffic was almost nonexistent.

Tye remained quiet as she huddled against the back of her seat. If it hadn't been for the biting cold, the day would have almost seemed like a bad dream. They had almost lost a calf, and Tye had to admit she had been afraid to see Preston saddle up and ride out into the storm for the third time. She tried to place the fear but she couldn't name it.

She had to admit that he had impressed her with his quick action. The way he had been able to lift the calf onto his horse and then ride with the shift in weight. It had been so easy for him, but she knew it wasn't easy. "You're going to make a great veterinarian," she said.

"I'm not so sure," Preston replied. "I never should've left that cow in the field in this kind of weather."

Tye wasn't sure what to say. She weighed her words. "I don't know enough about ranching to make that kind of a judgment call," she said. "I just know that the Thomases have a brand-new calf because you took care of him and his mother. I also know that the rest of their herd is okay because you went back out into the storm and checked them again as you brought them closer to the house."

Preston relaxed. He placed his hand on Tye's knee. "Thank you, Tye. That's a very kind thing to say. I'm glad you're my partner."

"Not as glad as I am that you're my partner." She placed her hand on his.

"Oh, I think I'm the happier one." He grinned. "Especially since you have now revealed to me that cows get tired of this snow."

Tye giggled.

Preston doubled parked in front of Tye's home and walked her to the door.

She wanted to invite him in and continue to feel the warmth of his company and the fire she now sensed in his blue eyes. But the weather discouraged her. The storm had intensified with the darkness. She waved him off her front porch as he began to back away.

"I'll see you Monday," he said as he tread down her porch steps.

"Drive carefully."

Preston gave her a final wave as he climbed back into the cab of his truck.

In spite of the raging weather, Tye stood on the porch and watched the tail lights fade into the snowy darkness.

Chapter Twenty-Nine

"My daddy's here again," Trista whispered as Tye buckled the cinch around Patches' belly.

Tye swallowed hard as she tried to push away the attraction she felt for Trista's father. It confused her, sometimes causing a stab of guilt. What would Preston think? But then she and Preston were only friends. There had been no declaration between them. For all she knew Preston dated lots of different women. No, that wasn't true. Still, there was no reason why she shouldn't pursue a friendship with Kenneth as well. But what would he ever see in her? He was a doctor, surrounded by professionals in his field of work. She was simply his daughter's riding instructor. The only thing they had in common was Trista, and that was for the best.

A few minutes later, Tye found Kenneth in the stands. He gave his familiar smile and wave. Tye waved back before turning her attention to Trista. She helped her young student begin Patches' warm-up program. Soon, they were working through elementary dressage routines.

"Your posting has definitely improved, Trista. I'll be glad when the weather warms up, and you'll be able to work more outside. You and Patches will both enjoy the change of scenery."

After the lesson was over, Triss asked, "Will you be here during the summer, Miss Jorgenson?"

"No. I have to go home and look after my own horse."

Trista looked stricken. "What am I going to do without you?" she asked.

"Don't worry, Triss. There will be someone here who can teach you."

"But I like you," Trista said. "You're the best teacher I've ever had. You're even better than my school teachers." Tears began to fill Trista's eyes.

Tye walked to where Trista sat on Patches. She patted the young girl's leg. "Triss, honey, don't fret. I'll be back in the fall. It'll be good for you to learn from someone else. Then when I come back you can show me how much you've improved."

"When are you leaving?" Trista asked.

"Not for a while. So, don't worry about it. In fact, right now, you should be worrying about dismounting and getting Patches ready for his stall."

"Yes, ma'am," Trista said as she dismounted.

As soon as Trista dismounted, Kenneth joined them in the arena. "You're doing better each time I see you, Triss. I'm really proud of you." He gave his daughter a hug.

Trista beamed.

The threesome walked the pony out of the arena where Trista began going through the now familiar motion of untacking and grooming. Kenneth helped her, giving Patches a soft pat on the neck. "He really is a nice pony, isn't he?"

Tye agreed. "He's gentle and patient with the kids," she said.

"I heard you mention that you have a horse. Is he like Patches?"

"Trapper? Oh, no. Trapper is sixteen hands and a full-blooded thoroughbred. He's a competitor."

"That must be a thrill. Competition, I mean."

"Yes," Tye said. "It was."

"Past tense?" Kenneth inquired.

"I don't compete anymore," Tye said. "Oh, I do some local shows in the summer, but since my mission I just haven't felt the same edge or desire to compete."

"Where did you serve your mission?" Kenneth asked.

"San Antonio."

"I served in Brazil. I was born in San Antonio, though. I've been back several times. I love that city."

"I've never been to San Antonio," Trista piped in.

"No. Grandma and Grandpa Brannon moved to Colorado when I was about your age." He mussed Trista's hair. "Maybe someday you and I can go to San Antonio. We can visit the city where I was born," Kenneth said. "And we'll go to the Alamo."

"Oh, yes, Daddy. I want to go to the Alamo." Trista became thoughtful. "What's the Alamo?"

Kenneth laughed. "The Alamo has been many things. It used to be an old Spanish Mission. Then it was a military fort."

"It's a beautiful spot, Triss. You'd enjoy it," Tye said.

"I'll talk to your mom and see what we can arrange," Kenneth said.

"Would Mommy come too?" Trista asked hopefully.

Tye noticed a look of sadness come into Kenneth's face.

"No, sweetie. It would be just the two of us."

Triss nodded her understanding before changing the subject. "Do you want to help me put the tack away, Daddy?"

"Sure thing, honey," Kenneth said as he lifted the saddle.

Tye led Patches to his stall. When Trista and Kenneth returned, Kenneth said, "May I speak to you privately, Miss Jorgenson?"

Tye nodded.

"It's not too cold," Triss said. "I'll wait in the car for you, Daddy."

The adults waited until they heard the car door slam. Then Kenneth looked at Tye. "I really appreciate all you're doing for Triss. She's blossoming under your care."

"I just teach, Mr. Brannon. Triss is blossoming under her own care."

Kenneth smiled. "Would you do me two favors? Would you please call me Kenneth, and would you be willing to have dinner with me tonight?"

Tye's mouth went dry. She had yearned for this invitation. Yet, she hesitated. She liked the bold way this man stated his intentions. Was he really an adulterer as Celia claimed? She had to admit that she found Kenneth attractive and interesting. She wanted to hear about his work as a doctor, and it would be nice to share her memories of San Antonio with someone. But did she want to get involved with Trista's family on a personal level?

"I don't blame you for hesitating," Kenneth said. "I'm sure Celia hasn't said anything pleasant about me. I know what she tells people."

"Oh? And what's that?" Tye asked.

"That all the nurses in Boulder, Colorado know me—in the biblical sense."

Tye blinked. "That's exactly what she says."

"I know."

"Is it true?" Tye asked.

Kenneth became thoughtful. "The truth is, there was only one nurse, but that is one too many. I understand that now. Like I said before, I've made some mistakes in my life. I wasn't exactly a stellar husband or father. Ceila has her reasons for being angry with me, and she didn't make them up. I'm sure you sense that." He paused. "I won't pretend that I've been the perfect return missionary, Miss Jorgenson. I'm sure you see a lot of young men in this area who live up to that expectation." He sighed. "Maybe I was out of line by issuing the invitation. I'm sorry. I didn't mean to put you on the spot. Perhaps I shouldn't have …"

Tye shook her head. "No. Kenneth," she said quietly. His name rolled on her tongue like sweet cream. "I would love to go to dinner with you." A new thought came to Tye. "I just don't want to interrupt your time with Trista. I know how precious your visits are to her."

"You wouldn't be interrupting. I have to take Triss back to her mother by five. Trista doesn't spend the night with me. I pick her up from Celia's on Saturday morning and Sunday morning after church. I bring her back by five in the evening. It would be different if I lived here. But that's the way things stand now."

Tye nodded. "Okay, Kenneth. I'll have dinner with you."

Kenneth smiled. "Thank you, Tye."

Tye blushed at the sound of her name.

He pulled out a piece of paper and a pen from his coat pocket. "Will you write down your address and directions to your place? I'll pick you up at six-thirty, if that's all right with you."

Tye wrote the necessary information and handed the paper and pen back to Kenneth.

Kenneth took her hand and gently kissed it before silently leaving the barn.

⌒

Later that evening, Tye stood before the mirror, taking extra care with her make-up. She never wore make-up to the barn, but she wanted to look special for this evening.

KayLee stopped in front of her bathroom. "This boy must really be something special, Tye. I've never seen you go to so much trouble."

"He's not a boy, KayLee," Tye said. "He's a physician in Colorado, and he has a seven-year-old daughter. That helps qualify him as a man."

"I would never date a man with a child," KayLee responded. "It usually means he has an ex-wife." KayLee made a face.

Tye gave KayLee a worried look.

KayLee continued, "Besides, if this man has a seven-year-old, he must be pushing thirty. Chances are he's way over thirty. Don't you think that's a tad old for you?"

Tye had not considered Kenneth's age.

"Oh, bug off, KayLee," Meggie said as she came from the bedroom. "Tye doesn't tell you who to date. Leave her alone."

KayLee gave Meggie a sour look. "Well, you don't have to get cranky, Meg. Just because Joel and I hit it off and you're not dating him any more isn't any reason to snap at me. I'm just worried for Tye, that's all. She hardly ever dates. I would hate to see her make a mistake her first time out."

Meggie scowled. "This doesn't have anything to do with Joel. Besides, I introduced the two of you, remember?"

Tye laughed. "Don't worry, KayLee. I've dated before." But in the back of her mind, she realized that KayLee's concerns were valid. Kenneth did have an ex-wife. He was older. What did that mean in terms of any kind of relationship they would have? Still, she couldn't deny the attraction she felt for him. The doorbell rang. "I'll get it!" KayLee said as she rushed down the stairs.

"She just wants to meet your date," Meg said.

Tye giggled. "Don't worry about it. I know KayLee irritates you ever since that little episode with Mark. But I don't care if she meets Kenneth."

Meggie scowled again.

Tye laughed. "Come downstairs with me and meet him yourself."

Meg followed Tye down the stairs as KayLee was rushing up. "Oh, I was just going to come and get you," KayLee said breathlessly. "Kenneth is here."

"Hi Kenneth. Did you have any trouble finding the house?" Tye asked from the stairway.

Kenneth shook his head.

Tye walked the rest of the stairs. "You've met KayLee. This is Meggie."

"Tye tells us you're a physician," KayLee gushed.

"Yes. I work in Colorado."

"My, that must be such interesting work."

Tye smiled at Kenneth, who grinned back at Tye. "It can be." He continued to look at Tye. "Are you ready?"

Tye nodded.

"Is this your jacket?" Kenneth asked as he pulled one from the coat rack.

"Yes."

He held it open, and Tye stepped into it.

KayLee almost swooned.

Out on the walk, Kenneth helped Tye down the icy steps. "The car is a rental, so it has that rental car smell. I hope that won't bother you."

"Oh, no. My truck smells like horse. Rental car will be a nice change."

Kenneth laughed as he held open the door.

⌒

Sitting in the booth of the Stratford's Restaurant, Tye pulled her legs under her as she ordered. The waiter took their menus after Kenneth ordered.

"You look lovely tonight, Tye," he said after the waiter left them.

"Thank you. It's good to see you outside of the barn. How did your day with Trista go?"

"It was nice. We had an early lunch and went to a movie." He changed the subject. "She's quite fond of you. She talks about you all the time."

"I'm sure that's because you happen to see her right after our lesson."

"No. I call in the middle of the week too, and she talks about you then. You're doing her a world of good."

"She's a good girl, Kenneth. She tries hard."

"This summer is going to be difficult for her."

"Oh? Why is that?"

"I won my custody fight," Kenneth said. "Trista will be moving back to Colorado with me after this school year."

"That's wonderful, Kenneth. You must be pleased."

Kenneth nodded. "I am very happy about this."

"How did Celia take it?"

"I can't say. She's not speaking to me."

"I see."

"That's part of the reason I've stepped up my visits. I want Trista and me to get to know each other as well as possible before the big move."

"Does Triss know she's moving to Colorado?"

"Not yet. I just found out yesterday. I'm not sure how to tell her."

Silence hung between them for a moment.

"Kenneth, may I ask you something personal?"

"Sure."

"Why did you get custody of Triss? Maybe I'm old-fashioned, but it seems to me that the mother gets custody most of the time." She hurried on, "Don't get me wrong. I'm sure the courts made the right decision. It's just that I want to understand."

"It's not because of my profession, if that's what you're thinking," Kenneth replied.

"The thought did cross my mind," Tye said.

"No. The fact that I'm a doctor would only make a difference in my child support payments if Celia were to get custody. Of course, having a steady job is important to being the custodial parent, but Celia is a hard-working nurse with a stellar employment record, so I don't think that played any part in the judge's decision." Kenneth shook his head slowly. "No, my being a doctor didn't weigh in with the courts. I think it was the fact that I've been in therapy with a licensed psychotherapist and my bishop, or clergy as the court calls them. That made the difference. Celia refused all therapy."

"I see." Tye looked outside. The weather was blessedly calm.

Then she turned back to Kenneth. "I think I'm a little out of my league."

Kenneth covered Tye's hands with his own. "Be grateful for that, Tye. You don't want to play in this ball game. It's been very hard on all of us." Kenneth leaned back into his seat, removing his hands from Tye's. She missed the warmth immediately.

"Tell me," Kenneth began. "How is San Antonio? I haven't been there in years."

"I love San Antonio," Tye began as a new warmth spread through her. In spite of her earlier hopes to talk about her mission, Tye rarely spoke of it. Now she could sense her eagerness to share it. Her mind welcomed the memories of San Antonio like bluebonnets reaching for the warm spring Texan sun. "I actually didn't mind the muggy summer heat, but my favorite time was March. The weather was mild and the wildflowers were out." She became thoughtful. "But it's the people that I really came to love. I thoroughly enjoyed the mix of cultures. Everyone is so warm and generous."

"But they're not real interested in the gospel, are they?" Kenneth said.

"No. We didn't have a lot of baptisms. I only had two that I taught directly."

"Tell me."

Tye flushed at a memory that she had not seriously considered since her breakup with Kyle. "We met a young woman named Rachel. Rachel was Catholic, but she had school friends who were LDS. She met with us at her best friend Clara's home, but her parents would never come. They weren't very happy about her involvement in the Church. When she decided to be baptized, her folks told her she could either continue to live at home or be baptized. They would not allow her to be a Mormon under their roof."

"What did she do?" Kenneth asked.

"She was baptized. She moved in with Clara's family. That wasn't the ideal circumstance either. I know it sounds wonderful; two best friends coming together because of the gospel and then living together for their senior year in high school. But it's rarely that easy. Clara was already sharing her room with her little sister. Now she had to share her room with Rachel too. It was very crowded and difficult but they persevered. It taught me a lot about sacrifice. The Juarez family gave up a lot to bring Rachel into the gospel. Their house was small, so when Rachel moved in they lost all sense of privacy. Rachel also lost all sense of privacy. She also lost her family. So, even though she was gaining the gospel, there was an incredible sense of loss for Rachel. Then there were the monetary issues. Rachel presented another mouth that needed to be fed. She was going through a lot of the typical teenage issues that girls go through. She was dating boys and trying to get ready for college. I learned a lot from the Juarezes. They never complained or resented Rachel's presence. If they needed help from the ward, they asked for it and others pitched in. They faced every day with vigor and humility. I was honored to be a part of that whole process. Before I left, both girls had graduated from high school and had started college in Austin. They were still roommates, and they were active in church and institute."

"That's some story, Tye."

"It kept me going on the days when our success was limited." She paused. "I bet things were different in Brazil."

Kenneth smiled wistfully. "Brazil seems like a hundred years ago. But yes, we baptized quite a few people in that mission. It was a wonderful experience."

"What happened?"

"You mean when I got home?"

Tye nodded.

"I just lost myself. I can remember waking up my first morning after coming home from my mission. I was so afraid. I was ashamed of that fear, and I didn't understand it. I mean I had just served a successful mission, why should I be afraid? Turned out, I had a lot of reasons to be afraid. I missed the structure that the mission afforded me. Without it, I felt lost. I started to drift away from the Church. It was a slow process, but thorough. By the time I'd been home for a year, I wasn't attending my meetings anymore. Still, I would've never considered myself inactive or without my testimony. I was in denial about a lot of things, and I was drifting spiritually. I was very focused academically, however. That's where my energy went. I would tell myself that as soon as I finished my schooling I would start going to church again. I met Celia during my residency. She was a nurse, and we were immediately drawn to each other. After a couple of dates, I found out she was also a less active member of the Church. We got married and immediately got pregnant. I was so overwhelmed by it all. I was a young medical student, with a young wife and child. The pressure was incredible. After I graduated, we moved to Boulder. I began working as a full-fledged cardiologist, but I felt so empty inside. I expected my work to fill me up, but it didn't." He paused. "I find it so ironic that I was a doctor for the heart, when my own heart was leaking lifeblood like a colander."

"As I look back, I wonder how my patients could stand me. I didn't have any compassion. I had no understanding of their fear and concerns. I was good at what I did, but I was thoughtless." He closed his eyes. "I wasn't much better at home. Celia and I fought constantly about money. Every year she would take off with a bunch of her friends and spend four days in Aspen. Aspen of all places! She would leave the baby with a sitter and leave me a note on the counter. She would pay for everything for everybody, and come home with credit card bills running into five digits. She'd think nothing of it. Then she would gripe because I was never there for her and the baby. I would try to tell her that I needed to work overtime just to keep up with the bills, but she never seemed to understand. You're a cardiologist, she would say. You make plenty of money. I would try to show her the bank statements, but she wasn't interested. I realize now that Celia must've felt pretty empty inside too. While I was trying to fill myself up with my work, she was trying to fill herself up with money. Neither one of us did a very good job."

He grew pensive. "It wasn't all bad. I remember after Trista was born, I took a month off to be with Celia and Triss. Celia's parents were on a mission when Trista was born, so they couldn't come. It turned out to be the best thing that ever happened to us. It was the honeymoon we never had. Celia never suffered from postpartum depression. It was as if the baby calmed her and brought her some kind of peace. She was relaxed and happy. I was thrilled." He laughed. "You know, we didn't even answer the phone for the first week. It was ringing off the hook with people wanting to congratulate us and wish us well. We just let the machine pick it up. In fact we turned the ringer completely off. Then I had to go back to work and the whole thing started all over again. Before I knew it, Celia was a distant memory. Trista was four, and I was involved with another woman."

Kenneth ran his hand over his face. "No wife should ever be a distant memory," he said. "When Celia learned about the affair, she moved out that very afternoon. She's been in Utah ever since. At first I was very angry. I felt I had worked just to keep her in Aspen, and now that my credit cards were saturated, she was deserting me. But slowly, I came to realize that even though our marriage was crippled, I was the one who amputated its legs. I shouldn't have turned to someone else. I should've found help—not an escape. With the help of a therapist I began to realize my own problems and take responsibility for them. I had to stop blaming Celia for everything. I started going back to church. I was beginning to put my life in order. I was counseling with my bishop. I began to feel that Celia did the right thing by leaving. She was allowing us the time we both needed to get our lives together. I finally came to a point where I knew what I wanted and what I had to do. I wanted my family. I came to Utah one day and took Celia out for dinner. I told her how sorry I was and I promised that it would never happen again. I told her that since our separation, I had learned so much, and I wanted to work on our marriage. I told her about my therapy, both with Dr. Curtis and Bishop Madsen. I asked her to come into counseling with me. She could stay here in Utah if she wanted, and we could take it slow. I offered to fly her into Colorado for the sessions. I wanted to try again." Kenneth shuddered. "She listened to all of it then told me that I'd be served divorce papers when I got home. I was devastated."

"I know she got a little thrill out of that powerful scene. It hurt me deeply, and I think she viewed it as a payback. She told me that I could be as sorry as I wanted, but it wouldn't change anything. She left me there, sitting in the restaurant completely stunned, but it didn't change my feelings. I was still sorry. I just knew she would never be coming back, and that hurt. It took me a while to work through that new reality."

The waiter came and placed their meals in front of them, but Tye ignored hers. "Where is Trista in all of this?" she asked.

"Trista is at the top of my life," Kenneth said. "She matters more than anything or anyone. I'm ashamed to say that it hasn't always been that way, but it is now."

"I'm glad to hear that. It's what Trista deserves." Tye turned to her meal and bit into a fresh ravioli.

"I don't usually do this on the first date," Kenneth said. "Tell someone my life story. I guess I just feel like you know Trista, and so you would understand. Besides, most people don't ask. You're the first person who has asked me about what happened. Most folks only want the glossy story about being a doctor. They watch those TV dramas and think my life is like that, and that everything is all wrapped up in a neat little package at the end of the season."

"I do understand, Kenneth. I'm very sorry about you and Celia. I'm mostly sorry for Triss though. She misses the benefits of an intact family."

"Someday I hope to change all of that. I hope to give her a solid, intact family."

"But it will never be the same without her mother and her father."

Kenneth put his fork down. "I know," he said. "Some things I can never change. I can simply do the best I know how." He brightened. "Tell me about your horse back home. What do the two of you do?"

"Trapper is a bay thoroughbred that stands about sixteen hands. He's a work of art. We used to compete in three-day-eventing."

"Was that before you started college?"

"No. I competed for OSU before my mission."

"OSU," Kenneth said under his breath. "Oregon State? Are you from Oregon?"

"Yes."

"Then why didn't you go back to it when you got home from San Antonio?"

Tye didn't want to talk about Kyle. "I lost my desire to compete," she said. "I doubt the trainer would've taken me back anyway. She wasn't very happy when I left the team to serve a mission."

"I see. So, you teach Trista how to ride instead?"

"It's what I've always wanted to do. I hope to have my own barn someday," she said.

"Trista would love to have a barn," Kenneth said. "She doesn't think she gets enough riding time with weekly lessons. Do you want to settle here in Utah?"

"No. I believe I'll go back to Oregon after my schooling." She sighed. "There's too much about my home state that I love. It's already spring there, and the crocuses are beginning to bloom."

"Do you like crocus?"

"They're my favorite flower. They come in so many different colors and sizes. And they're the first flowers to bloom in the spring. That means a lot to me. Every year I start looking for the bright spots of purple, yellow, and white that usher in the beginning of spring."

Kenneth sat back in the booth. "It must be hard for you to be in this snowbound state."

"It is."

"How much longer do you have to go?"

"This is my junior year."

"My college years are nothing but a big blur. What kind of classes are you taking?"

Tye began telling Kenneth about her classes. She warmed as she talked about Elsa and her nearing delivery date.

"That sounds so interesting," he said. "Maybe I could come out and meet your cow sometime. I've never been around cows; only horses."

Tye immediately thought about Preston. It didn't feel right to think about taking Kenneth out to the barn where Elsa lived. That place belonged to her and Preston. It was private and special. She changed the subject. "So, what do you and Trista do on Sundays?"

"Well, it's hard, because it's the Sabbath, and I don't like to do a lot of activities. I usually keep the hotel room until my flight leaves. Then after church, I bring her to the room. I ask her what she learned in Primary. I tell her what I learned in the ward I attended. Then, we read some scriptures together. She'll bring board games from home, and we'll play with those. Sometimes we'll go for a long ride or a walk, if the weather is nice. If she wants, she can invite a friend. She's only done that a couple of times. Last week, she wanted me to ask you to join us on Sunday."

Tye warmed to the idea. "Maybe I can have you and Trista over to my house for Sunday dinner sometime."

"I would enjoy that, Tye. And I know Triss would love it."

The waiter brought the dessert tray, but Tye turned it down. "I really need to go and get some studying done tonight."

"Oh, of course. I'm sorry for keeping you so long," Kenneth said. He paid the bill and hurried Tye to the car. The drive to Tye's home was silent and comfortable. Tye enjoyed the warmth of Kenneth's company. She appreciated his honesty about his past, and she admired his courage in dealing with his own mistakes and shortcomings.

Kenneth pulled the car in front of Tye's home. "May I call you sometime?" he asked. "From Colorado, I mean."

Tye's heart fluttered. "Yes."

"Will you give me your phone number?"

Tye wrote it down on one of his business cards.

Kenneth placed the number in his coat pocket. Then he hurried out of the car and walked Tye to the door. "Thank you for a lovely evening," he said. "And for letting me tell you my story. I haven't felt this comfortable with anyone since Celia left."

"I'm glad for that."

Gently, Kenneth caressed Tye's cheek and hair. He bent over as if to kiss her, then he stopped and simply pressed his cheek to hers in a warm embrace. "I'll call," he whispered.

"I hope so," Tye replied gently.

Kenneth broke away and walked down the steps while Tye turned into the warm light of her home.

he following Tuesday afternoon, Tye sat on the bed and watched Meg dress in several layers. "So, who's the lucky guy tonight?" Tye asked.

"I'm skiing with Calum tonight."

"I don't think I've ever met Calum," Tye said.

"No, I don't believe you have. Mark met him last semester on the slopes, but Calum has never been to the house. Last semester we had the same Book of Mormon class. This year we're both taking the Old Testament. We decided there must be a reason we ended up together in the same religion class for two semesters in a row. We figured we were meant to ski together." She changed the subject. "I am so glad we had that weekend storm. It probably extended the skiing season by two weeks at least and with today's dusting there will be some fresh powder tonight."

The doorbell rang.

Meggie clenched her jaw. "I'll get it," she mimed as KayLee yelled those same words from downstairs.

"It's probably Calum," Meggie said.

"Tye!" KayLee yelled from downstairs. "The door is for you."

Tye and Meggie exchanged looks as they walked down the stairs.

A delivery man was standing in the living room holding a cobalt ceramic bowl that was full of blooming, yellow, white, and purple crocus. Tye gave a cry of delight.

"I'm to deliver these to Tye Jorgenson," the delivery man said. "Are you Tye?"

Tye nodded as she took the flowers.

The delivery man smiled. "Enjoy them. They're beautiful."

"Yes, I will. Thank you."

The delivery man found his way to the door as KayLee and Meggie crowded around.

"Who are they from?" KayLee whispered.

Tye searched for the card and pulled it out. "Thank you for the loveliest evening I've had in years. Kenneth."

Tye's heart fluttered like a caged butterfly as she touched the silky petals. She was awed by his ability to hear what was important to her. She had only mentioned her longing for an Oregon spring once. And now he was doing his best to provide a small token of that glorious season.

"Oh, Tye," KayLee gushed. "You sure know how to pick them. He's the handsomest man I've ever seen in my life. I mean, he's gorgeous. Then he sends you flowers! This is so romantic."

"I thought you said you would never date a man with a child," Meggie said.

"I take it all back. If I could find myself a Doctor Kenneth Brannon, I'd be dating him tonight. I see the difference between men and boys."

Meggie and Tye exchanged looks.

The doorbell rang again but KayLee was too intrigued to bother answering it.

Meggie went to the door.

Calum stood in his ski suit. "Are ya ready?" he asked.

Meggie nodded. "Let's go. I've only been night skiing once, and I loved it."

"Have a good time," Tye said.

"You should come with us," Calum suggested. "My friend, Josh is in the car. He'd be happy to help you learn."

"Thanks for the offer," Tye said. "But tonight I'm going to a play with Mark; something warm and safe."

Calum laughed. "I can tell you're not a skier."

Meg became thoughtful. "A play sounds fun. Tell Mark I said hello. Maybe we can all go again later this week."

"I'll ask Mark if Thursday night is good for him."

Meg pulled her skis from the wall. "Okay. See you later."

Several minutes later, Tye placed her flowers on the window sill of her bedroom. They brightened every corner of the room, bringing the Oregon springtime closer to her heart. The doorbell interrupted her thoughts. She hurried downstairs.

"You're looking so much better," Tye exclaimed as she greeted Mark.

Mark smiled. "My strength and stamina are starting to come back. I went to all my classes today and still feel strong enough to see this play. Thanks for coming with me, Tye. My drama class requires that I attend."

"Thanks for asking. It sounds fun."

She and Mark huddled together against the clearing cold as they made their way to the theater. They selected their seats. Soon the curtain was raised on a three-act play about dating experiences at BYU.

After the play Mark and Tye wandered to the Cougar Eat for some hot chocolate to help ward off the chilly walk home. Once they were seated Mark asked, "What were Meg's plans for the evening? She never told me. She only said she couldn't come with us."

"She and Calum went skiing," Tye said.

"Who's Calum?"

"I just met him for the first time tonight. She said you met him on the slopes."

Mark furrowed his brow. "Oh, yes," he began slowly. "I do vaguely remember running into some guy from one of her classes. He wanted her to stay on the slopes to go night skiing with him."

"Well, it looks like she finally got her chance." Tye changed the subject. "Hear from KayLee lately?"

Mark grinned. "Nope. I think it was the chicken gizzards that chased her off."

Tye laughed.

Mark grew serious. "I wish I could go skiing," he said. "And I wish Meggie would've come with us tonight."

Tye gave him a puzzled look. "Is it bothering you that she's choosing to go out with other men?"

Mark hedged. "No. I just wish she was here with us. That's all. You have to admit that the evening isn't the same without Meggie."

Tye agreed. "She said that maybe we could all go again later this week—maybe Thursday."

"Maybe," Mark said as they threw away their trash and started the short walk home.

THE RIVER HOME   229

"How are you feeling?" Tye asked as they stopped in front of Tye's home.

Mark sighed. "I'm okay, but I think I'll turn in. I'm tired. Goodnight, Tye." He waved as he began to walk to his home.

Tye returned his wave before walking into the house where she found KayLee on the couch with a young man. KayLee was talking animatedly about her high school cheerleading squad, where she had been the head cheerleader.

"What have you got there?" Tye asked.

"Oh, it's my high school album."

"You brought that all the way from home?"

"Sure. I think it's important to stay connected to one's roots." She looked at the young man. "Don't you?" she asked.

He was obviously besotted. "Absolutely," he said.

KayLee put the book down. "I'll show you a cheer," she said. "Sit down, Tye."

Tye sat next to the young man, who didn't even bother to introduce himself; he was so enthralled with KayLee's lithe beauty.

Tye watched as KayLee went through the motions of a cheer from her senior year of high school, yelling at the top of her lungs. Her blonde hair flew in all directions as she jumped and then landed in the splits.

"That is so impressive," the young man said. He turned to Tye. "Don't you think?".

"Oh, yes," Tye agreed.

KayLee scrambled from her position on the floor. "I hope to be a cheerleading coach when I get out of school. I'm studying to be a teacher, but all I really want to do is teach young girls how to cheer. And I would love to prepare squad teams for competition."

"Are there scholarships available for cheering?" Tye asked.

KayLee nodded. "They're hard to come by though. I tried for one but didn't get it."

"Oh, I'm sorry," said Tye. Then she rose from the couch. "Well, I should let the two of you continue with your evening. By the way, KayLee, where's Dianna?"

"Oh, she's probably studying in our room. Ever since she and Doug broke up permanently, she's turned into a hermit. I can't get her to do anything fun." KayLee motioned to the young man by her side. "Chad here had a friend, but she wasn't interested."

"Well, I think I'll hit the books myself," Tye said as she walked up the stairs.

It wasn't long after Tye had settled in with her business plan that Meg walked in the bedroom door.

"Did you have a good time?" Tye asked

Meg propped her skis up in the corner of the room. "It was okay. Calum is a better skier than Joel, and he was more interested in skiing with someone than in impressing everyone around him." She looked at Tye. "Still, it isn't the same as when I'm with Mark. Did you guys have a good time?"

Tye nodded. "The play was really funny. Then I came home and saw the whole thing acted out again with KayLee and her date."

"What do you mean?"

"The play was about dating at BYU. It was a spoof on how men and women interact. You should've come with us, Meggie. You would've loved it—especially after that little encounter with KayLee and Mark. Mark said it reminded him of how the two of you were always talking about love vibes." Tye giggled.

"How is Mark?"

"He's feeling pretty good. He missed you though."

Meggie sat on her bed and began removing her boots. "You know, I missed him too. I wish he could go skiing. We only went once, and I had the most fun. Every time I go skiing with someone, I keep wishing Mark was there."

"He wishes he was there, too. I think he misses you, Meg. Since he's been sick the two of you haven't been able to cook like you did last semester."

"I know. He just doesn't have much stamina for long detail in the kitchen. Part of it is my fault, I guess. I get so worried about him getting sick again. I don't make myself available for anything that isn't strictly required for his classes. Even when we're in the kitchen for some assignment, he gets tired. Consequently we don't spend as much time together as we used to." She sighed. "He really scared me, Tye."

"I know, Meg."

Meg had stripped to her long underwear before grabbing her pajamas. "Did he say anything about going out later this week?"

"Not much. You'll have to talk to him about that."

Meg nodded. "I'll do that tomorrow. Right now, I'm getting in the shower, then I'll be in bed."

"Goodnight." Tye called after her as she turned out the light.

ayLee yelled from the hallway, "Tye, phone."

Tye put her business plan down before picking up the extension in her room.

"Tye? Kenneth Brannon here."

Tye smiled into the phone. "Well, Dr. Brannon, you sound ready for surgery."

Kenneth sighed. "Actually, I just got out of surgery so my day has been long. We had an emergency angioplasty this afternoon."

"What's an angioplasty?" Tye asked.

"It's when we insert a small balloon through a patient's artery and thread that balloon into the arteries leading into the heart. The artery is blocked and needs to be cleared so that the heart can get enough blood supply. Otherwise the heart will go into arrest."

"You mean, like a heart attack?"

"Yes. A heart attack. We insert this balloon to press the blockage against the artery wall. Then we insert a tiny piece of mesh to keep the plaque from breaking off or falling back into the artery."

"Sounds like it can be tricky."

"Sometimes. If the blockage is in a difficult spot, it can be a little dicey. But all went well with my patient this afternoon. He should be home by tomorrow afternoon and playing in the snow with his dogs by the weekend."

"Congratulations, Dr. Brannon."

"Thank you. Yes, it's satisfying work; healing people's hearts."

Tye could tell by the warmth in Kenneth's voice that he was pleased with the day's events.

"I received the flowers," Tye said.

"I hope you like them."

"They're lovely, Kenneth. Thank you for sending them. I have them in the window sill, and they brighten up the whole room. This afternoon the sun came out, and it almost looked like spring in here." She paused. "Thank you again."

"It was my pleasure, Tye." He was quiet for a moment. "I wanted to let you know that I'm going to come down to Utah this weekend. Perhaps we could go to dinner on Saturday?"

"I have a better idea. Why don't you and Trista come for Sunday dinner?"

"That would be wonderful. My flight leaves at seven-thirty. Can we plan for an early meal?"

"Absolutely. I'll see if Meggie and Mark will cook for us. If not you'll be stuck with my version of macaroni and cheese."

Kenneth laughed, then said, "I remember meeting Meggie last Saturday. Who's Mark?"

"He's a good friend of ours. Mark and Meg are culinary majors. They're good cooks."

"Yes, but surely they cannot afford to feed extra people."

"Usually, we all chip in."

"I'll send a check in the mail tomorrow morning."

"Thanks, Kenneth. That would be great."

"I may not remember much about my college days, but I do remember a lot of pancakes and bottled spaghetti sauce with tons of pasta."

Tye laughed. "Yeah, it can be a tight budget."

"Tye?"

"Yes?"

"Thanks again for last Saturday. I'll look forward to seeing you at Triss's lesson and then on Sunday. It'll be my last weekend for a month or so."

Tye felt a stab of something she couldn't name. "I'm sorry, Kenneth. I'll miss you," she said.

"And I'll miss you too, but I'll call. I promise."

"Let's not worry about that until Sunday."

"I'll see you then. Triss will be thrilled."

Chapter Thirty-Two

Tye read Preston's business plan slowly. "I had no idea there was such overhead involved in a veterinarian practice," she said slowly without looking up from the page.

"I know," Preston said. "I knew there would be a lot of expense, but I didn't figure this much."

Tye turned another page. "There's labor, of course. You have to have people working for you: vet techs, receptionists, maybe another veterinarian to split some of the night and weekend emergency hours." She settled deeper in her chair. "But look at this. I never would've thought about x-ray equipment, intravenous fluids, and an echo cardiogram." She stopped. "What's an echo cardiogram?"

"It's like ultra sound for the heart. I'll be able to look at the heart muscle of an animal without invasive surgery."

Tye thought of Kenneth. She wondered if he had an echo cardiogram in his office.

"That's the thing about a veterinarian practice," Preston said. "I'll have to run it like a small, independent hospital. There's no such thing as pet hospitals; not in the same sense as human hospitals, anyway. The veterinarian's office is the hospital. So, I have to have almost everything that a hospital has."

Tye looked up at Preston before turning another page. "And I suppose it has to be state-of-the-art. I mean, I know when Trapper sees the vet, I expect him to get the very best of care and have access to the latest technology."

"Exactly."

"You're looking at a six-digit investment before you even open your doors," Tye said.

Preston nodded. "That doesn't include the schooling debt. So far I've been able to pay as I go. Once I get into vet school though, I may have to take out loans. It's sobering."

"Are you changing your mind?"

Preston shook his head. "No. I may change my method though. I've been thinking about going into a partnership with someone. Or I may buy an existing practice. That would mean the same investment but it would come with an established client base and materials."

Tye bit her lip as she read the rest of the paperwork. "Have you considered insurance?" she asked.

"Gosh, no! I should call an agent."

Tye nodded as she handed the report back to Preston, who scribbled a note on the first page.

"Let me see yours," Preston said.

Tye dug around in her bag before producing a multi page document. She handed it to Preston. "It's not near as involved as yours. I split mine into two categories."

"I see," Preston said slowly as he read the first page. "You could own your barn or work for someone else."

"Owning my own barn would mean quite a bit of overhead."

Preston agreed. "First of all you have the investment in the land and buildings. That can be pricey." He flipped the page. "You'd need plenty of land so you could give your boarding horses pasture time and maybe grow some of your winter feed."

Tye blinked. "I never thought about growing my own feed."

Preston looked up from the papers. "If you owned your own place, it would be a good idea. It would be cheaper than buying it and you could insure the quality."

Tye took the papers back and scribbled in a note. "I'll have to look into that," she said.

Preston continued, "You'd have to decide if it was worth the land investment. Then there would be the cost of seed and harvesting and possibly irrigating; depending on where you live and what you grow. In my opinion it would be worth the investment. That's how we do it on the ranch. We grow as much of our own feed as possible. It's an absolute necessity for us."

Tye nodded thoughtfully as she handed the papers back to Preston. He continued to read.

"Wow! You sure would have to pay a lot of insurance."

"I know. If someone gets hurt on my property, I may be liable."

"I never thought of that," he whispered to himself. He turned the page. "Do you have to worry about insurance if you don't own the property?"

"I still have to carry liability, in case someone gets hurt on my watch, but it's not the staggering amount the barn owner should have."

"Have you decided what you're going to do?" Preston asked.

"I hope to start out working for someone who owns a barn. Then I'll save my money, and if I still want to own a place I'll think about buying. I don't think I want this hefty debt coming right out of school."

Preston handed her the papers. "I don't blame you."

Tye put her papers away then placed her hand on Preston's knee. "Thanks for looking this over."

Preston covered Tye's hand with his own, squeezing her fingers for a brief moment. "It's been fun, and you've given me some really good ideas. I'm glad we're doing this together." Tye changed the subject. "How is our new calf?"

"He's fine," Preston smiled. "He's growing fast. Three other cows have dropped their young in the last week, so Martin and Lorena are really busy right now. I wish I could help them, but I've been tied up here with school. I haven't been out there since that morning."

A sense of relief washed over Tye. She liked to think that Preston would take her with him if he went to visit the Thomases. "Have you seen Elsa lately?" she asked.

"Not for anything more than the perfunctory visits. I think we're going to have to start checking more often though. We should set up a schedule so at least one of us sees her every day."

Tye agreed, and soon they had worked out a calendar.

"I guess we should go," Preston said. "It's getting late."

Tye checked her watch. It was nine-thirty.

Preston stood and offered Tye his hand. She took it, and he helped her out of her chair. His roughened palm lingered on hers. Then he took her hand firmly in his as they walked out of the library. "I'll walk you home," he said.

"Thanks, I'd like that."

They trudged through the falling snow in a comfortable silence. She enjoyed Preston. It was different than her time with Kenneth.

Preston was more of a partner; a comrade. They shared equal footing. They worked together and considered it play. There was an innocence about Preston that Kenneth lacked. But life had thrown different experiences at Kenneth, and he was tackling them with courage and humility. He seemed to have learned from his mistakes, and he was pursuing a course that would ultimately bring him and his family happiness. Tye admired him for that.

Preston's fingers tightened around Tye's as they came to her house. "I'll let you know if I see any changes in Elsa."

Tye returned Preston's squeeze as she looked into his eyes. "Thanks for walking me home."

The porch light was softened by the snow, giving a luminous glow. Preston's blue eyes flickered with warmth. It was as if they had a fire of their own. She had seen it before during their visits with the Thomases. Tye was beginning to believe in that fire and the gentle passion that accompanied it.

No words were spoken. Instead, Preston caressed Tye's face with a tender gesture before retracing his steps.

Tye watched until he was swallowed up by the falling snow.

Chapter Thirty-Three

eggie pulled the lasagna out of the oven.

"Could you please keep the oven on?" Mark asked. "I'll wait twenty minutes before I put in the parmesan garlic bread. We want the lasagna to rest."

Tye was cutting tomatoes for the salad when the doorbell rang. "That must be Kenneth and Trista," she said.

"Are you nervous?" Meggie asked.

"A little."

"Whatever for?" Mark asked. "We're serving up a meal fit for an Italian king."

"Kenneth isn't Italian," Tye said.

"Well, pardon moi," Mark said. "Perhaps you would prefer French."

Tye laughed at his accent. "It's not the meal. You guys are great. He'll probably want to take you home."

"And you prefer that he take you home?" Mark asked.

Tye blushed. "No. That's not it, exactly. I'm just well …

nervous, that's all." She threw a dish towel at Mark.

The doorbell rang again. Tye hurried out of the kitchen and opened the door. Her nerves disappeared as Trista flung her arms wide, hugging Tye. "Hi, Miss Jorgenson."

Tye pulled Trista close. "Hi, Triss."

Tye looked up at Kenneth, who reached around Trista and gave Tye a kiss on the cheek. "Hello, Tye."

Tye warmed under Kenneth's kiss. "Kenneth," she said softly. "Please come in. Let me take your jackets."

Trista dumped hers on the floor before walking into the living room.

"Wait just one minute, young lady. You don't live here. Come get this jacket, and hand it to Tye properly."

Trista scurried back and picked up her jacket. She turned it over to Tye. "Sorry, Miss Jorgenson."

Tye smiled as she took the jacket. Kenneth placed his on the coat rack and then pulled out a bottle of sparkling cider. "I hope this goes with the meal."

"Sparkling cider goes with everything," Tye said. "Thanks for bringing it."

"Dinner smells wonderful," Kenneth said.

"Meggie is making vegetable lasagna. It's one of her best creations," Tye said.

"Hey, Miss Jorgenson, can I see your room?" Trista asked.

Kenneth spoke, "No, Triss, you cannot see Miss Jorgenson's room. That's not a polite question to ask. Her room is in a private part of the house."

"But I can show you the kitchen and introduce you to Mark and Meggie," Tye said.

Trista beamed, reaching for Tye's hand as they walked into the kitchen.

Tye made introductions. Mark and Meggie both shook Trista's hand. Mark introduced himself with an Italian accent, making Trista giggle.

Several minutes later, Mark and Meggie came out of the kitchen. Tye made more introductions. "You've met Meggie. This is our good friend, Mark."

Mark and Kenneth shook hands. Soon, everyone was sitting around the table. Tye asked Kenneth to say the prayer. She loved the sound of his deep voice as it resonated in the dining room.

After the prayer, Meggie dished up everyone's plate.

"So, what kind of doctoring do you do?" Meggie asked.

"I'm a cardiologist," Kenneth explained.

"He heals hearts," Trista announced.

"Yes, it sounds like that's exactly what he does," Mark said.

"I'm going to live with my daddy starting this summer," Trista announced.

Tye shot Kenneth a look.

"Yes," he said. "Triss and I have talked about it, and she wants to come back to Colorado."

"My grandparents have a pony for me. I'll be able to ride as often as I want!"

"Well, probably not that often," Kenneth said. "But you will be able to ride more than just weekly."

"What's the pony's name?" Meg asked.

"Bluebelle. Daddy told me that I named her when I was really little, but I don't remember."

"Do you still like that name?" Mark asked.

Trista nodded. "Yeah. I can't wait to ride her."

After dinner, everyone pitched in. Trista and Kenneth cleared the table while Meggie, Tye, and Mark washed, rinsed, and put the dishes away. It didn't take long. After they were finished, Meggie announced that she and Mark were going to take a walk before going to Mark's home for the evening. Tye was grateful for the thoughtfulness of her friends.

"I brought some games," Trista announced. "Can we play?"

Kenneth and Tye agreed. Trista hurried to the car and brought out the game of *Life*.

"I should let you know that Trista is the high champion in the game of *Life*," Kenneth said before beginning. He was right. Trista won both games.

Kenneth glanced at his watch. "I really need to get Triss back to her mother so I can catch my flight," he said. "I regret having to leave so early, but I really must."

"Yes, I understand," Tye said.

Kenneth turned to Trista. "Can you take these games out to the car?" he asked. "I'll be along in a minute."

Trista obediently put all the game pieces together. "Thank you for dinner, Miss Jorgenson. I had a nice Sunday."

"Thanks for coming, Triss. I'll see you next week for your lesson."

Trista gave Tye another hug before picking up the board game and going out to the car.

Kenneth watched from the window as Trista settled into the front seat. "I am so glad the custody battle is finally over." He turned to Tye. "I didn't hide from Celia the fact that this is where we were spending our Sunday." He shook his head. "No, that didn't come out right. What I mean is; Trista may tell her mother. I never ask Triss to keep anything from Celia. That's too big of a burden for a little girl. So, just be prepared. If Celia hassles you in any way, please tell me. I'll take her to task over it."

"I'll be fine, Kenneth."

Kenneth walked to where Tye stood. He placed his hands on her arms. "I wish I didn't have to go," he said. "And I wish I could tell you exactly when I'll be back, but I'm not sure. I'll call."

"I'm glad we had this afternoon. Thank you for coming."

Kenneth tilted Tye's chin. "May I?" he asked.

Tye smiled into Kenneth's hazel eyes.

He placed his lips on hers and gently pulled her to him. Tye allowed the tender power of his warm embrace to envelop her.

Kenneth pulled away. "I'll call," he said.

Tye caressed his cheek. "I'll be here," she replied. Then placing her arm through his she walked him to the door. Kenneth turned and kissed her again. This time there was a sense of urgency. "I'll miss you." He pulled away again and opened the door. Tye waved to Trista. The young girl waved brightly as her father walked down the steps.

Chapter Thirty-Four

*T*ye walked into the arena with Triss by her side. Trista was leading Patches. When she got into the center of the arena Tye glanced into the stands, even though she knew Kenneth wouldn't be there. Her heart jumped when she saw Celia. She was dressed in jeans, a black knee length coat, and a scarf. Her hands were shoved into her pockets. She still looked cold.

"Mommy!" Trista said.

"Hey, Triss. I came to watch your lesson. Now get to it. It's freezing in here."

"Okay, Mommy!" Trista mounted and began to warm up Patches.

Soon, they were in the heart of their lesson when they heard Celia yell, "Don't get so close to the wall, Triss. That horse will squish you!"

"Mom!" Trista yelled.

Tye walked to where Celia was standing. "Mrs. Brannon, we have everything under control. Please, don't distract Trista. It could prove dangerous."

A cold look came into Celia's eyes. "Don't you Mrs. Brannon me," Celia said. "I can tell she's getting way too close to the wall."

Trista rode over. "Mommy, please," she said. "Miss Jorgenson knows what she's doing. We do this all the time. This is only your first time watching. It's okay."

Celia sat down. "Well, fine. If you say so. I just don't want you cracking your knee cap on that wall when that pony decides to give himself a rubdown. These arenas are really safety hazards."

"If Patches misbehaves, Trista can correct him. It's part of what she learns in here, Mrs. Brannon," Tye said.

Celia folded her arms but said nothing more during the rest of the lesson. After it was over, she stumbled out of the stands and followed Tye, Trista, and Patches to the crossties. "My legs are numb," she murmured.

"You should ride, Mom. It keeps you warm."

"No thanks. I had enough of horses when I was married to your father." She looked at Tye.

Throughout the rest of the work, Celia was surprisingly silent as Trista finished up with Patches. After the young girl led the pony to his stall, she looked at her mother. "I'm ready to go, Mommy," Trista said.

Tye could feel Trista's anxiety, and she felt bad for the little girl.

"You go and sit in the car for a minute, Triss. I need to speak to Miss Jorgenson."

"Please, Mommy, can't we go now?"

Celia turned to Trista. "Quit whining. I'll be out in a minute."

Trista gave Tye a desperate look.

Tye smiled. "Go on ahead, Trista. Your mother needs to speak to me. It's okay."

The sound of a car door slamming resonated through the barn. "I know about you and Kenneth," Celia said. "Trista told me that she and my ex-husband spent Sunday afternoon at your place." She sneered. "That's just like Kenneth. He likes young women."

"I am young," Tye replied.

Celia gave her a hard look. "You should be concerned about the age difference, Miss Jorgenson. Kenneth must be ten years older than you."

"Lots of things concern me, Mrs. Brannon."

Celia began to pace. "He has full custody, you know."

"Yes. He told me."

"I supposed he gloated over his win. That stupid judge. Just because Kenneth is a doctor doesn't mean he can be a decent parent. He's always been a good doctor, but he's been a poor husband and an even poorer parent."

"Have you talked with Kenneth lately, Mrs. Brannon?"

"More than I care to."

"No. I mean have you really talked with him?"

Celia stopped pacing and gave Tye a long, reckoning stare. "Oh, I get it. I suppose he told you about the day I told him I wanted a divorce. How repentant he was and how sorry for all the stupid things he had done. Well, no amount of repenting could change what he did."

"Being sorry is the best he can do, Mrs. Brannon. And he truly is sorry. He's changed his way of thinking. Doesn't that count for anything?" Tye asked.

"Not in my book," Celia said. "I put him through medical school, and how does he repay me? By having an affair with one of my peers. I knew that nurse. We had worked together." She shook her head. "No amount of sorry can make up for that."

Tye nodded. "Yes. I can understand. I don't blame you for being mad, but it was a long time ago. People change."

"I don't care how much time passes," Celia said. "I will never forget what he did."

"You know what else he told me?"

Celia leaned forward.

"He told me that he took a month off after Trista was born. He said it was the honeymoon you never had."

Tears came to Celia's eyes.

"Mrs. Brannon, talk with Kenneth."

Celia gave her a strong look.

Tye could read many emotions before Celia blinked. Then without a word, Celia turned and walked out of the barn.

Chapter Thirty-Five

*T*ye stared at the open page of her religion manual, but she had quit reading thirty minutes ago. Kenneth had called since Tye's talk with Celia, and she had told Kenneth what was said.

"I can call and tell her to leave you alone," Kenneth said.

"No," Tye replied. "Leave it be. I think everything is fine now."

Tye enjoyed Kenneth's calls. She enjoyed listening to him talk about his practice and his patients. He told her funny stories about some of his co-workers and shared his frustrations over hospital politics. She told him about her classes and Trista's lessons. She kept silent about Elsa and Preston.

Meggie walked into the bedroom. "You look like you're studying hard."

Tye shut the book. "Meg, when do you tell people about other people?"

Meg sat down on her bed. "What do you mean? Oh, you mean Kenneth and Preston."

Tye nodded. "They don't know about each other." She paused.

"And neither one of them know about Kyle."

Meggie scooted across her own bed and leaned against the wall. "Have they asked?"

"No."

"There's your answer."

"Is it really that simple?"

"Sure. Have they volunteered any information about their dating habits?"

"No. I don't think Preston is seeing anyone, though."

"What about Kenneth?"

"I honestly don't know about Kenneth."

"Maybe there's more to this question. How do you feel about each one of them?" Meggie asked. "And how does Kyle fit into your relationships with these men? Why do you feel it important for them to know about him? You haven't seen him since last July. It's almost been a year."

Tye's heart constricted with the mention of his name. No matter how long it had been or how many evenings she spent with someone else, Kyle was always a consideration. She pushed that away and contemplated Kenneth and Preston. "I enjoy both men but for different reasons."

"Do you feel closer to either one of them?"

"Kenneth, I guess."

"Why?"

"Because what's happened between Preston and me has simply been through a course of events. Kenneth has sought me out." She grew quiet. "But there's something about Preston. He spends so much time alone. I want to break through that and get close to him. I want him to choose me."

"And if he did choose you, what would you tell Kenneth?"

Tye blinked. "I don't know. I haven't thought of that." She was silent for a moment. Then she asked, "Did you ever tell Calum and Joel about each other?"

Meggie shrugged. "There's nothing to tell. I didn't start seeing Calum until I quit seeing Joel. Besides, Calum and I have only gone skiing once." Meggie sighed. "I do wish Mark could go skiing. The doctor told him he couldn't ski for the rest of the year. The cold wind and weather would be too hard on his respiratory system."

"I doubt he has the stamina for it," Tye replied. "He makes it through his classes, and he's all caught up, but he gets really tired."

Meggie agreed. "The doc said he had a very bad case. Still, I miss him on the slopes." She changed the subject. "I wouldn't worry about Preston and Kenneth, Tye. I would worry about Kyle."

"What do you mean?"

"It's been almost a year. He shouldn't even be a part of the equation. I guess I just wonder why you consider him so much."

"I think I will always consider him." Tye folded her hands in her lap. "I loved Kyle deeply, and he was attached to Trapper. It makes the situation unique."

"Yes, I suppose it does. But I don't think it's right that he should be with you for the rest of your life. Someday you're going to have to make room for someone else."

"I wonder how long that will take."

Meggie shrugged. "I don't know, Tye." She paused. "I'm real sorry about Kyle. I know there wasn't any closure to that relationship. It ended badly."

"Sometimes it still feels like it didn't end at all," Tye whispered. "Ever since Christmas vacation I've been able to realign my relationship with Trapper so that I can love him completely and without any thoughts of Kyle. I've been happy about that." She paused. "And I know that Kyle is not coming back, but there's something that won't quite turn me loose. I can't name it, and I don't understand it."

"But don't you see the progress you've made? There was a time when you couldn't separate your relationship with Trapper from Kyle. Now you're able to do that."

Meggie continued, "I would seriously worry about you, Tye, if after your breakup with Kyle you just launched into another steady relationship. You've been wise in allowing yourself time to heal. And you're right, what you and Kyle had was unique, and I suspect it will be a slow process in letting all of that go. But already things are beginning to change. You're seeing Kenneth. You and Preston have developed an honest working relationship. I guess I see all of these things are progress towards completely letting Kyle go."

Tye stood and gave Meggie a hug. "Thanks for understanding, Meg." She walked out of her room and down the stairs, stepping out onto the front porch. Folding her arms across her chest, she breathed deep and shivered. She had forgotten her coat. The fading afternoon was blue and motionless.

This is what Kyle brought out in her; a paralysis that made her want to retreat into the blueness, no matter how hard she struggled against it. She glanced up at the sky. The clouds hovered low in the disappearing afternoon light. She wondered what the canyon felt like now. Was it still and blue? A soundless, sharp wind scraped at Tye's skin and pulled the hair away from her face.

It was hard not to turn away from winter; to get in her truck and drive to Arizona or maybe even further away. Just some place sunny and warm. Sighing, she turned and walked into the house. It didn't matter how far she drove or what climate she discovered. Winter wasn't just a season. It lived within her.

Chapter Thirty-Six

ye's teeth chattered more from nerves than the cold as she dialed Preston's number. When she heard his familiar voice answer the phone she felt better.

"Preston, you'd better get down here. Elsa is on her way."

"Okay. I'll be there soon."

Tye put the receiver in the cradle and pulled her jacket close to prevent the shivers. She hurried back to Elsa's stall. The cow looked fine.

Still, when Preston walked up to Elsa's stall ten minutes later, Tye was relieved.

"What have we got here?" he asked softly as he let himself into Elsa's stall.

"She's very fidgety, and I've noticed that in the last few minutes she's started to strain."

After the next contraction Tye turned to Preston. "What do we do?"

"Nothing, yet. She'll probably just handle it herself. We'll just stick around and watch to make sure that she doesn't run into any trouble."

Tye nodded and began pacing the diminutive stall. It had always seemed big enough, but now with two people and a pregnant cow in the process of giving birth, the walls seemed to close in on Tye. After several minutes Preston took her by the arm. "Why don't you sit down and relax. It won't be a long wait."

Sitting down, Tye pulled her knees to her chest and waited silently. Preston sat beside her.

An hour passed. Elsa had stopped making progress. She seemed tired and quit straining even though the hooves of the youngster had appeared. The cow laid down on her chest.

"This isn't a good sign," Preston said. "The calf is presented correctly or we wouldn't have seen the hooves. Maybe the head is bent or something, but I don't think so. I'm going to have to feel around in there and see if there's a problem."

Tye stood. "What can I do?"

"Bring me a bucket of hot water, some soap, and a latex shoulder glove. I'll need some towels and a rope too."

Tye hurried out of the stall. A few minutes later she returned with the items Preston had requested. She watched as he stripped to the waist and washed his arm up to the shoulder.

"I hope she doesn't strain while I'm feeling around in there," he mumbled to himself.

"Does it hurt?" Tye asked.

"It feels as if your arm is going to pop off at the shoulder." He spoke as he lowered himself to the ground, and inserted his arm into the cow. After a minute he pulled himself out of the big animal. "It's like I said, the calf is presented correctly. She's just gotten tired." Preston looked at Tye. "Do you want to feel?"

Tye nodded and scrubbed her arm. She put on a latex shoulder glove before kneeling onto the stall floor that was slick with dung and blood in spite of the straw. Tye ignored all of this as she inserted her arm into Elsa's birthing canal. At the end of her reach, she could feel the hooves of the calf, but she couldn't grasp them. That was far as her arm would go.

After Tye had risen from the floor, Preston grabbed the rope and made a slip knot. He put on a fresh glove and with the slip knot in his fingers placed his arm back into the cow's body.

Tye watched as he maneuvered the rope until he was satisfied.

"Okay. It's around the front hooves."

"Now what?"

"We'll just gently pull him out as if she were straining. Meaning that we'll pull for a minute, then we'll rest for a minute."

Tye nodded as Preston gently picked up the slack of the rope and began to pull the calf to its birth. After he had pulled several times he handed the rope to Tye. "You try."

She grabbed the rope giving Preston an uncertain look.

"Pull gently. Don't jerk."

Tye gently pulled. After a few minutes of work the front hooves began to show again. Tye panted heavily. "That's hard work."

"Yes, it is. It's nice to have two of us to share the load," Preston said as he began his turn.

At the last minute Elsa decided that she would help out. She gave one final heave. A wet and wiggly calf sprawled out on the ground, much to Tye and Preston's delight.

Preston handed Tye a towel, and the two of them began rubbing the young creature. They started with her face, making sure the nostrils were clear of the birthing sac. The pungent, musky odor of the birth filled the stall, and the floor became slick with water and more blood. Still, this was different than Tye's earlier experience in the Thomases field. There was no bone numbing wind or heat robbing snow. She was grateful for the warm stall.

Soon, they were pushed out of the way by Elsa. The mother began licking her calf with enthusiasm. She lowed softly. The calf answered with a bleat of its own. They noticed the tired look had left Elsa's eyes as she focused on her newest addition. The bond between mother and baby had begun. After Elsa had done a thorough job cleaning her, the calf instinctively began to look for its first meal. It didn't need any help in the search. Preston and Tye allowed the calf to do its own exploration on shaky legs.

After everything appeared in good condition, Preston and Tye began cleaning the stall. They worked fast, each shoveling out the evidence of the birth and replacing it with fresh straw and sawdust. When they were finished, they looked at each other. Both of them were covered in muck and dried blood. Although Tye was aware of the smell, it didn't offend her. It had become a part of her work with Elsa. But she was sure it would overpower her roommates.

"I guess we should clean up before heading out," Preston said.

"You first," Tye said. "You're the dirtiest."

"I don't know about that," Preston said. "I think we make a matched pair."

Tye laughed as she waved him off to the bathroom. A few minutes later it was Tye's turn. She washed up the best she could and changed her sweatshirt before returning to the stall, where she sat next to Preston. They looked at each other and Tye caught the fire in Preston's eyes. It warmed her.

"Well, what do you think?" he asked.

"I think new life is wonderful," she said. "I don't get to do this very often, but I think it's something that would never get old."

"Well, it isn't always this easy."

"I didn't think it was easy at all," Tye replied.

"It is compared to the calving season on the ranch. For one thing, Elsa was gracious enough to have her baby early in the evening. Most cows drop their young in the middle of the night. Calving season on the ranch doesn't always happen at convenient times, but it does happen all at once. For several weeks during the early spring, I just know I'm not going to get any sleep. I've been awakened at three in the morning to help a struggling cow. Some nights, I don't get any sleep at all. Sometimes you'll get two cows giving birth at the same time, and it can be pretty hectic and messy. This was a relatively clean birth." He paused. "But it never gets old for me. In spite of the sleepless nights, the mess, and hard work, calving season is my favorite time of the year."

He began picking up the soiled towels as he stood. "Well, our little one has had its first drink of milk. Our job is finished here."

"I'm not really ready to go home," Tye said. "Somehow this has left me feeling invigorated."

Preston agreed. "Why don't we drive up to Sundance? It's a fairly warm evening, and the mountain will be all lit up for night skiing."

"I'd like that."

Preston offered his hand to Tye. "We should both wash up at home. We've been crawling around in the hay and muck. Even though we've changed our clothes, I doubt we're fit for society. I'm sure we don't smell very good." He reached over and picked out several pieces of straw from Tye's hair.

Tye looked down at her jeans. They were smeared with blood, dung and the afterbirth. She hadn't thought to bring an extra pair. She looked at Preston. He didn't look any better.

Preston continued, "How about if we both go home and I pick you back up in thirty minutes."

"Good idea," Tye said. Then she turned to Elsa and gave her an affectionate scratch.

～

Forty-five minutes later, they drove Provo Canyon in silence until they reached the ski resort, allowing the warmth of the evening's events to be enough. For Tye, this silence was different from the silence she shared with Kenneth. This was more than comfortable. It was full of the partnership that comes from mutual exploration. Part of her felt as if she had known Preston all of her life, while another piece of her explored the idea of opening to the newest of possibilities.

Once they arrived at Sundance, Tye was awestruck. She had never been to the mountain. Its beauty surpassed her expectations as the white, jagged peaks pierced the star-spangled sky. The ski runs were brightly lit, illuminating the snow and surrounding area with a glow, creating a delicate blend of fire and ice. Light spilled onto the nearby snow clothed trees giving them a sparkle that looked as if they were dressed in white sequins. But all of it looked insignificant compared to the fierceness of the mountain night with its sky full of stars keeping company with the moon. Tye had forgotten how bright the sky could be on a moonlit night. When she and Preston moved away from the brightly lit resort, she could see the light of the moon reflecting off the snow, casting long shadows of trees and mountain peaks.

Unbidden memories came to Tye. She recalled cool, moonlit summer evenings at the beach with Kyle. The foamy white waves would dance with the light of the moon, always in motion and never quite attainable. This was different. During Tye's beach evenings with Kyle, everything had been in noise and motion; the steady and pulling rhythm of the ocean, the sand that was drawn to the sea only to be thrown back onto shore. Here, in this winter clothed land, snow muffled all sound. Tye was drawn to the stillness. Winter was offering one of its many gifts, and for the first time, Tye was drawn to it.

Tye pulled her coat close. In spite of the warmer valley temperatures that promised spring, the mountain held a tinge of frost in the air. It bit at her and heightened her senses. Winter had always seemed so dead, but tonight it was different. Elsa's calf was fine and warm on this winter night. And the mountain, with its dark, rugged beauty and brightly lit snow enraptured Tye. The many skiers added a festive feel to the evening. Winter had never looked like this; alive and inviting.

Tye turned to Preston. "Isn't this beautiful? I've never been here before. Have you?"

Preston nodded. "I've been up here a couple of times since school started in the fall. It reminds me of my mountains at home."

Hand-in-hand, they wandered the grounds before finding a place to sit. They huddled against each other in the cold. Everywhere they were surrounded by skiers, but none of them paid any attention to Tye and Preston. After several minutes the cold forced them to walk inside. They walked through the old country store before settling in at The Foundry Grill for dinner. They both ordered grilled chicken with light cream sauce sprinkled with rosemary and garlic. Tye thought of Meggie. She would have to tell her about this wonderful place. The room was rough with wood and a large slab rock fireplace. A wood burning fire crackled and spit as it gave off its cheery heat. A small candle flickered on the table; a symbol of the larger fire that was keeping the room cozy. A murmur of conversation added to the warmth of the room.

After they ordered, Preston asked, "What drew you to three-day-eventing?"

Tye was surprised at the question. She told Preston of her passion to ride and how she had worked for a scholarship at Oregon State University.

"What are you doing at BYU then?" Preston asked.

"I went on my mission and made the trainer at OSU unhappy." She became thoughtful. "Besides, after I got back from my mission, I didn't have the same desire to compete. So, I never went back. Kyle, on the other ..." her voice trailed off.

"Kyle?"

"Kyle was the man you saw in the photo of Trapper." She pulled out her purse and showed Preston the new snapshot of Trapper. "My mom took new pictures while I was home for Christmas."

Preston looked at the picture. "He really is a beauty. What happened to Kyle?"

A new desire to share this tender part of her welled up inside of Tye. But something else was happening; something new and wonderful. In her desire to get close to Preston, she was allowing him to reach a part of her that she had tried to close off. Maybe sharing her story of Kyle with Preston would help in the healing process she and Meggie had discussed.

Putting her fork down, Tye said, "I met Kyle at OSU. He was a senior and the captain of the competition team at Oregon State. I was brought onto the competition squad as an alternate rider in my sophomore year."

"What does that mean?"

"Most alternates are juniors. It gives them an opportunity to get used to the competition circuit. Usually the alternate will move into the captain position during his or her senior year."

"It sounds like it was quite an honor for you to receive that distinction during your sophomore year."

"It was. And the junior team wasn't happy about it. The trainer picked two alternates that year. I was one of them."

"So in essence, they created a position for you."

Tye nodded.

"Where does Kyle fit in all of this?"

Tye looked at Preston as she considered her words. How much should she tell him? The expression on his face was open and patient. She settled back in her chair and pushed her plate away. She would tell him everything. "Kyle and I fell in love," she said gently. "When I told him I was going to go on a mission, he wasn't very happy." Tye paused. "But I went anyway. Kyle took Trapper back east with him. He paid me for that privilege, which helped pay for my mission. He didn't have to pay me for Trapper, but he did. Then when I came home we just picked up where we left off."

"I don't see the catch."

"Kyle isn't a member of the Church. He took the missionary discussions, but he refused to join. Then he asked me to marry him, promising that as soon as he got through with the Olympic Games in four years he'd join the Church so we could be married in the temple." Bitterness rose up in Tye's throat, but she pushed it down. She wanted to be finished with that. It had no place in her relationship with Preston. Tye waited for Preston's next question, which she was sure would be about Kyle's Olympic goals.

He asked, "Do you still love him?"

The question took her completely by surprise. It took her a minute to focus. Then she answered, "It's not quite that simple for me because my relationship with Kyle involved Trapper. But during the Christmas holidays I came to realize that it was over between Kyle and me, and I started trying to put it all behind me. My first step was to reclaim Trapper. Because Kyle had been such an integral part of my relationship with Trapper, it was hard for me to be around my horse. But since Christmas I've been able to recover my relationship with Trapper. Still, I think these things take time."

Preston nodded. "I haven't been involved with anyone since before my mission. There was a girl in Montana who promised to wait for me, but I got a letter nine months into my mission where she told me she was dating other men. It didn't bother me so much. I was so involved in the work of the mission that it was easy to let her go. But nothing has been easy since."

"I understand," Tye said.

"I'm not very comfortable around women," Preston said. "I've spent too much time alone while I was growing up, and I came to like it." He paused. "But you're different, Tye. You understand my love for animals. You encourage me in my pursuit of a vet practice. Most girls think it's romantic until they find out what dirty, sweaty, smelly work it can be. Then they don't want anything to do with it." He continued, "I don't think I've ever told you this before, but I'm really glad that Professor Gates brought us together. I'm glad you're my partner because it feels like we share equality." He shook his head. "I'm not explaining this very well. I guess I like the way we work together. I've learned a great deal from you."

Tye laughed. "I have no idea what you could be learning from me. I've never worked around cows before."

Preston smiled. "Well, you did tell me that cows get tired of the snow."

Tye laughed again. "Oh, I see, you just want to tap into my psychic powers. Is that it?"

Preston laughed with her, then grew serious. "No. It's not that. You've tapped into something in here." He pointed to his heart. "There's a part of me that I didn't even know existed until I met you."

Preston placed his hand over Tye's. Was he choosing her?

They finished their meal, and Preston paid the check. They walked slowly along snowy pathways that were illuminated with soft lights. Preston spoke first. "You did a great job tonight."

Tye smiled. "You are the one who knew what needed to be done. I would've had to call the vet."

Preston grinned. "I am the vet. Or I hope to be the vet. Nevertheless, you did your share. I'm glad you were there." Preston stopped and turned to face Tye. Gently, he caressed her face. "Every time I see you, I'm surprised that you prefer to spend your time in barns and blizzards."

"I like barns," Tye said. "But I can't say the same for blizzards." She put her hand over his.

Slowly Preston pulled Tye closer to him and cradled the back of her head with his hand. He drew her into a kiss.

Warmth exploded inside of Tye that she could not remember ever experiencing. Just minutes ago she had been chilled. Now the fire burst forth from within. No one had ever unleashed such power and desire in her before. It overwhelmed her with its strength. She put her hand to Preston's face and responded to his kiss. The safe feeling that had been with her all evening enveloped her as he folded her into his arms. Everything else dropped away.

Tye didn't know how long they stood in their embrace. The warmth never left her, even as she drew away from Preston. He kept his arm around her as they both watched the water of the mountain stream play over the rocks.

Preston placed his fingers under her chin and raised her face. Their eyes met again. More was said through their silence.

Preston spoke, "Someday, Tye, I want to take you to Montana and show you the land. We can ride up into the mountains and explore all Montana has to offer."

Tye smiled. Yes. She longed for that very thing. She wanted to learn of Preston through his surroundings. He was offering her something grand; entry into his private places, his personal retreats.

Tye also wished to throw the doors of her own wonderland wide open. She longed to take Preston to Oregon so she could introduce him to her parents, her home, and Trapper. Then there was the great Pacific; her special place with Kyle. But maybe soon, she could reclaim that as she had reclaimed Trapper. Tye hoped to open up that part of herself; to present to Preston her beloved ocean, with its foamy white and crashing waves that met miles of sandy beaches. No longer did the great deep blue of the ocean need to be her secret treasure that held only memories of Kyle. Was she ready for that? She thought of the trace of bitterness that had risen in her throat like a sour apple during dinner. Maybe not quite yet, but she could prepare for it.

"Preston, I want to go to Montana with you. And I want to show you Oregon."

Preston returned Tye's smile. "We have a lot to learn, don't we?"

"Yes."

"I think we can teach each other a lot, Tye." He took her elbow, then said, "C'mon. Let's go back to the barn and make sure our calf is okay."

The drive to the barn was quiet. Nothing needed to be said. When they arrived at the barn, they checked on the new mother. The calf had settled down in the deep straw and was sound asleep. Tye let herself into the stall. She knelt beside the youngster and gently stroked her head. She loved young animals.

"Being born is hard work," Preston said as he motioned to the calf.

Preston followed her into the stall and stood beside her, laying his hand on her shoulder. "Tonight was very nice."

She turned and looked at him. "It was."

Preston knelt beside her. "I know this changes the relationship," he said.

"I hope so, Preston. I hope it changes everything," Tye said as she entwined her hands with his.

Chapter Thirty-Seven

*T*he morning dawned clear and warmer. Tye was anxious to go to the barn and leave the city behind. She wanted to see Elsa and the calf; to be reminded that last night had not been a dream. Once she reached her destination, she stepped out of the truck and allowed the morning to fill her. Birds, long silent through winter's reign, now tentatively began taking delight in the hopeful sign of the valley spring. As the sun rose, Tye could see the black silhouette of the mountains etched against a golden sky. The birds weren't alone in their hope. The morning was soft and clear and it mirrored Tye's feelings.

Once in Elsa's stall, the calf Tye had brought into the world ignored her completely as she ate her own breakfast.

"What should we name you?" Tye asked in a soft whisper.

Footsteps came down the aisle, and Tye rose. She hoped it was Preston, coming early to look at the little miracle they had helped to bring into the world. The footfalls didn't sound like Preston though. After spending years in barns, Tye could identify people just by listening to them walk down the aisle. No, this wasn't Preston. But it was familiar …

Quickly, Tye unlatched the stall door and faced the man making the distinctive sound as he walked.

"Hey, Tye. Meggie told me I could find you here. I hope that's okay."

"Kyle? Kyle, how can this be? What are you doing here?"

"I came to see you, Tye. I have something to show you."

Kyle walked closer. Then he reached into his back pocket and brought out a piece of paper. He unfolded it and handed it to Tye. It was a baptismal certificate.

Tye looked at Kyle. She was speechless. In her hand she held her dream of last summer. Kyle stepped closer, gently caressing Tye's cheek. "I think I understand what you meant when you said I'd be willing to make room for the gospel if I truly believed in it."

Kyle's hand dropped to Tye's neck as he pulled her close. Tye went to him as he kissed her with hunger and passion.

"I've missed you," he whispered in her hair. "Oh, I have missed you."

～

Later, Tye sat with Kyle in a quiet booth at the Meadow Lark Café. She looked at the menu but the words were only a blur. When the waitress came by, Tye ordered toast and hot chocolate. Kyle ordered the same.

They had stopped at Tye's home before making the short trip to downtown Provo. All of the girls were anxiously awaiting Tye's arrival and had hurried to her room when she appeared.

"I told him where you were," Meggie said. "I hope that was okay. I didn't know if I should just ask him to wait. But then I realized you could be all morning, and I didn't know how much time he had. Oh, Tye, I hope I did the right thing."

"Of course you did the right thing, Meg. It's fine."

KayLee had been excited. "This is just the most romantic thing I've ever witnessed," she said. "This mysterious man has come all the way from the east coast to win your heart. It sure doesn't get any better than that."

"Kyle isn't all that mysterious and don't jump to conclusions," Tye warned.

Now as Tye sat opposite of Kyle she was trying to take her own advice.

Tye spoke first, "How is life back east?"

"Good. I'm not at Willoughby stables anymore. I've moved on to Seven Gables in Virginia. I have a string of horses that are under my care now, and a couple of them show international potential. I'm to meet everyone down in California next week."

"I see. And how's Ben?"

Kyle broke into a grin at the mention of his own horse. "He's better than ever. I'm giving him and all my horses a week off before we start on the California and then the Florida circuit. I'm hoping it will make them keen when they start competing."

Tye nodded. "That's a good strategy."

The waitress brought the hot chocolate and toast before moving away.

Tye turned her attention to the cup of steaming chocolate, using her spoon to play with the whipped cream.

"How is school?" Kyle asked.

"I'm enjoying my classes. Last night we helped a cow give birth."

"That's how we met, remember?" Kyle asked. "We brought Gypsy into the world."

Tye nodded.

"Who's 'we' Tye?"

Tye thought about Preston. He seemed far away and completely disconnected from her. "There's somebody else. Isn't there?" Kyle asked.

Tye looked at him. "I don't know, Kyle. I do have a partner in animal reproductive physiology. We were responsible for the birth of a calf. He's a vet major. We've grown close …" her voice trailed off.

He nodded. "I appreciate your honesty, Tye. Now I'm going to be honest with you. I was wrong to walk off and leave you after I proposed. It took me a long time to understand it, but I realize now that I shouldn't have done that. I won't even give you an excuse for it because there isn't any. All I can offer you is an apology." He paused. "And a promise. I'll never do that again. If you ask me to leave, I will. And I wouldn't blame you. But I'll never walk away from you again."

Tears stung her eyes. "I never thought I'd see you again, Kyle. I've made room for other things. And I don't know what your visit means."

"I know it would be impossible for us just to pick up from where we left off. We've had a lot of separate experiences since we've been apart. But I was hoping you'd be willing to spend part of your summer with me on the circuit. We sure could use your help and expertise, and it would give us the opportunity to work together and get used to one another again. We've always made a great team, Tye, and I think you might enjoy it." Kyle placed his hand over Tye's. "I can't tell you how sorry I am, or how good it is to see you."

The warmth of Kyle's hand melted into Tye's cold skin, thawing memories Tye had wanted to place on ice. "I have no doubt that I would enjoy it." She sighed. "We had some good times didn't we?"

Kyle returned the smile. "We sure did."

"Our last summer together was magical," Tye said. Then she sobered. "It wouldn't be like that though, would it?"

"Why not?" Kyle asked.

"It felt like one long vacation since you weren't working, and I wasn't in school. It was a dream world of four lovely months together. We rode together on the beach and in the mountains. We competed at the local shows. We sure played a lot."

"Play is healthy in any relationship."

Tye nodded.

"What is it, Tye?"

"I don't know if we could ever recapture that again, Kyle."

"I'm not so sure we should, Tye. I want to build on it. We'd wait a while, of course. It'll be a year before I can go to the temple. Nothing would happen before that." He grew pensive. "I know I deserve to be turned out, Tye. After all, that's what I did to you. But please, don't turn me out."

Silence grew between them. Did Tye want to turn him away? What about Preston?

"I still have the Book of Mormon you gave me at Oregon State. I brought it with me. I've read it a couple of times already."

Tye was touched that Kyle would still have the small, sturdy book she had given him so many years ago.

After Kyle paid the check, they walked to his rental car. Slowly, he drove Tye home. He parked on the street and shut off the engine, then turned and faced her. "I'm staying at this motel on University Ave." He gave her a business card with his room number penciled on the back. "This is where I can be reached if you need to talk." He paused. "May I see you again?"

Tye thought for a moment. "Tomorrow is Sunday. Church is at

eight-thirty. Do you want to come?"

Kyle nodded. "Yeah. I'd like that."

Tye made a move for the door handle, but Kyle gently took her arm. She turned and looked at him; the memory of his brown eyes took her breath away. She looked down, no longer able to hold his gaze. Kyle placed his hand under her chin and lifted her eyes to his once again. "No matter how long we're apart, Tye, there isn't a day that goes by that I don't remember your face. My memories of you are clear."

Tye was at a loss for words as Kyle leaned over and placed his lips on hers. She responded to him as memories washed over her. They had a history together. Even her mission was bound up in Kyle. He had taken care of Trapper and sent her money every month. Everything about him brought back bittersweet thoughts— his kind generous nature and his bitter abandonment. But was that fair? Hadn't she left him first to serve a mission? But now he was here, asking for another chance; nothing more, just another chance.

Everything about him besieged her. His touch, the clean smell of his hair and his warm embrace knocked away all defenses. Then the question came to her in looming clarity. Did she love him? She drew away from him and hurriedly brushed a tear away. "It's been a long morning," she said in a shaky voice.

Kyle nodded as he caressed her cheek one last time.

Tye stumbled out of the car and waved goodbye from her front porch. As she watched Kyle drive away she wished the answer had been as clear as the question.

Chapter Thirty-Eight

*P*reston walked into Martin's barn and found the older gentleman saddling the gelding. "Hi, Martin."

Martin stopped his activity and looked closely at Preston. "Why Preston. What a surprise! We weren't expecting you this weekend."

"I know, but I'm kind of at loose ends. I was hoping you'd have some work that needs to be done."

"Well now, I think we can accommodate you," Martin said good-naturedly. "It's calving season you know. And I've got some cows that need to be brought closer to the barn." He looked beyond Preston. "Where's that young lady that's been out with you the last couple of times?" Martin asked.

"She's busy," Preston said with finality.

Martin slowly nodded. "Well, let's tell Lorena you're here."

The two men moved toward the house.

Lorena looked genuinely pleased to see Preston. "Let me cook you some breakfast."

Preston shook his head. "No thanks. If Martin will just point me in the direction of the work that needs to be done, I'll get out of your way."

"Right this way," Martin said as he opened the door and began to walk back to the barn, followed by Preston. Quickly, Martin set Preston up with Sergeant. "Just check the cows," he said. "And if any look like they're about ready to drop a calf, just ease them on this way. Oh, and could you check the fences and troughs while you're out? The troughs should be fine, but this melting snow is showing wear on the fences."

Preston mounted Sergeant and nodded as he pushed the horse into a slow trot.

Quietly, Preston rode over the slushy fields, looking over fences. The snow drifts that had held some of the posts in place were now melting and there were places where the fence sagged or the post had snapped off completely. He looked over several cows and pegged a couple he would move in closer to the barn after he was done with the fence work. His thoughts remained strictly on his work. It eased his earlier shock of seeing Tye kiss another man. Whenever the image would come before him, he would push it away and concentrate on barbed wire, wooden posts, and pregnant cows.

After he finished his work for the morning he rode back to the house and tied Sergeant in his stall.

He walked into the house. "I'm looking for Martin. Do you know where he is?" Preston asked Lorena.

"He went into town," Lorena said.

"Can you tell him I brought in two cows that look like they're about to drop? They're in the near field with the lean-to."

"Why don't you sit down," Lorena said. "I'll tell Martin when he comes home."

Preston wearily sat as Lorena placed homemade soup and bread on the table. Lorena joined him with a cup of soup of her own. They ate in silence for a moment before Lorena gently placed her question. "What's happened between you and Tye?"

Preston put down his spoon. "How did you know?"

"I didn't raise four kids without learning a thing or two," she replied seriously.

Preston looked at his bowl. "Last night we shared a special evening. We've been friends right along, you know, and last night I really believed that it was turning into something else. We brought a new calf into the world. That bonded us together. I've never experienced that with a woman before. Then later, we went out to dinner at Sundance lodge. Then this morning I go out to the barn, and I find her kissing another man. And I don't mean just kissing. I mean kissing. There was all this passion and hunger between them." Preston shook his head as if to dispel the memory.

"Do you know this other man?" Lorena asked.

"I don't know him, but I have a pretty good idea who he is. He's not from here. I think it's an old boyfriend of hers."

Lorena sighed. "I see." She was quiet for a moment. Then she asked, "What are your feelings for her Preston?"

He shrugged. "I don't know anymore. Last night was magical and we both acknowledged that our relationship was changing. She talked about Kyle for the first time. I've thought about that conversation a hundred times since last night. She never did say she was completely over him. She said that these things take time."

"Do you think Tye was expecting a visit from him?"

Preston didn't even have to think. "No."

Lorena put her hand on his arm. "Maybe you should give her an opportunity to explain."

"What's to explain?"

"You'll never know unless you ask. His surprise visit is a very good reason to hear an explanation," Lorena reasoned. "In some ways this may be the best thing for both of you."

Preston gave Lorena an impatient look. "Just how do you figure that?"

"She's being presented with an opportunity to work through her feelings for this man. And you're being given the chance to work through your feelings for her. Don't run away from this, Preston. Face it. And I promise you, no matter what the outcome, it will serve you in the end."

"I understand what you're saying Lorena, but right now she's the last person I want to see."

Lorena patted his arm and returned to her soup. "You think about it."

∽

Preston walked into Monday afternoon's class a few minutes late, stealing a seat in the back. He saw Tye looking for him. He gave her a brief smile.

After class Tye hurried to catch up with Preston. They walked down the hallway together.

The silence was uncomfortable. Preston spoke first, "I saw you with Kyle."

Tye turned and faced him. "How? When? When did you see me?"

"I went to the barn Saturday morning to check on Elsa. The two of you were in the aisle."

Tye stopped and leaned against the wall. "Kyle came for a visit," she said.

Preston nodded. "I figured as much." He paused then continued, "Look Tye, you don't owe me an explanation, but if you want to tell me about it, I'll listen."

Dear, sweet Preston, Tye thought. How could she ever explain the intensity of that brief moment with Kyle in the barn? She barely understood it herself.

They continued to walk toward her home in silence. When they reached her front porch, Tye placed her books on the steps before facing Preston. "He's been baptized. He showed me the certificate."

Preston involuntarily sucked in his breath. "Well, that is good news, isn't it? Is he still in town?"

"He's going to be here for about a week," Tye said.

Preston nodded slowly. She hadn't sent him packing. "Maybe that's all I need to know," he said. "I wish you and Kyle much luck, Tye." He changed the subject. "Now that Elsa's had her calf we won't have to be meeting at the barn. We can write our essays separately."

Panic clamped around Tye's throat. "Don't leave me Preston," she said. "Don't go."

"What would you ask of me, Tye? You want me to stay out of sight and wait for you to pick one of us? Or maybe I can be your cowboy when Kyle isn't being your horseman. Is that what you want?" Jealousy and anger laced his words. "I could never offer you what he obviously can; Olympic medals, money and excitement. He's way out of my league." Preston paused. "You don't owe me anything, Tye. We can leave it now and make a clean break. Wouldn't that be better than making a mess of things?"

"I don't know if I love him anymore," Tye said as tears came to her eyes. "I feel like I should, because I've wished and prayed for his baptism for so long." She looked at Preston. "During the Christmas holidays though, I started to ease out from under the burden of my relationship with him." She grew still, then whispered, "And I liked it." She brushed the tears away and sat down on the porch steps. "Kyle and I have always been like oil and water. We don't mix unless something is shaking us up. I don't want to spend my life all shook up, but then I know that if I turn him away this time—it'll be the last time. He will never come back. I don't know if I have the strength to do that."

Preston sighed, his anger dissipating. Tye was truly in pain. He sat next to her and put his arm around her. She buried her face in his chest and sobbed. Gently, he caressed her hair as he gently rocked her. She needed a friend right now. And isn't that how the two of them had started; as friends? He could be her friend again. It wouldn't be easy to retrace their steps. But she needed him, and he loved her. He pulled her in tight and kissed her forehead. Yes, he loved her. "I can't give you that strength, Tye. It's not mine to give. You'll have to find it within yourself—if that's what you truly want."

Tye sat up and wiped her eyes. She nodded. "Sometimes I think it's what I want, but then when I think about the reality of it; how low I was when he first left, the history we have together, how he took care of Trapper while I was away and how he helped me with my mission, I wonder if I should give him another chance."

"Out of guilt? Because you owe him? Or because you love him?"

"I don't know," Tye whispered.

She laid her head back on Preston's chest. Closing her eyes she murmured, "This is so nice."

Preston knew what he had to do. This was going to be hard. Harder than anything he had ever done before. Before he could change his mind, Preston quickly kissed her forehead again and gave her a squeeze around the shoulder. Then he stood.

"What are you doing?" Tye asked.

Preston shook his head. "I won't be your distraction, Tye. I won't have you leaving Kyle for me. You'll have to do that for yourself."

Tye looked stricken.

"I don't mean to be harsh," he said gently as he knelt on the step in front of Tye. "I can't give you the reason or the strength to leave him. I need to leave you now so your decision will be clean. If you stay with Kyle, you stay because of the merits of that relationship. If you leave him, you do it because your relationship with him doesn't hold any merit for you. Not because I'm here holding your hand. I can offer you friendship and understanding, but the rest is up to you. If you need me, call. I'll help you talk it through if you want. But you'll have to bind up your own wounds. I can't do it for you."

Preston took Tye's hand. "Don't you see? I can't be the crutch that allows you to leave Kyle. I would not be serving you well in that capacity."

Slow understanding came to Tye. Preston had to leave. She nodded.

"Give Elsa a pat for me and name her little one well," Preston said as he stood. Then before Tye could scramble to her feet, Preston was gone.

Chapter Thirty-Nine

ye and Kyle met Tuesday afternoon at the Spencer W. Kimball building. Kyle was familiar with that landmark since they met there on Sunday for church. Today, Tye and Kyle had no plans, other than to spend the day together. She gave him a short tour of the campus before they settled into one of the trendy restaurants near school for something to eat. The weather had turned cold again. Fits of snow blew in on the disgruntled wind.

Tye shivered elaborately in her coat as she watched the swirling snow. "Just when I was getting used to the idea of spring," she said.

"Winter can't give up without a final stab," Kyle said.

The waitress came and deposited menus at their table.

"How are you liking it here?" Tye asked.

Kyle shrugged. "It's okay. It won't hurt my feelings when I go down to California though. It's about sixty-five degrees down there today."

"You're just trying to make me jealous," Tye said.

"I'm hoping you'll meet me there after the semester is over," Kyle said.

In some ways it was a delicious thought. It would be warm and she could help Kyle work the horses under his care. They could easily fall into the familiar patterns of their relationship. But what about home? What about Trapper? She had been looking forward to spending her summer months with him, basking in Oregon's fertile season. And since Kyle's surprise visit, the pictures of her home and her horse were the only clear images on which she could rely. What about Preston? The clarity left. Preston had made it obvious that he would support her as a friend, but all other bets were off.

"I don't know Kyle …" Tye countered slowly.

"You wouldn't have to stay the whole summer," Kyle said as if reading her mind. "You could go home whenever you wanted. Or we could ship Trapper to California and take him with us. If you didn't want to do that you could help me ride and work my string of horses. The weather would be great. We could even sneak off for some riding in the California countryside."

"How would Meggie get home?" Tye asked. "I usually take her home."

"Maybe her folks could pay for an airline ticket this one time."

That was a possibility. Meggie's parents wouldn't hesitate to pay for Meg's transportation if Tye had other plans.

"You could bunk with a bunch of girls at the show grounds," Kyle said.

Tye laughed. "Yeah. I know the routine. When Thelma and I used to go to shows together we stayed in her old Winnebago. The owners of some of the horses would show up in these fancy custom-made buses but not us. We'd show up in Thelma's beat-up RV from the seventies."

"Well, nothing has changed. What do you say, Tye? Will you meet me in California? You could come as soon as you're finished with your finals."

Tye grew serious. It sounded fun but it wasn't home, and Tye wanted to go home. More than ever, since Kyle had arrived, Tye longed for home. She gave Kyle a careful look. Did she want what he offered? He was handing her so many wonderful options, but Tye wasn't sure she wanted to put on the scratchy coat of their relationship. "I don't know, Kyle," she repeated. Part of her wanted to tell him the very things she had cried out to Preston just yesterday. But she held back. How would Kyle take it? Was that her responsibility? It felt like it was.

Kyle covered her hands with his own fingers. "Just think about it. We've got plenty of time. Maybe you would prefer to wait a while and meet me down in Florida."

"I'll think about it," Tye said.

The waitress returned and glanced at the unopened menus. "Should I give you a few more minutes?" she asked.

Kyle grabbed them and quickly handed one to Tye. She scanned the daily specials and finally settled for a bowl of hot soup and a spinach salad. Kyle ordered a warm deli sandwich.

After the waitress left, Kyle picked up the conversation. "Oh, and you'd get to meet some really great riders. John Thurgood will be there. Deborah Maler will be there with her husband, Michael."

A flame of excitement brightened in Tye; top riders in the sport of three-day-eventing who were well-known celebrities in the horse world. Tye only knew them from magazines and the cable channels that broadcast her sport. It dazzled her to think she would meet these people, and that Kyle would introduce them.

"Deborah is bringing along her favorite horse named Spinning Top. He's six now. In four years he's going to be peaking just in time for the Olympics. I think she's a shoo-in for the team."

"Do you know Deborah?" Tye asked.

"Yeah. She and Michael are great horse people. They are very personable. John Thurgood is a little bit aloof, but no one can doubt that he knows his job."

"How do you think the Church is going to fit in all of this?" Tye asked.

Kyle became intense as his voice dropped a notch. "That's a good question, Tye, and I don't exactly know the answer. During the competition season I won't be able to attend my meetings since I would be competing on Sundays. I would be able to go fairly regularly during the off season. Does that bother you?"

"A little bit. It's part of the reason I chose not to pursue a competitive career in this sport. Taking the sacrament is really important. It helps us renew those covenants we made at baptism."

"I understand that."

That scratchy feeling was coming back. "Do you ever think about how that would affect a family?"

"What do you mean?"

Tye grew pensive. "You asked me to marry you at one time, Kyle. And if we were to pursue a relationship it would be with the understanding that it would lead to marriage."

"A temple marriage," Kyle said.

Tye smiled and all scratchy feelings left her. She squeezed his hand. "Yes, a temple marriage."

"Wouldn't that be something?" he asked.

"Yes, it would."

"You don't know how hard it is for me not to ask you again—right this minute."

Tye's heart beat faster. "Or how hard it would be for me to say no."

"Would you say no?" he asked.

Tye became pensive. "It scares me, Kyle. And I'm not so sure love should be scary."

"What exactly scares you?"

"The whole idea of you and me getting married. We are so different. We want different things out of life. You want to follow the horse circuit and compete. I want to settle down and teach. That doesn't even get into the realm of children. I think it would be difficult to bring little kids on the circuit. It's easy now. You board with the guys. I board with the girls. If we were married, that would be easy too. We would have our own Winnebago from the seventies, and it would just be the two of us. But this isn't any kind of life for children. It doesn't give them any stability as they're dragged around the countryside while their parents work with horses."

"We would give them that stability, Tye. As parents that's our responsibility anyway no matter where we live, don't you think? We'd have our own RV by then. We'd be a family unit. Nothing could take that away from us."

"But the Church would simply be a seasonal influence. And what would happen when the kids got old enough to attend school? Would I stay home with them while their daddy traveled for months at a time?"

"People in professional sports and the military do it all the time. Michael and Deborah Maler have two little children. Seth is four and Mattie is two. Right now they're bringing their children with them. The barn they work for pays for a nanny who accompanies the family. I don't like the idea of leaving you and children behind. Maybe we could home-school or do as the Malers and bring a nanny or a tutor when they're old enough."

Tye could tell that Kyle was making up his answers as he went along. "You haven't thought about these things, have you?" The scratchy feeling returned.

"No," Kyle said honestly. "But I do believe they can be worked out as we meet them. We don't have to tackle the whole marriage right now. We can take it one day at a time. Besides, I wouldn't be competing forever."

"Maybe so, Kyle, but all we have to work with are our present-day circumstances. Right now, competition is a big part of your life." She paused. "Personally, I don't see that changing anytime soon."

"Tye, if we love each other, we can manage through anything."

All grew as still as a tomb inside of Tye. Nothing spoke. Did she love Kyle? She listened. Nothing.

The waitress came and placed their meals in front of them. Tye was grateful for the distraction. Slowly she stirred her soup as Kyle turned his attention to his sandwich.

"This smells good," Kyle said. "I'm glad you suggested this place."

Tye pulled her thoughts back to the present. She looked outside. The snow was beginning to stick and the wind grew from fitful gusts to a constant push; an uninvited late spring storm. California sounded nice. Participating with Kyle and his horses on the riding circuit wouldn't be a bad way to spend a summer. She would be surrounded by a community she knew and loved. Already she could smell the dust and hay and see the sun filtering through the cracks in the barn. It would warm everything it touched, including the horses, bringing out their earthy aroma. She would work hard from dawn until late. Her body would be tired and her soul satisfied in a way that could only come through working with the horses.

She shivered as she watched the snow cling to budding leaves. In the cold, even a scratchy coat feels good.

ark sat next to Meggie on the couch. "Why don't you cancel your date and come with me?" he asked. "This is the last play of the season. We'll have fun."

"I can't do that. I already told Calum I would go skiing with him."

"Calum? Oh, yeah, Calum. I met him on the slopes didn't I?"

Meggie nodded. "I wish you could go skiing," she said. "I've had the most fun with you, and we were only able to go together once."

The phone rang. KayLee rushed to answer it.

"Whenever she's home I never have to worry about the phone," Meggie said. "It's the nicest thing about her."

KayLee came out of the kitchen. "It's for you, Meggie," she said as she pulled on her coat. "I'm meeting Kirk on campus. I'll see you later." She handed Meggie the phone and waved to Mark as she walked out the front door.

Meggie put her hand over the receiver, giving Mark a smile

before rising from the couch to move into the kitchen. "I'll be right back."

"No doubt penciling in another date."

Meggie threw him a grin that irritated him.

A few minutes later, Meggie came out of the kitchen.

"Dare I even ask who that was?" Mark said.

"It was Calum. He was just confirming our ski date tonight. He also asked if I wanted to go later in the week. I don't know where he gets his money." Meggie sat down next to Mark. "I told him no."

Mark's heart skipped a beat. "Why?"

"I don't know. For one thing I can't afford it. Besides, I guess I just don't feel like it. He's a nice guy, and he's a better skier than Joel...." Meggie's voice trailed off. "I guess he's just not my type."

"Then why are you even going with him tonight?" Mark paused. "Meggie, what is your type?"

Meggie walked to the window. She pulled the curtain back and looked at the afternoon snow. "I don't know," she said.

"Was Joel your type?" Mark probed.

"Joel was nice enough, but he definitely wasn't my type. He had no concern for food or what he ate. He always acted so bored when I tried to tell him about my kitchen experiences. I could never see us together for very long."

"Not everyone understands that kind of passion for food and cooking."

"I wish you hadn't gotten sick. I have the most fun when we're together. I mean, Calum is a nice guy, but he isn't someone I would ever take seriously."

"Why not?"

"He's a slob for one thing," Meggie said. "You should see the inside of his car. It's so dirty I'd be afraid to get inside during the summer. It must be a haven for every six-legged critter known to the area." She sighed. "I know I make fun of KayLee, but sometimes I think I'm the one who has it all wrong."

Mark followed Meggie to the window. He stood behind her. "What would make you say such a thing? Do you want the same thing KayLee wants? Do you want a diamond?" He grinned as he whispered in her ear. "All this time I thought you were only interested in lift tickets."

Meggie stayed serious. "No, I don't want a diamond. Not like KayLee wants one. I'm not like that."

"Do you want to be married? Don't you think we're pretty young?"

Meggie laughed. "That's the Catholic priest in you speaking."

Mark chuckled. "Yeah. You're right. But I've always believed in friendship first. I want to know someone before I marry her. I want her to know me."

Meggie agreed, then asked, "Why don't you date, Mark? How are you ever going to get to know someone if you don't go out on a date?"

Mark placed his hands on Meggie's shoulders and drew her close. Meggie softened under his touch.

"We've been good friends, Meggie," Mark whispered into Meggie's hair.

Meggie turned and looked at Mark with surprise as Mark encircled her in his arms.

"I have been dating. You just didn't know it."

Meggie placed her fingers lightly on Mark's chest. Then she pressed her palms into his body and moved her hands to his shoulders.

"Come with me tonight, Meggie."

Meggie pulled Mark into a new embrace. "I think I'll call Calum, and tell him I can't go skiing tonight," she said gently.

Mark gently cupped Meggie's face in his palm as he drew her near in a sweet and slow kiss.

⌢

"Meggie?" Tye began. "Do you think your folks would mind buying you an airline ticket for the trip home?"

"No. I don't think that would be a problem. Why?"

"Kyle has asked me to meet him in California. I'm considering it."

"And I'll be taking Mark home to meet my parents."

Tye blinked. "Mark? What—Meggie? What happened?"

"While you were out earlier today, Mark and I talked. I think we're going to start dating." She stopped. "It feels kind of weird, but it also feels just right. I've missed him, Tye. We're going out to a play later tonight."

"I wish I could come with you," Tye said.

"Of course you can come. Do you have any plans with Kyle? He could come too."

"Kyle and I don't have any plans. We had an early dinner. He needs to call back east and check on his horses before it gets too late. We're finished for the day."

"Then why don't you come by yourself?"

A tiny spark of envy flashed inside of Tye before she snuffed it out. Why would she be jealous of Meggie and Mark? She loved Mark as a friend. And didn't she have enough problems with Kyle? No, it wasn't Mark. It was the way things had settled. There was none of the turmoil and anxiety for Meggie that Tye fought when she was around Kyle. "You're lucky, Meg."

"Yes, well … Mark is a wonderful man. I've always known that. Our relationship kind of eased to this place. It's as it should be for us."

"Maybe that's how it should be for everyone."

"What do you mean?"

Tye flopped on her bed. "I'm not sure. It's just that when I'm around Kyle, everything is hard."

"Oh, I don't know. I saw the two of you saying goodbye a little bit ago, and it looked pretty comfortable to me."

"Don't you find that a bit ironic? We're at our best when we're saying goodbye," Tye said wryly. "No, my relationship with Kyle has never had the ease that exists between you and Mark. I wish it did."

"The two of you have a different relationship. It works on a different level."

"And what level is that, Meggie? I don't have a clue how it works." She shifted on the bed. "I'm sorry. I shouldn't be snippy with you."

"Aren't you happy, Tye? I would think Kyle's return would've thrilled you. He's been baptized. Everything is in order. What more do you want?"

"That's a good question. When I'm with him, I feel this pull towards him, but it's also like two opposing magnets. We push at each other."

"Come with Mark and me tonight, Tye. It'll take your mind off these things and maybe things will be clearer in the morning."

"Thanks, Meggie. I think I will join you."

∽

Later, in the theater, Tye sat with Meggie and Mark. She appreciated the quiet tranquility that surrounded their newly discovered love. But it wasn't all that new. They had been working and playing together for months. They were friends first. Their relationship had always been soft and gentle and reminded her nothing of her relationship with Kyle, which felt prickly and uncomfortable.

It was easy for Meg and Mark. They wanted the same things. Tye sucked in her breath. That was it! That was why she had found her friendship with Preston so peaceful. He wanted to settle down, start a vet practice, and raise a family. He didn't want to go traipsing all over the country, following the horse circuit. Tye needed to be honest and frankly admit that she didn't want that either. She would have to be honest with Kyle too. That would be hard because she did love him. Closing her eyes against the drama before her, Tye realized her own drama was unfolding. All along she had been asking herself if she loved Kyle. That was the wrong question. She did love him. She always had. But she didn't want what he wanted and love would not be enough. It wouldn't make up for the unsettled life and divided loyalties that simply existed when someone devoted themselves to the sport of Kyle's choice. Could she invite him into her dream? She wanted to settle down, have a family, and teach children to appreciate horses. It didn't even come close to what Kyle was choosing. Kyle was a good man but he had never been her man. He belonged to the horses. The very thing that had brought them together was now tearing them apart. Would he leave the glory of competition for her? Would he walk away from the temptation of gold, silver and bronze? She had not wanted him to be baptized for her but did she want him to leave his dreams of gold medals behind for her? Was that fair?

At intermission, Tye pulled Meggie aside. "I need to go," she said. "I need to see Kyle. I'll meet you at home."

Meggie pulled Tye into a silent embrace before Tye walked into the frigid night. She hugged her coat close and found the nearest pay phone. Digging around in her purse, she found the business card with the motel name and Kyle's room number written on the back. She dialed the number and was connected to Kyle's room. He answered on the second ring.

"Kyle, do you have a minute?" she asked.

"Of course, Tye. I always have a minute for you. What is it?"

Her heart hesitated. "Maybe we could meet at the Meadow Lark."

"Sure. I'll be there in a few minutes."

Tye hurried to the restaurant. The lights were dim and inviting as she and Kyle found a booth near the heater. Tye took off her coat. The waitress came and handed them menus. Tye waved them off. "Just a hot chocolate for me," she said.

Kyle agreed.

"What is it?" Kyle asked. He smiled. "Have you decided to come to California with me and beat this cold weather?"

Tye took a shaky breath as unbidden tears came to her eyes. "I can't meet you in California, Kyle," Tye said quietly.

"Why not? Did you talk to Meggie about getting an airline ticket?"

"Meggie isn't the problem. Please let me finish."

Kyle grabbed Tye's hands, and she knew he was sensing the importance of what she was about to say.

"I love you, Kyle. I have loved you since our time at Oregon State. I loved you for taking care of Trapper and for helping me on my mission. You are one of the most generous and gifted souls I have ever known."

"Somehow I don't think this is leading to a good place."

Tears spilled on to Tye's cheeks. She let them go unchecked, and hated the publicity of their environment. She grasped his fingers. "It can be a good place, Kyle," she said hopefully. "I can't follow you around while you work a string of horses. I can't live in an RV with children. I've told you that. I want to settle down. I want to have a house, a barn, some horses. I want children, Kyle, and they need the Church in their lives. I need the Church in my life. Not just in the winter but in every season. I admire you for joining the Church and for having the strength to do both. But I don't want to do both." She put her hand to her mouth unable to finish.

Kyle threw a few bills on the table before helping Tye out of the booth. "Let me walk you home," he said.

Once outside, the bitter cold hit Tye. She huddled against Kyle who put his arm around her as they silently walked through the new snow.

When they reached the end of her block, Kyle stopped and turned to Tye. "I won't try to talk you into something you don't want, Tye. I just hope you understand that I can't keep doing this. I can't keep checking in with you every year or so to see if you'll change your mind. I need to get on with my life."

Fresh tears came to Tye. It was the very thing she knew he would say.

Tye grabbed Kyle's coat, allowing her invitation to spill out with her passion and hope. "We could settle down together," she said. "We could raise a family in Oregon and train and teach together while we competed locally. It could be like it was last summer. Remember how peaceful and joyous our time together was? You've always loved the way we've worked together as a team. This would be our team, Kyle. Not team USA but you and me." She paused. "Please, say yes."

Kyle smiled. "Well, Tye, did you just propose?"

New tears came to her eyes as she nodded.

"Oh, Tye," Kyle whispered as he brushed away her tears with warm fingers. "Last summer was simply an intermission for the two of us. You said yourself we could never go back to that place. It was a time for me to be close to you and figure out how everything fit." He looked away into the darkness. "I need to earn my medal," he said. "I will never be able to rest until I do. If I were to leave my dream now I would always wonder. I couldn't live that way. You wouldn't want me that way."

"We could work that out," Tye said. "If we love each other, don't you think you would be able to find enough joy in what we created?"

"I'll always find joy in you, Tye. And I know I'd find joy in the family we would raise, but I need to go up against this thing. I can't explain the drive behind it. It's just something I must do." He pulled her hand towards his chest. "I don't blame you for not wanting to live out of an RV. It's not for everyone. It's hard. It's a life without roots. I won't want it forever. But I know I'll want it for the next four years. After that I can't say."

Tye ran her sleeve across her face. "This first Olympics will just be a taste, Kyle. It doesn't matter what color of medal you bring home in four years. You'll never give it up."

Kyle shuffled in the snow. "I guess you know me well, don't you, Tye?"

Tye nodded.

"Come on, let me walk you the rest of the way home," Kyle offered his arm.

Tye shook her head. "No," she said quietly. "You go on back. You're already blocks away from your hotel. I appreciate you taking me this far."

Kyle took both of her hands in his as he searched her face in the dim light thrown off from a nearby porch. He reached over and kissed her. Tye pulled herself to him. She wanted to remember this kiss. She wanted to gather up all the passion that was between them and explore it in this moment. With intensity, she embraced him. "Please, Kyle. Please come home to Oregon with me," she whispered.

"I can't, Tye," Kyle whispered back. He pulled her into an embrace. "I love you, Tye. I'll probably always love you." He pulled away. "Oh, I'll find someone else, and I'll fall in love again. I know people heal. I'll marry just like you will. But you'll always be with me somehow."

Tye saw tears in his eyes as pain came into his face.

He looked away for a moment, and then he looked back at Tye. "You don't know how hard it is for me to walk away from your invitation," he said.

"Then don't walk away from it. Come home with me." She took his hand and whispered, "Please, come home."

Kyle shook his head. "I can't," he whispered again. Then with a final squeeze of her hands, Tye watched as he walked out of her circle of light. She listened until the sound of his muffled footfalls disappeared and then turned slowly toward her house. Her teeth chattered in spite of her coat and her fingers were stiff with cold. She had never been so icy in her life. It would be hard to live without her scratchy coat.

Chapter Forty-One

*T*ye sat in class and tried to nurse the headache pulsing between her temples. The night before, she had cried until Meggie had arrived home. Then she had shared the events of the evening with Meggie and had cried more, all the while debating over whether she should call Kyle. It was no use though. She rubbed her forehead, willing the ache to go away.

Preston sat beside her. Tye gave him a wan smile.

"Rough morning?" Preston asked.

"Rough night," she replied. "Kyle's gone."

Preston nodded. "I'm sorry, Tye."

"Me too, but it's for the best," she said.

The professor came into the room, announcing that this would be the last lecture before the final exam. Everyone would be getting a custom test, depending on what their project had been for the semester. Unbidden tears rose in Tye. She couldn't stand it. She gathered her books and left the class as the professor began his lecture.

It wasn't until she felt Preston's hand on her shoulder that she realized he was even walking near. It startled her. For a moment the tears dried as she sucked in her breath.

"I'm sorry. I didn't mean to scare you."

Tye smiled. "Don't worry about it. It's a nice change from the other emotions I've been feeling."

"Want to talk about it?" Preston asked.

Tye hugged her books. Slowly, she nodded.

"I'll drive," Preston said. He took Tye's elbow and guided her to his truck where she dumped her books on the floorboard and leaned her head against the seat, closing her eyes. Preston drove in silence. It wasn't until they reached the barn that Tye opened her eyes.

"Have you seen Elsa and her calf lately?" Preston asked.

Tye shook her head.

"I haven't been here either." He helped Tye out of the car and they walked down the aisle. "Have you thought of a name for Elsa's calf?"

Tye shook her head again as they stopped at Elsa's stall. It was empty.

"She must be in the field," Preston said. "It's a lovely day for a romp." Taking Tye's elbow they walked toward the fence where they spotted Elsa and her young calf. Elsa was happily munching on the new spring grass. The calf was imitating her mother but with little success.

Tye smiled. "I love young animals," she said as she propped herself against the fence. The company of Elsa and her calf in this spring morning softened the edges of Tye's pain.

"That's part of the reason I want to go to vet school," Preston said.

The silence grew between them. It was comfortable and easy.

"It's hard to imagine that we don't have all day to just sit here and watch the calf," Tye said.

"We do have all day, Tye. We have as much time as we need. Why don't you tell me what happened."

Tye bit her lip. "It's very simple," she said. "We don't want the same things. He wants to ride for the Olympics. It's a goal within his grasp. I want to settle down and have a family."

"You do love him though, don't you?"

Tye looked out over the field. "Yes, but I won't always."

"How do you know?" Preston asked.

"Because I don't want to." A sudden urge hit Tye. "I could love you, Preston."

Preston nodded. "And I could love you, Tye."

"It wouldn't be right though, would it?"

Preston shook his head. "Not now."

"You deserve better than this wounded part of me."

"And you deserve to be whole without me," Preston said.

She paused. "Sometimes I'm mad at Kyle."

"Why?"

"What business did he have coming here now and reopening all of this pain? He walked away from me once. He should've stayed away. He ruined everything that could've been between you and me."

"He didn't ruin anything, Tye. If you had truly been free of him you would've sent him packing, but you didn't. You needed to work through whatever he was offering you." He stopped for a moment, then continued, "You and I would've fallen apart anyway if you still loved him." Preston moved toward Tye and gently brushed a stray strand of hair from her face. "But now there's hope. You can clean out the wound Tye, and when you love again—it'll be a fresh start. You won't be carrying any suitcases with Kyle's name written on them." He paused. "I don't want to wonder if we're together simply because I was the next man in line. I can't be your rescuer Tye. I can't rescue you from the pain of Kyle. I want you to choose me, not a set of circumstances."

"But maybe when I'm ready you will have moved on. Or maybe I'll heal in a way that distances us."

Preston became thoughtful. "Yeah, I suppose that's the risk. That would hurt, wouldn't it?"

"It would hurt me."

"It would hurt me too."

"I'm so sorry," Tye whispered. "This whole thing has probably been painful for you."

Preston placed his hand over Tye's. "Yes," he said softly. "It's been hard. Just learning about Kyle was difficult but then when I came to the barn and saw the two of you …" His voice trailed off.

Tye closed her eyes. She wasn't sorry for the moment between her and Kyle. It encompassed everything she felt for him. Still, she could only imagine Preston's shock. She was sorry for the hurt.

"It wasn't just the kiss." Preston continued, "It was the passion behind it."

Tye nodded. "Yes, I can understand. It may be difficult to trust me after witnessing something like that."

Preston grabbed Tye's hands. "Which is why I would need you to be whole before we try again. Someday I want you to kiss me like that—not because you're projecting your feelings for Kyle onto me, but because you feel that kind of familiarity and passion for me. That can't happen now."

"Maybe you have some healing of your own, Preston."

Preston agreed. "Oh, yes, Tye. I need some time. But I also owe you a great deal."

"How is that?"

"You say that I have taught you a lot about cows. Well, you have taught me a lot about life—my life." He looked out over the pasture. "I know now that it isn't always better to be alone. You've opened up my life in ways I never considered."

Tye looked down for a moment and then she met Preston's blue eyes. "So, what does this mean, Preston? Are we friends?"

Preston pulled her into a close embrace. "We're the best of friends, Tye," he whispered into her hair. "The very best of friends."

Fresh tears came to Tye as she breathed in the scent of Preston. He smelled of young spring grass and a fresh new river. Tye closed her eyes. She loved young things. This friendship was young. She pulled Preston close for a moment, then they moved apart.

Chapter Forty-Two

"Tye!" KayLee shouted from downstairs. "Kenneth is here to see you!"

Tye swallowed. Kenneth. She thought back to their last phone conversation. They hadn't spoken since Kyle's arrival.

Swallowing again, Tye walked out of her room. She met KayLee on the stairs, who whispered, "I'd give my eye teeth to have your dilemma."

"Then you'd be making a bad trade," Tye whispered back.

Walking down the stairs, Tye focused on Kenneth who was smiling up at her.

His smile disappeared as she got closer. "Tye, you don't look at all well. Are you all right?"

"Kenneth."

"Come here, let me look at you."

Tye stood before Kenneth.

Kenneth looked at her with a cold, diagnosing eye. "You've lost weight, child. Have you been sick?"

"Kenneth, I'm not a child."

"Oh, I'm sorry, Tye. I'm just shocked to see you. You look so drawn and well, you look young."

"I am young."

"Right. I know. I suppose we'll have to talk about that someday. But right now I want to talk about you. Are you eating?"

"Yes, but nothing has any taste."

"What's wrong?" Kenneth led her to the couch.

"Can we go someplace?" she asked. Tye didn't want KayLee eavesdropping on their conversation.

"Yes, of course. I planned on taking you to dinner, if you were free. Are you free?"

Tye nodded.

Kenneth helped her into her coat. He drove to a nearby restaurant. Tye was glad for his choice. It was quiet and exclusive. When the waiter came with menus, Tye tried to wave him away, but Kenneth took them. "You need to eat," he said as he handed her a menu. He looked at the waiter. "Can you wait while we decide?"

The waiter stood by the table.

Nothing sounded appealing. How was she going to tell Kenneth about Kyle? What was she going to say? Finally, she ordered fish. Kenneth placed his order. The waiter left with the menus.

Anxiously, Kenneth placed his hands over Tye's. "What's the matter, Tye? Trista told me that you called in sick last Saturday, and that someone else taught her lesson. I've tried to call, but you haven't been home. I've left several messages, but I haven't heard from you. I know you don't have the money to call me back. Still, I've been so alarmed. It's only been a couple of weeks since we last talked, which isn't all that bad. I know you've got classes, and our schedules don't always match. But when Trista told me you'd been sick, I became concerned. Something just didn't seem right."

"Is that why you're here?"

Kenneth nodded. "I took a late afternoon flight out of Denver. I only have a couple of hours."

Gratitude and sorrow mixed together in Tye. She would do her best to be honest with this good man. He deserved that. "Kenneth, something unexpected has happened."

Kenneth squeezed her fingers. "Go on."

"Do you remember when I told you about my tenure at OSU?"

"Yes. You rode for the equestrian team."

"Right. Well, I met a man during that time. It was before my mission to San Antonio." Tye began to tell Kenneth about Kyle. She shared everything. Then she took a deep breath. "Kyle came back."

"What do you mean? Is Kyle here in Provo?"

"He was. He's gone now."

"But you said you hadn't heard from him since last July. What brought him back now?"

"He's been baptized." Tears came to Tye, and she bit her lip. "But it doesn't matter. Kyle and I want different things. I begged him to come home to Oregon with me; to leave the Olympic Games behind, but he wouldn't."

Kenneth flinched.

Tye swallowed. "I'm sorry," she said quietly. "I don't mean to hurt—."

Kenneth shook his head. "I've learned to prefer truth over illusion, Tye. It's better that way. It's okay."

"I have no interest in the Olympics," Tye continued. "I lost my desire to compete while I was on my mission. Other things became more important. I want a family; roots. I want a home and a barn. I want to teach children to love and respect horses. I can't reconcile what I want with what he wants."

Kenneth rubbed her arm. "I know," he said. "You deserve a home and a settled family, if that's what you want."

"It is what I want," Tye said passionately. "I've always wanted that. Kyle knows it." She brushed the tears away.

"Listen to me for a minute, Tye. I'm sorry about Kyle, but let me offer you something else. Let me help you forget him. I know we've only begun our relationship, and there's no certainty about how it will turn out. But will you come to Colorado this summer? We'll ship Trapper to Boulder. We can find you a teaching job. It wouldn't be all that hard." Kenneth grabbed Tye's hands and brought them to his lips. "Let me help you heal."

Tye hesitated. Kenneth was offering her sweet distraction. "Trista told us that you heal hearts."

Kenneth squeezed her fingers. "It's my job. Let me heal yours."

"I can't go to Colorado, Kenneth. I need to go home."

"Make a new home in Colorado. Triss and I will help."

The waiter brought their meals. Tye pushed hers aside. "It's not that simple." She became thoughtful. "When you heal hearts, don't you first have to introduce a certain amount of trauma?"

Kenneth blinked. "Yes, I supposed you could say that."

"This is my trauma, Kenneth. The healing will come later. I don't know when or how, but I know it will come."

"I won't lose you, Tye. I won't lose you to some haunted memory of a man who can't give you what you deserve, when I'm right here, willing to give you what you need."

Tye sucked in her breath. Quietly, Preston's words echoed in her heart, and Tye drew strength from them. "My healing is not your job, Kenneth. It's mine. Let me do my job." Tye closed her eyes.

Could it be that she was beginning to heal already? For the first time since Kyle's departure, Tye knew she could mend the torn chambers of her heart. It was within her power.

Kenneth grew quiet. "I understand what you're saying, Tye. I do."

"And I appreciate your offer, Kenneth. But I can't take it. Ultimately, I would be cheating all of us." Tye leaned back in her seat.

Kenneth sighed. "What would you like me to tell Triss?"

Tye considered her student. "Nothing should change from Trista's point of view. She knew I was going home this summer. Besides, she'll have so many new adventures she'll hardly think about me."

"I'm not so sure," Kenneth replied. "She's wanted me to ask you to come to Colorado for a visit during the summer. She wants to show you her pony and go riding with you outside. She'll probably have questions."

"I'll tell her that I need to stay home this summer to look after my own horse. She'll understand that."

"If you ever need to talk, Tye, just call me." He paused. "And please, let's not say goodbye. I understand your desire to come to terms with your own trauma and become whole. But when you feel ready to step outside of that experience, I hope I can call you."

Tye thought about Preston. Best of friends, he had said. Could she love Kenneth like she loved Preston? No. But maybe she could love Kenneth for who he was. Slowly, she nodded. "I hope you will call, Kenneth."

Kenneth smiled. "Trista will see to it. Now, can I interest you in some fish?" He placed Tye's plate in front of her. "Please, eat," he said gently.

Tye placed her hand in Kenneth's and smiled into his eyes. Then she reached for her fork and tasted food for the first time in over a week.

Chapter Forty-Three

*T*ye glanced at her watch as she parked the truck in the lot of Bridal Veil Falls. She took a deep breath. She had plenty of time before Trista's lesson. It would be Tye's last teaching assignment before she left for home.

Pulling herself out of the truck, Tye stood in the new spring sunshine that spilled around her. So much had changed since her last cold visit to Bridal Veil Falls and the Provo River. Standing in the soft, clear air she expected silence. Then she heard it; the sound of flowing water. Hurrying from the truck, Tye walked to the river. As she arrived at the footbridge, she looked down to see the riverbed filled with life-giving water. It was sun dappled as it lapped at the banks in its hurry to feed the valley below. She jogged the short distance to Bridal Veil Falls; the sound of rushing water growing closer with each step. Standing at the foot of the falls, she stared with warm reverence. The new season had released the falls from the icy grip of winter. Now, water flowed and tumbled freely over the rock as it played with the sun, sending prisms of light through its graceful descent. The heavy scent of freshly released water filled Tye's lungs as tears spilled onto her cheeks. She brushed them away impatiently. She didn't want her vision to be blurred by tears.

Drying her eyes she looked up at the mountainside. Patches of snow still clung to the landscape, but even that would soon be gone. It would have to withdraw its frozen grasp with the onslaught of a warming sun that bathed everything it touched. Still, the snow had its purpose in all of its frigid sterility. It cleansed. It fed and nourished.

With deliberate steps Tye hiked up the short distance up the wall of the mountain. She found rest at the side of the falls. She remembered her first dusty and dry hike to this place. Oh, the difference of a season! Now the water bathed her in the cold mist that drifted from the abundant harvest of winter. She moved closer and let the heavy mist envelop her with its sweet snow fed waters. It was cold, but she didn't shiver. The sun also managed to reach her skin, kissing it with the benevolent rays of spring.

As Tye raised her face to greet the sun and water, she realized that this coming summer would be different from the last. This season the sun would not be alone. It would have a friend to help temper its heat. This summer there would be water in the rivers.

Chapter Forty-Four

"Daddy says you can't come for a visit this summer because you have to look after your own horse," Trista said after she mounted Patches.

"Yes, you're daddy's right. Trapper needs me for the summer."

"So, I guess this is our last lesson," Triss said.

Unexpected tears came to Tye. "Would you like to ride outside?"

Trista nodded her enthusiasm. Then she dismounted and with Tye's help led Patches outside.

"My mom called my dad the other night," Trista volunteered. "But they didn't fight this time."

"That's good."

"They talked about their honeymoon. Mommy cried. Then, after she got off the phone she hugged me real tight."

Tye felt an inkling of joy and hope.

"Do you think my mom and dad could live together again, someday?"

"I don't know, Trista. That'll have to be between the grown-ups."

"But you're a grown-up."

"I mean your mom and dad."

"Oh."

"Now, let's warm up this pony," Tye said.

Trista began putting Patches through his warm-up routine. "This arena is much bigger than the one indoors."

Tye could hear a niggling of fear in the young girl's voice. She walked closer to where Trista was riding Patches. "Are you okay, Triss?"

Triss nodded. "It's a little scary out here."

Tye moved closer but as the lesson progressed, she distanced herself from the youngster and her pony. After the lesson was over, she moved in close again. "You did well, Triss. After a few minutes I was able to move away, and you were riding by yourself."

Trista blinked as she realized the truth in Tye's statement. "You're right," she said. "I rode by myself, outside! Now, I can go meet Bluebelle."

"Yes, I think you're ready."

"Daddy said he'd take one of the bigger horses, and we'll go riding together." She dismounted Patches. "I hope you can come for a visit and go riding with us someday."

"Maybe someday."

Walking back into the barn, Tye saw Celia waiting in the aisle.

"Hi Mommy! I rode outside today."

"I know. I watched you. You were wonderful."

"Want to help me take care of Patches?" Trista asked.

Celia gave Tye a pained and helpless expression. "Sure, honey."

Tye stepped out of the way as mother and daughter worked over the horse. Finally, he was ready to be led to his stall. Trista led the pony with her mother by her side.

Trista came to Tye and threw her arms around her. "I'm going to miss you, Miss Jorgenson."

"I'll miss you too, Triss," Tye said as she embraced her young student. Tears began to form in her eyes.

Trista pulled away, and Tye noticed the young girl's cheeks were wet.

Celia came forward. "I guess this is goodbye then, Miss Jorgenson."

Tye nodded. Celia held out her hand. Tye took it. The grip was firm and dry. Celia's face was soft and open.

"Come on, Triss. Let's get you home and cleaned up."

Mother and daughter walked down the aisle together. As they reached the door, both turned and looked back. Tye waved. Trista waved back. Then she was gone.

As the afternoon drew to a close, Tye fed the horses their afternoon alfalfa before turning out the lights. She would be back, but it wouldn't be the same without Trista, Kenneth, or even Celia. Already she missed them.

Stepping out into the fading afternoon sun, Tye was pleased to see Preston sitting in his truck. She smiled and walked to where he was parked. He opened his door.

"What are you doing out here?" she asked. "You could've come in."

"I didn't want to disrupt your lessons."

"I was just feeding. You could've helped."

"Ahh, now I've been caught."

Tye grinned.

"Have you seen Elsa lately?"

"Not since you and I were there last."

"I thought I'd take one more look before I left in the morning. Do you want to join me?"

Tye nodded.

"Hop in."

Preston leaned over and opened the passenger door. Tye settled in, buckling her seat belt. Preston started the truck, and they drove in silence to Elsa's barn.

Once at the barn, they walked directly to the pasture. In the soft spring afternoon Tye could see the Elsa's calf was growing fast.

"I call her Lil. I hope that's okay," Preston said.

"I think it's a perfect fit," Tye said. Then she raised her eyes over the pasture and looked toward the mountains. Even though there hadn't been a snow storm in weeks, a white blanket still covered the mountain tops. The snow caught the spring sunshine and seemed to reflect the light back into the sky.

Even winter had its purpose. Its frozen starkness would feed the valley for the coming summer. "My folks are coming into town tomorrow," she said. "We're going to be sealed together in the Salt Lake Temple."

"I know. You've waited a long time for this."

"My whole life."

"Maybe compared to that wait, our healing doesn't seem so long."

Tye looked at Preston. "I hadn't thought of it like that."

"Tye, I was wondering, could I possibly come visit you in

Oregon this summer? I've spoken to my folks. I feel the need to look into the veterinarian program at Oregon State University. I'm going to visit the campus this summer. I thought maybe we could spend some time together. I hope you don't think I'm being too bold."

"Not at all. I'd be disappointed if you came all the way to Oregon and didn't visit."

Preston smiled. "I don't know when I'll be coming just yet. Can I e-mail you?"

"Yes. I'll expect it. I'll have the same e-mail address at home that I have here."

"Then I'll find you," Preston said.

They both turned their attention to the calf, which had given up on the spring grass and was nursing from her mother. Tye pulled in the lengthening afternoon. The sun shone like liquid gold across a deepening azure sky, softening the feathery breeze that played across her skin. A quiet stillness breathed life into her soul.

Tomorrow she would kneel across the altar from her parents, and through priesthood authority she would be sealed to them. Preston was right. She had waited a long time for this. But now that it was here, the long years felt as weightless as a songbird.

Tye looked at Preston. It would be the same for them. There was much they had to examine alone, but hopefully that would only bring them closer together.

"Look! There's a finch!" Preston said as he pointed to a nearby tree. "The first one I've seen all season." The bird's call rose into a melodious song. Preston continued, "They're coming home to raise their families."

Tye followed Preston's outstretched hand; a flash of red met her eyes as the bird flew off against the backdrop of the still and snowy mountains. She recalled the last time she had seen red against white. The snowy storm she had shared with Preston when red blood had covered the white snow. Birth was hard. Even the birth of spring from winter's grasp seemed to be slow and arduous in the recession of cold. But it would be winter's dormant frozen starkness that would replenish the drought stricken land.

Tye looked back to the mountain tops. If she was careful and paid attention, she could choose the rebirth of spring; deepening her river with a new understanding that flowed from the harvest of her winter.

If you enjoyed this book, please send your positive comments, along with your mailing address to: gift@shellyjohnsonchoong.com, and we will send you a free gift.